Thomas stared down at Laurentia, struck as he had been from the beginning by her beauty, so full of innocence and goodness. "Shall I tell you what would suit me?"

"I think I know," she responded on a whisper, lifting her face to his.

He kissed her full, ripe lips and reveled in the warm feel of her body against his. He had never known love before. This he admitted now as feeling after feeling, of affection and passion, washed over him. Somehow, in the nearly twenty days they had been together, Cupid had shot him full of golden arrows, and his only object anymore seemed to be in what way he could be of service to his wife.

As he searched her lips and explored the gentle softness of her mouth, he sought for some way to express the depths of his feelings for her, to explain that in his journey to Gloucestershire he had intended only to refuse their betrothal on principle . . . and instead had married and fallen deeply in love with the very woman he was supposed to have wed.

A CHRISTMAS MASQUERADE

Valerie King

Zebra Books
Kensington Publishing Corp.
http://www.zebrabooks.com

ZEBRA BOOKS are published by

Kensington Publishing Corp.
850 Third Avenue
New York, NY 10022

Copyright © 1999 by Valerie King

First Printing: November, 1999
10 9 8 7 6 5 4 3 2 1

Printed in the United States of America

One

"But, m'lord, the team has been kept in all this wind for nearly three quarters of an hour. If you be wishful of postponing the journey, what with the clouds coming in so dark to the west . . ."

From the porch of his childhood fort, built atop a thick-trunked Spanish chestnut tree, Lord Villiers glanced down at his manservant. His faithful valet, Coxwell, stood shivering from head to toe even though he wore a thick, burgundy wool scarf wrapped tightly about his neck. He was a thin fellow with scarcely enough meat on his bones to protect him from the wind, much less the snow-laden storm which certainly seemed to be looming somewhere off the westernmost coast of England. The tree fort was as sturdy as ever, a sanctuary of his own making, a relic of a fanciful, imaginative childhood gone by many, many years ago.

In his right hand Villiers held the letter that had kept him in a state of some agitation for the past fortnight, an offer of marriage to one of the wealthiest heiresses in the kingdom. The lady's uncle, recently deceased, had requested him ostensibly because he was a quite distant relative of his wife's, a lady who had passed away several years prior. He was honoring her request that Miss Cabot be married to a member of

her family—quite an odd request, he thought, given that there
were no blood ties between Mrs. Cabot and her niece.

In a moment of complete despair, Villiers had succumbed
to the temptation of accepting Miss Cabot's hand in marriage.
He had even replied that he would be arriving forthwith at the
village of Windrush in the Cotswolds, for the purpose of fulfilling his promise to marry the lady. However, from the time
he had posted the letter from London until now, which was
the very hour of his departure from his home in Somerset, he
had had the gravest regrets at having sent the deuced letter in
the first place! He had been kicking himself for days, now,
and yet still his mind was undecided as to what he ought to
do.

He watched his valet shiver once more and stare up at him
with a desperate expression on his thin face.

"Oh, very well!" he cried. He descended the ladder quickly,
then jumped the remaining few feet to the leaf-strewn ground.
"We shall leave now, if you are so anxious to be going."

Coxwell sighed heavily. "I don't wish to be going at all.
'Twill be very cold in Gloucestershire. I had much rather you
had accepted Lady Trent's invitation to spend Michaelmas in
Brighton, or even Whitehaven in Kent with the Marquess of
Chalvington. Now *there* is a house where the servants are
treated like royalty, more than sufficient coal for even the
bleakest of winter days.

"I have spoiled you," Lord Villiers responded, his spirits
rising dramatically. Something about his valet always kept his
thoughts turned in a direction less inclined to the doldrums.
If only Mr. Cabot's offer had not brought him so much distress.

As he marched along the path toward the lane where the
coach and pair were awaiting him, he saw the distant outlines
of his ancestral home through the limbs of the chestnut trees.

His heart ached at the sight of it, gone to rack and ruin as
it was for want of funds to repair the roof. Mildew had crept
in at every turn. The smell alone was enough to keep him on

his usual rounds of visits—either to the Metropolis as the guest of one of his numerous friends, or to a string of country houses, where he would make up his hostess's proper numbers. He was a welcome guest, the skills he brought to the drawing room his current mode of employment.

Of late, however, the life he had been forced to lead for so many years had begun to pall severely. At two and twenty such a vagabond existence had not been entirely without its interest and pleasures. But at one and thirty, with little hope of his fortunes changing in the near future, the constant shift of environment as his carriage rolled from the northern wilds of the land to the mild south and anywhere betwixt, he had grown restless in the extreme.

At the very moment he received Mr. Cabot's letter, he had been at his weakest. His feet had itched to be returning to Somerset for good with Miss Cabot's fortune in hand. He had been prepared to fold in the cards which had been dealt to him in exchange for a fortune not of his making. He had written an acceptance of Mr. Cabot's offer and posted it, with the strong rationalization that he was doing just what he ought to do for his title and his lands, for the sons and daughters he longed to have, for future generations.

Yet the very next day he had thought better of his decision. He had penned several more letters to refute his first impetuous one, yet had mailed none of them. Never in his life had so much indecision dogged him, so much so that he found himself at the eleventh hour in the worst position, having to travel personally to Windrush in order to inform Miss Cabot that he could not wed her, that in a thousand years he would never marry in order to solve his financial dilemmas.

"But do you think we shall actually outrun this storm?" Coxwell asked, shivering yet again.

"How the devil should I know!" he snapped, still irritated by the nature of the situation.

"You needn't come the crab," Coxwell reprimanded politely.

Lord Villiers sighed. "I beg your pardon," he murmured, glancing up at the sky. "By the looks of it, we shall have snow before we reach the Cotswolds. Don't fret. I have sufficient laid by to pick up an extra pair in Bath, and we'll overnight in Gloucester, which should place us at the Tump and Dagler in Windrush by nightfall tomorrow."

Another long-suffering sigh followed this speech. "The Tump and Dagler," Coxwell muttered. "With such a name I cannot imagine the supply of coal will be in the least sufficient."

Windrush, Gloucestershire

The following evening, snow swirled in a frightening halo about Laurentia Cabot's head as she dropped lightly to the innyard from her carriage doorway.

"Stable the team!" she called to her postilion. "We shall have to spend the night here!" Snowflakes spattered her face, and a frosty wind whipped at her skirts.

"Wery good, Miss!" her servant called back.

She ran toward the door, the glow from the windows of the inn the only guide to the ancient stone building. Snow had built up quickly in soft drifts. Even the path to the door was ankle deep. She should not have ventured forth in the storm, yet her haste to meet her betrothed before ever he set foot in Evenlode House was far too great to allow her anxiety to give way to her common sense. Her nose prickled as she breathed in the cold, forcing her to pull her red velvet cloak over her nose and mouth.

Reaching the door, she shoved her way inside and watched the astonished innkeeper, Mr. Newnham, nearly drop a tray of tankards as he caught sight of her. "Miss Cabot!" he cried, his brown eyes wide. "Be ye travelin' on a night like this!"

"I know!" she cried. "It is the greatest foolishness. I shall require a room and accommodations for Will, who is even now stabling the horses." She paused, her heart slamming wildly against her ribs. "Has he come?" she asked breathlessly.

Everyone in a five mile radius of Windrush knew that Laurentia Cabot's betrothed, the infamous Lord Villiers, would be arriving today from London.

"I don't know that 'e 'as, miss. There be a gentleman in the parlor, a stranger—"

"Then he has come!" she cried impetuously.

She whirled around, unheeding of the innkeeper.

"But, Miss—!" he protested.

Laurentia knew every chamber of the inn, having spent her entire life marching to and from the village. She did not listen to the end of Mr. Newnham's warning, but instead crossed the hall, and without the smallest hesitation gave the door of the parlor a shove.

The gentleman, presumably her betrothed, for she had never met him before, was sitting in a chair by the fire reading a book. Well! That was a novelty! A gentleman, reading! Her uncle, in all the years he'd been alive, had never so much as glanced at a cover, or even opened the pages to discover what might be hidden within. He had enjoyed brandy, gaming with friends from childhood, and counting his groats one by one. The finer occupations were lost to him.

"You there!" she called out as the man turned slightly toward her, an amused frown furrowing what she could see was a distinctively handsome brow. "Are you to wed me tomorrow?"

Until the words had actually left her mouth, Laurentia had not so much as wondered at either their sense or propriety. However, when the stranger's lips began to twitch and yet he did not open his mouth to give her answer, she felt a blush instantly suffuse her cheeks. What a perfect ninnyhammer he must think her, bursting into his parlor and demanding to know if he was Lord Villiers. If he was Villiers, though, her conduct might give him such a disgust of her that he would break off the engagement, in which case that would not be a bad thing. On the other hand, if he was not Villiers, he might feel obliged to summon the constable and have her committed to an asylum for the insane.

She dropped a ridiculous, hurried curtsy, took a step forward, and began again. "I do beg your pardon, sir, but I must know. I have been expecting Lord Villiers to arrive this evening. Are you his lordship?"

He smiled slowly at that. "I wish I were, of the moment," he responded gently in what she felt was probably the finest voice she had ever heard. The timber was ideal—the vibration, surely, of the midtone of a violincello.

She blinked and watched him curiously. "Who are you, then?" she queried. Again a blush rose up her cheeks. "Oh, do forgive me. I am being quite impertinent. It is undoubtedly from having grown up in the house of a widower who had no interest in teaching a little girl about proper manners and the like. And Grandmama would not interfere in the least!"

He closed his book and rose to his feet. "You must come to the fire. Your nose is still pink from the cold." He extended his arm in an inviting manner toward her. "Won't you?"

How could she refuse such an affable invitation? "Yes, thank you. I should like that very much. The temperature outside is abominable, and I can feel that the snow is beginning to melt on my hair and face." She shoved back the hood of her scarlet cloak and fluffed her thick, red locks, which were decidedly frizzed from the damp and not at all dressed as they ought to be for a young lady of quality.

She had waited and waited for Villiers to arrive. When he did not come, she knew she must rush to the village and see if he had yet made his appearance. Besides, how much better to speak to him here, at the Tump and Dagler Inn, rather than at home. Surely, once Villiers was actually ensconced within the walls of Evenlode House, she would never get him out!

"I can see the snow melting even now," the stranger said.

"And you shall be needing this." He drew a perfectly ironed square of cambric cloth from the pocket of his coat. The white-work about the edges was uniform and neat.

She took it gratefully. "Thank you ever so much. I know I must look a fright." She dabbed at her cheeks and chin and moved toward the fire.

"May I?" he queried, taking her cloak at the shoulders but waiting for permission to remove it.

"Yes, of course. You are very kind."

The cloak slid away from her as she drew close to the blazing warmth of the hearth. She heard his footsteps moving toward the door where the cloak-hooks resided, and chanced to glance at the kerchief. A beautiful, scrolled *V* was embroidered in one corner. She frowned down at it, and for a moment wondered if the stranger had humbugged her and was Villiers, after all.

"Do you care for a little wassail?" he inquired. "I have ordered a small bowl, and should be delighted to have you join me—unless, of course, you have certain apprehensions about sharing a cup with a stranger."

She turned toward him, the firelight catching his face in full relief. She gasped and blinked. He was deucedly handsome, by heavens, wasn't he! His hair was a raven's black, his eyes a deep blue, his cheeks molded, surely, by the heavenly chisel of Michaelangelo. His nose, though slightly irregular, was not in the least unattractive, and his lips, though curled in some sort of permanent amusement, quite perfection. Something within her began to quiver in the nicest way as she looked upon the stranger. She reminded herself, however, of the embroidered letter on his kerchief. "So you are not Lord Villiers?" she inquired again.

He smiled, but shook his head.

She lifted the kerchief to him. "Then what is your name, sir, for there is a *V* embroidered on your kerchief. I find the coincidence striking, for I have been expecting Villiers for *hours.*"

He seemed conscious of a sudden, and for that moment she was certain she had caught her betrothed in a terrible whisker—pretending not to be her husband-to-be! Why would he do such a thing?

She waited, however, for his answer.

"Oh, dear," he murmured. "I'm 'fraid you've found me out. I should never have kept that kerchief. What a gross indiscretion." He seemed utterly mortified as he continued. "You will have to forgive me if I don't explain the presence of a conspicuous *V* on my kerchief. The only explanation I could offer you would, by courtesy, have to be a lie."

Valencia? Victoria? Valenzuela?

A lady must have given it to him at one time, undoubtedly a Cyprian. She was astounded, and dropped the kerchief as though it were a living creature that had suddenly bitten her. "Oh! Now it will be soiled!"

He retrieved the kerchief with a quick snatching movement and hastily jammed it back into his pocket. "Forget, I pray, that you have seen it at all."

"Yes, of course," she whispered, her cheeks flaming. She felt irritated suddenly that she was embarrassed. She was four and twenty, yet had been kept wrapped in wool-linen for so long a time that she hardly knew how to conduct herself. Surely any other female of her age wouldn't have twitched even an eyelash at the hint of such a thing as a gentleman's paramour having given him a kerchief.

Well, at least now she was certain he was not Villiers.

She felt oddly dashed, suddenly, at the knowledge that the man before her was not her betrothed, after all. Something about him, the lightness of his expression or perhaps the amused glint in his extraordinarily blue eyes, appealed to her mightily.

At that moment, a serving maid entered bearing a bowl of

steaming, aromatic wassail. Her stomach rumbled in a most unladylike manner as she watched the maid settle the bowl and pewter mugs neatly upon a small round table in the corner of the room. Christmas greens had been arranged in a pleasing manner on a fine square of linen, and bunches of holly berries brightened the entire arrangement.

The traditional Christmas beverage, consisting of ale, eggs, roasted apples, sugar, nutmeg, cloves, and ginger beaten together and cooked over a slow fire, smelled of heaven. The aroma put her forcibly in mind of the fact that, given her state of nerves throughout the entire day, she had had but a cold slice of bread at nuncheon. She found she was decidedly hungry.

When the maid left, she recalled that the stranger had asked if she would care to partake of a cup with him. "As for the wassail," she murmured, eyeing the hot beverage with a famished eye, "I daresay I should be happy to share a cup with you—in the spirit of the Yuletide season, of course—but of the present I do not even know your name. I don't think it would be at all proper to lift a cup to you without first being introduced."

He thrust his hand forward and stated bluntly, "Adolphus Swinfield, at your service, Miss, er, Miss—?"

She was charmed, pure and simple. His ease of manners, the funning light in his eye, his outstretched hand . . . oh, she was quivering again! She took his hand in a firm clasp. "Miss Cabot, Laurentia Cabot of Evenlode House. I am very pleased to make your acquaintance." A certain remarkable thought struck her in that moment, a blinding solution to a most perplexing problem—one that had been deviling her from the day her uncle's horrid will had been read to her. Still holding his hand, she tilted her head and blurted out, "Will you marry me?"

His brows shot up in some surprise. "I beg your pardon?"

She fairly tumbled into her speech. "I know it must sound

positively ridiculous, and for all I know you could be married already, yet somehow as I look at you I know you are not. You are far too relaxed and congenial to be a man with a wife, and certainly not a man with children. Am I correct in this?"

He nodded as one who had been struck with a splash of water on his brow. She felt obliged to continue. "I am in a terrible fix, if you must know. I need a bridegroom for a month's time, and the one my uncle chose will not do at all, because I have little doubt that *he* will wish to remain married to me, since he hasn't a feather to fly with and only agreed to wed me because I happen to be quite wealthy—or will be, once I have been married for a month. Yes, well you may stare, but those were the conditions of my uncle's will. And you know what the laws are! Once I am wed to Lord Villiers, he and he alone will have command of my fortune. I will not see a farthing of it. You see, this fellow, Villiers, has the worst reputation as a gamester. It is even widely known that he used up his own entire fortune before his twenty-second birthday. Were such a man to gain control of my inheritance, I'd soon be in the poorhouse, no doubt!"

She was a little surprised that Mr. Swinfield lost some of his good-naturedness during her speech. If anything, given his charming demeanor, she had anticipated a little sympathy. Instead, his expression had become rather cloaked. Feeling she had made a dreadful mistake, she added hastily, "I should pay you quite handsomely for your services for the month, though I would insist that my solicitor draw up the appropriate papers—which you would, of course, be obliged to sign."

He turned away from her and moved to the table upon which the wassail bowl sat patiently. "I will confess I am utterly astounded, Miss Cabot. Your proposition is without precedence. Are you suggesting that once I wed you, in a month I would then be required to divorce you?"

"Precisely," she stated on a heavy sigh.

"But you know nothing about me. I am a perfect stranger

to you and yet, upon bursting into my parlor and flashing a shock of amazingly red hair at me, you beg for my hand in marriage. don't know what to think, either of you or of your ability to make sound judgments."

She wasn't in the least overset by this bit of plain speaking. She had grown up with her uncle, who had been a veritable crosspatch, always combing her hair for the smallest offense. "I know I must sound like a madwoman," she said in her defense, "but I beg you will believe me when I tell you I am not. I am merely *desperate*. And—I hope you do not mind my saying so—you seem to be just the sort of gentleman who would willingly help any lady out of a scrape."

He eyed her curiously as he ladled a cup of the steaming brew into one of the mugs. "Are you perchance in the habit of reading novels, Miss Cabot?"

"Why yes, I am," she responded ingenuously. "How did you know?"

He shrugged and began to smile. "Now that you know my name, and we are a little acquainted," he said, "will you permit me to serve you?"

"Oh, yes," she gushed, her stomach rumbling anew. "If you would. I haven't had but a slice of bread all day."

"Ah," he murmured, for the moment settling the ladle back onto the edge of the bowl. "Perhaps you would care to dine with me, then?" When she hesitated, he added quickly, "A pleasant meal together would offer the advantage of giving us a little more time with which to discuss your interesting proposition."

"Yes, it would, wouldn't it?" She eyed him for a moment, again taking his measure. She felt certain she could trust this man, stranger though he was. Also, he was not quite so pricklish about her idea as he had been a few moments earlier. "In that case, I shall accept of your invitation."

He bowed to her and moved to give a tug on the bellpull. When the innkeeper arrived, he requested an additional place for Laurentia. "Wery good, sir," the innkeeper responded with a worried frown between his brows.

Laurentia met his gaze, and was not surprised when the good Mr. Newnham gave her a meaningful stare. She returned his forceful look with one of her own. The landlord rolled his eyes and expressed his disapproval of her dining with a complete stranger by muttering incomprehensible things as he slowly moved from the chamber.

"One of your champions?" Mr. Swinfield queried, his eyes glinting with amusement once more.

"Yes," Laurentia breathed, grateful that he had understood the situation so swiftly. "You can see why I feel perfectly safe running amuck through our village. Everyone sees to me. I have been underfoot since I was a child."

He placed a dramatic hand over his heart. "Am I in certain danger, then, from vengeful innkeepers and the like?"

She smiled and giggled with utter pleasure. "Only if you were to kidnap me." She watched him pour the wassail into a second cup and quickly moved to stand beside him. She took the cup gratefully, surrounding the pewter vessel with both gloved hands. She was still chilled from the drive to the village.

She took a sip and closed her eyes, savoring the hearty, steamed concoction. "I believe from the time I was a child I loved the Christmas season best. My uncle was not nearly so irascible during Yuletide, for everyone came to call and gave him presents. He was never so happy as when he was being flattered and fawned over. Then he was kind to me, even pleasant at times. He never knew of my secret life, of course, that I had from the time I could remember made fast friends with his every tenant, and with all the shopkeepers of the village. She took another sip. The warm ale heated her throat, and the taste of apples, cinnamon, and nutmeg pleased her every sense.

She opened her eyes and met the stranger's stare firmly. "As to my ability to make proper judgments, I am in some ways untried. On the other hand, I have a natural sense for what is good and true. You, sir, seem to me to be both. Tell me I am mistaken, and I will withdraw my offer."

He seemed greatly struck. "As to that, Miss Cabot, I would like to think you were right on both counts."

She nodded. "Then, will you marry me? I absolutely refuse to wed Villiers. I have for so long a time planned precisely how my inheritance would be allocated that the thought of losing even a particle of it—nonetheless the whole of it—to a rogue is more than I can bear."

"I will admit that I have heard the same rumors of Villiers these many years and more, and I can understand your reluctance therefore to wed him. Any female ought to be warned against such a man. I can only wonder that your uncle permitted the arrangement in the first place."

She carried her cup back to a companion chair by the fireplace and took up her seat. She stared into the blaze and watched the reddening logs bristle with heat. "I don't know whether or not my uncle was warned of Villiers's past. According to his will, he had promised my aunt that I would be married to a member of her family, and upon writing a number of letters he discovered that a lord, distantly connected to her, was interested in the match. I am in no way of knowing, however, whether he had been informed of Villiers's reputation."

"I see. Your uncle, though, could not have been unhappy about seeing you wed to a Peer."

He had moved to stand close to her chair. She looked up at him and smiled faintly. "You may be right. As I said before, I truly do not know what his thoughts were. I, on the other hand, do not give a fig about being a lady this-or-that."

"But you do want your uncle's fortune."

"Yes," she stated decidedly. "More than anything else in the world. You see, there is so very much to be done. My uncle was a woefully negligent landlord whilst he was alive, and fairly ruined the wool-making industry here in Windrush. I have every intention of rectifying his many wrongs." She sipped her wassail a little more and glanced toward the windows as a series of snowy gusts played a gentle tune on the glass. "I daresay Lord Villiers is snowbound somewhere, which was precisely the kind of good fortune I've required these many days and more to see my way out of this wretched tangle."

"I am puzzled on one point," Mr. Swinfield said.

"And what would that be?"

"Did not your uncle inform you of your betrothal before he died?"

She shook her head. "He knew me too well to do anything of the like. I should have set up a caterwaul, and though I doubt I could have persuaded him against the marriage, he never was able to tolerate even the smallest complaint from me."

"I think it abominable," he said, a serious frown on his brow. "I should never have—I mean, I must presume you are one of his few living relations. Am I right?"

"His mother survives him, as well."

"I simply cannot credit how he could have done something like this. I, myself, have no one. Had I had a niece to follow after, I should have treasured her and done everything in my power to make certain her future was settled to her satisfaction."

"I should have done the same, Mr. Swinfield."

Thomas Michael Adolphus Swinfield, fifth Viscount Lord Villiers, looked into the face of a beauty such as he had never seen before. Her complexion was so serene as to be lit with a warm light from within. Her face was a perfect heart-shape, her eyes luminous and a glittering green in color which put him in mind of emeralds. Her lips were full, a delicate rose, and of just such a shape that demanded kissing. He wondered if it would be possible to steal a kiss before the unexpected evening drew to a close. Mistletoe hung from one of the ancient oak beams which supported the ceiling. If he was careful, perhaps he could claim a kiss as his rightful due for even considering her absurd proposal.

She shifted her gaze back to the fire and fell silent as she sipped her wassail. He was heartily glad of it, for now he could observe her almost unawares. What great, good fortune it was that he habitually traveled under his surname. His impoverished state made the use of his title more of a burden than a blessing, for whenever it became known that a *milord* had come to dine or to stay the night, he would be given the finest and most expensive of rooms, the rarest and dearest of wines, as well as the best and most costly of fare. He had learned early on, once his fortune had slipped away, that anonymity was a better friend to a poor man than an exalted station without funds could ever be.

So, he was here, with his betrothed, and pretending to be mere Mr. Swinfield. What a rare good fortune, indeed!

Only, how was it that such a great beauty, with simple, attractive country manners, great style in her fashion, a woman of some heart, had escaped matrimony until now? He felt it was a mystery of some moment. Had the young woman never left Gloucestershire? He felt it was possible, given the secluded nature of the village and of Evenlode House. Both were tucked away in the depths of the lovely Cotswolds. Yet, why had not some equally ingenuous country gentleman stumbled upon the lovely, red-haired beauty and made her his wife beforetimes? Mr. Cabot may not have taken his niece to Bath, where she could undoubtedly have made a great match, but how was it possible she had escaped wedding any of the local bucks? Surely, there had been a few to pass through Windrush now and again and stumble upon her existence.

Perhaps in time, he might discover the truth.

For now, however, he was content to watch her, to admire her, and to plot just how he would take the innocent beauty into his arms before she retired to her chambers for the night.

Of course he couldn't marry her. That was impossible. Ah, but to feel her perfect rosy lips beneath his own, to take her young body in his arms, to hold her against him, these were things he could do.

Laurentia had never enjoyed a meal so much as the one she shared with Mr. Swinfield. His manners were open, warm, and engaging. Any awkwardness she might have felt because of the simple fact that he was a stranger to her had dissipated by the time the first course of pigeon pie and rabbit stew had been removed and some fine, thinly sliced Yorkshire ham was placed in front of her. A bottle of East India Madeira accompanied the tidy feast, and Mr. Swinfield's anecdotes, of which he had a vast store, kept her in giggles throughout her peas, salad, potatoes, and sliced apple.

He was a knowledgeable man, and spoke of the beauties of the English countryside as though he had walked them all, from the cherry orchards in Kent to the smugglers' haunts along the coast of Cornwall, from the limestone caverns of Derbyshire to the wilds of Yorkshire and the exquisite beauty of the Lake District in Cumbria. She had long since settled her elbows on the table, her chin in hand, in order to soak up every word he could utter about *other places*.

Oh, once she was in possession of her fortune she would visit them all! She would make Mr. Swinfield compose a list of every hamlet in Albion she should visit. Then she would begin her own tour of her native land, and see all the places she had been dreaming of since she was a child.

When he had fallen silent, his own gaze fixed to hers in a wondering manner, she whispered, "So, Mr. Swinfield, will you do me the honor of becoming my husband?"

Once more, he was taken aback. He settled himself into his chair and folded the linen on his lap. "I could think of no greater honor," he responded with obvious sincerity. "But I do believe I should turn the matter over in my mind at least once or twice more before venturing into so unusual an arrangement. Would you mind if we discussed your proposition in the morning? I will have an answer for you then."

His mention of morning made her think of her bed, and she covered a sudden yawn, then apologized. "I am sorry. I expect the hour is late."

"It cannot be much past nine."

"That is late," she murmured.

He coughed and sputtered a little.

"Oh, you are laughing at me, but we keep country hours. My uncle preferred the household to be bustling from dawn until dusk, then early to bed. Although, I know what your hours in London must be. Do you sleep 'til eleven every morning?"

"I am not so indulgent as that," he responded, "but I confess I hardly arise as the cock crows."

"No, I wouldn't suppose you would." She rose to her feet. "Thank you for a delightful dinner. You were so very gracious to have invited me, especially after I shocked you with my outrageous proposal. Indeed, if you feel it to be wholly inappropriate and a notion you cannot embrace, pray do not trouble yourself overly much. I shall manage, somehow. A simple note would be sufficient to end the discussion."

She offered her hand to him and was a little surprised when he drew very close and lifted her fingers to his lips. The feel of the kiss that followed sent gooseflesh popping up all down her arm. "Oh, my," she murmured.

He lifted his gaze to hers as he slowly released her hand. How blue his eyes were, stunningly so. And he was standing so very close. Oh, my. Was he leaning toward her? Were his lips on hers?

She felt stunned, like a small animal caught in lantern light. His lips were warm, soft and moist. She had been kissed before, but this was strangely different, somehow, perhaps because it had been entirely unexpected. She felt him draw closer still. His arm slipped about her waist. Was she caught in a dream? She settled her hands on his arms, and heard the softest moan from his throat—or was it from hers? He pulled her tightly against him, and she lost all sense of time and place. She knew nothing except the feel of him against her and the soft search of his lips on hers.

After a long moment, he released her, albeit quite slowly. He seemed not to know where he was. "You see," he began by way of explanation, his voice husky and low, "you were standing beneath the mistletoe."

She slowly lifted her eyes to the ancient oak beam above her. She smiled. "I was, wasn't I?" she responded on a whisper.

"I shouldn't have taken advantage of you."

"No, you shouldn't have. But then, I shouldn't have asked you to marry me, so I suppose turnabout is fair play."

At that, he smiled. "Where have you been all these years?" he queried teasingly.

"Buried in the Cotswolds," she returned with a sad little smile.

Two

The next morning, Viscount Villiers awoke to the sound of complete quiet. The storm had passed, leaving behind a blanket of snow which seemed to have dampened every noise possible. The hour was quite early and the chamber cold, since the coal fire had dwindled substantially during the night.

He glanced toward the window and saw that the sky was a soft, wintry blue with yellow-gray dawnish lights streaked throughout, an effect which put him strongly in mind of Turner's unusual watercolors. From belowstairs only the faintest rumblings and scrapings could be heard to inform the guests that the inn was awakening.

His thoughts turned swiftly to the evening prior. He recalled vividly the very moment when Miss Cabot had burst into his parlor and he had turned around to find out what manner of hoydenish female had disturbed his reading.

What a shock he had experienced when he discovered that a creature as lovely as Aphrodite had so suddenly entered his life. When she had thrown back the hood of her snowflake-dotted cloak and her red hair had fairly shouted at him, he had felt entirely bowled over.

Who could have blamed him for wanting to take such a maiden in his arms? He could still feel the soft velvet of her dark-blue gown, the curve of her back, and the smallness of her waist. The kiss she had given him, withholding nothing, had been magical and intense. He felt certain she had been kissed before, which again led him to the mystery that she was as yet unwed.

When a scratching sounded on his door, he suspected his valet had arrived. "Come," he called out, thrusting his hands behind his head and staring up into a white-plaster ceiling, his mind still full of his betrothed.

The door opened quietly and Coxwell entered on a soft tread, prepared to mend the fire. Crossing to the fireplace, and protecting his knees from debris, he set about scraping out the dead coals and replacing them with fine, black, living chunks that would soon have the chamber warm and comfortable once more. "Good morning, Sir," he said, glancing his direction.

"Good morning, Coxwell." Lord Villiers was grateful his servant remembered to address him as, "sir," instead of "m'lord." Given his conversation with Miss Cabot of the night before, he was more intent than ever upon keeping his identity a secret, at least until he decided what he should do. "I have a matter of some import to discuss with you."

"Indeed?"

"You may well 'indeed' me, for last night my betrothed presented *Mr. Swinfield* with an offer of marriage. It would seem she holds *Lord Villiers* in considerable disgust, and has no intention of wedding him.

At that, Coxwell turned around and eyed him carefully. "And are you considering the proposal?" he queried.

"I find myself intrigued by the proposition. You see, Miss Cabot is in something of a fix, and does not intend for the marriage to *Swinfield* to continue beyond a month."

"How extraordinary. She wants to be married only a month? You would divorce her then?"

He nodded. "She only inherits after being wed a month, and she wants control of her fortune. Apparently, she has no desire to be married—to anyone."

"Again—how extraordinary. However, I cannot like it. Divorce would mean a terrible scandal, and how could you sustain masquerading as *Swinfield* the entire time? No, I do not like it by half."

"Nor I, to own the truth," he responded. "Ah. I see the inn has plenty of coal."

Coxwell grunted. "I have been agreeably surprised by the accommodations," he admitted. "My chambers were comfortable and warm, which is not to say I wish to remain here." He cleared his throat as he continued to remove the ashes from the grate.

"I must say I am in agreement with you. Every instinct tells me to flee at once. However, I have begun to think there is something havey-cavey about the whole business. You see, Mr. Cabot did not tell his niece of her approaching nuptials before he died. He let his solicitor inform her of her betrothal upon the reading of the will."

At that, the valet paused in his scraping. His sharp nose twitched. "One could only suppose then that Mr. Cabot did not possess sensibilities of a refined nature."

"One could most definitely suppose that he did not."

"I believe there is something I should tell you," Coxwell said, shoveling fresh coal over the heart of the previous night's fire. "Something I heard from belowstairs."

"Yes?"

"It would seem Sir Alan Redcliffe has been residing in the vicinity of Windrush for nigh onto five years, and was a friend to Mr. Cabot—a good friend as well as a business associate."

At the mention of Redcliffe, Villiers threw back the covers and slid his legs over the side of the bed. "That brute has another house? Here?" he cried. "In Windrush?"

"Evidently."

"How many homes does that deuced fellow own?" he cried, outraged.

"I'm sure that with your fortune properly invested he can have acquired a dozen. The mansion here, apparently, is quite large, even vulgar, a word employed by one of the undermaids when describing his house."

Villiers chuckled bitterly. "I would not be in the least surprised. He may behave the gentleman in society, but I always suspected he had the discernment of a pig's snout."

Coxwell nodded, then continued. "There is more. Miss Cabot's name was connected to the baronet in one particular remark I overheard. It would seem Redcliffe has offered for Miss Cabot,"—here he paused—"on more than one occasion."

"Offered for her! Why, he must be twice her age! I suppose he cannot be content with my fortune. Now he must have hers, as well!"

Villiers slid his feet into warm slippers and drew near the growing fire. Coxwell took up a thick, amber dressing gown and offered his master a sleeve. The room was still cold, and Villiers accepted it gratefully, sliding one arm in and then the other in a familiar rhythm of manservant and master.

Staring into the glowing coals, Villiers frowned heavily. So, Redcliffe had actually offered for Miss Cabot. The very thought of it made his stomach boil. Was there no end to greed in a greedy man?

Villiers turned around and stared at his valet, who was settling the coal bucket near the door. When he met his gaze, he saw a familiar, resigned expression in his valet's eyes. He felt obliged to say, "No, Coxwell, I have not decided to stay."

"But you will."

"I suppose, then, you are so perfectly acquainted with me that you know my every thought?"

Coxwell offered him a generous half-smile. "Very nearly so, I believe."

"Well, in this you are mistaken. I am inclined to leave Windrush quite soon. Redcliffe is nothing to me anymore, and Miss Cabot's scheme I find utterly unacceptable. Haven't I enough scandal attached to my name that next I would add divorce to it, and that involving a perfect innocent? No, I shan't stay. Whatever trials have attached themselves to Miss Cabot, they are of no concern to me, however pretty she might be."

Something In Coxwell's eye brightened. "Indeed? Is this truly your intention? Then, have I your permission to discharge the bill? We could be in Tewkesbury by noon, and Gloucester by nightfall. Another day and we would be in Bath, dining at the White Hart. You always were fond of Bath."

"Yes," he responded firmly. "See to it at once, and have coffee sent to me with a little bread and butter and some local jelly, if there is any available. Oh, and some writing paper and a pen.

"Very good, *m'lord.*" Coxwell hefted the bucket, readying himself to depart, when a scratching sounded on the door.

"Who might that be?" Villiers queried.

Coxwell was about to open the door when a muffled yet decidedly feminine voice spoke from beyond the white-painted wood. "Mr. Swinfield? Have you risen? I . . . I must speak with you at once. Oh, pray, will you open the door to me? I know it is quite early, but something rather urgent has just transpired."

Villiers adjusted his dressing gown, and nodded to Coxwell. "Open it a mite," he murmured. "And suggest I call on her in a few moments when I am not *en deshabille.*"

Coxwell did so, but Miss Cabot pushed the door the rest of the way, and without ceremony rushed into the room. "Mr. Swinfield," she cried hurriedly. "Oh! You are still in your nightclothes. Well, it hardly matters if we are to be wed. But, I do beg your pardon." When he advanced quickly on her and moved to take hold of the door, she added, "Yes, yes, please do shut the door. Something untoward has occurred. A few moments ago, I had just descended the stairs when I noticed that a rather large conveyance had drawn into the innyard—a fine coach, coachman-driven, in fact—and a gentleman of some stature emerged. His cloak held more than eight capes, and I felt certain—oh, Mr. Swinfield, I am convinced it is

Villiers, himself. He must have waited until the snows stopped some time last night, then traveled through until he's just now arrived. You must give me your answer, and I pray that you will not refuse me. As I said last night, I am become quite desperate. I had rather marry anyone than Villiers."

Lord Villiers glanced at Coxwell, who met his gaze with an astonished stare of his own. He addressed his valet, "Will you go down and discover the traveler's identity?"

"Oh, yes, please, would you?" Miss Cabot added, turning toward Coxwell herself. Villiers watched his man meet Miss Cabot's pleading gaze and saw without the least degree of surprise that a flush crept up his cheeks, matching the burgundy muffler still wound about his neck. In the early morning light, even a nodcock could see she was a diamond of the first water. "Y-yes, Miss," he stammered. "Of course I will."

"You'd best go at once," Villiers murmured.

Coxwell took a step toward the door, then glanced back at his master. "And what about *the other matter?*"

"Belay that order, at least for a few minutes."

Coxwell looked him up and down, obviously registering the most improper fact that Villiers was still in his dressing gown and entertaining a young lady who was to all effects a stranger to him, in his bedchamber, *alone*. Villiers said, "Yes, I know. But we shall get it all sorted out later."

As Coxwell left the chamber, Miss Cabot stuck her head through the doorway, peeking into the hallway. She sighed and drew back into the chamber, closing the door with a soft snap. "No one is there. Thank you so much for seeing me in this wretched manner, but I am utterly disconsolate. Have you considered my plight? Will you help me? If you will agree, even if Villiers has just arrived we can escape from the inn unnoticed. Using my traveling carriage, we can go directly to Tewkesbury and call upon my solicitor. We can have the entire matter arranged in a trice."

Villiers wasn't certain what prompted him to do so, but he

said, "I will need to see your uncle's will first, to see if what we are about to do—*if* I should agree to your completely madcap scheme—will comply with your uncle's intentions."

"But . . . but what about that scoundrel, *Villiers?*"

"If Villiers has indeed arrived, I shall deal with the fellow myself. After all, he cannot force you to marry him, not when you are surrounded by so many who would champion you."

A smile softened the anxious wrinkles on her forehead. "I knew that was how it would be with you. I knew I could rely on you completely. And see, I wasn't wrong, was I?"

The compliment had precisely the effect it would have had on any person of the male gender. He felt flattered by and proud of her assessment of his character. He certainly liked to think of himself as the sort of man any young woman in distress could rely upon. On the other hand, she couldn't know that his bold words were meaningless since he was, himself, *that scoundrel, Villiers.*

He cleared his throat. "Now that that is all settled, I do beg you will excuse me while I dress." He had spoken firmly, but she seemed disinclined to leave.

"Oh, that." She dismissed his dressing gown with a wave of her hand. "I don't give a fig for it. Please permit me to stay until your man returns. You cannot imagine how distressed I am."

He was astonished, yet she had spoken truly, for there was nothing in her manner that indicated even the smallest embarrassment. He should have been shocked, but something about her sweetness, her naivete, simply charmed him, and the unusual nature of being in his dressing gown somehow warmed his heart. Whenever he had thought of marriage, this was how he had believed it would be—comfortable, easy, and innocent.

"Of course you may stay," he said.

She released a deep sigh, thanked him, and moved to stand by the small window of his bedchamber, where she pushed aside the old lace curtain that she might better see the innyard below. The sight of her, framed by the winter's morning light, pulled strongly on his heart. He found himself longing for her, not as a man might lust for a woman in such a circumstance, but for the homey, relaxed quality of the arrangement. He could see himself wed to her, even for a month, and enjoying a similar existence, perhaps reading to her or hearing her pleasant voice marking the prose of Shakespeare, Pope, or even— God forbid, but-wouldn't-it-be-delightful—Lord Byron.

"Do you enjoy Byron's works?" he asked on impulse.

She turned back to him and smiled. "What do you think?" she asked, teasingly.

"I think you may have memorized "The Corsair" by now."

She lifted her chin and appeared utterly adorable in her attempt to assume a pose of *hauteur*. "Only parts of it, so now I trust I have brought you down a peg or two."

He laughed and rocked on his heels. Where had she been all his life, this darling creature?

At that moment, Coxwell returned with the news that the stranger wasn't Villiers at all, but a man by the name of Alexander Quince.

"The London financier?" he asked.

"Yes, so it would seem."

Miss Cabot, whose hands had been pressed dramatically to her chest from the moment Coxwell returned, cried, "Then he is not Villiers! Oh, thank God!"

Villiers shifted on his feet. The tug of quagmire and a muddy scrape seemed to be pulling at the soles of his slippers. She certainly had no good opinion of *Lord Villiers*. What on earth had the chit heard to have so given her a disgust of him? Or had Redcliffe somehow learned of her uncle's scheme and poisoned her against him? Possibly. He addressed his valet. "Did you happen to hear what Mr. Quince is doing in so small a village? Does he mean to stay? Does he have a purpose here?"

Coxwell seemed slightly distressed. "Apparently, he's come to do some work for Redcliffe."

"Ah."

"Do you know Sir Alan?" Miss Cabot asked.

Villiers turned to her. "Yes, I am slightly acquainted with him."

"Then if you wed me, you will know someone in our little neighborhood," she responded cheerfully. "He was a friend of my uncle's for many years, and a good friend to me, as well. He is one of the kindest men I have ever known."

Her words, so sweetly spoken, tore through his past like a swiftly thrown spear. He was drawn back to the age of sixteen, to losing his parents in a terrible coaching accident. He remembered how gently Sir Alan had spoken to him the day of the funeral, told him how his father had many, many years earlier appointed him guardian and that he intended to do everything he could to be a good friend to him in the coming years.

He had trusted Sir Alan in a naive manner, just as Miss Cabot did now. All had seemed so secure.

When he had come of age, he discovered that Sir Alan had supposedly made several unwise investments, and all but a pittance of his large fortune was gone. Sir Alan had appeared absolutely sick at heart at his mismanagement, and for a time he had believed the baronet's story. What remained of Villiers was a few acres of land and his house, Fairwood Hall, which he had had to keep boarded up because he could not afford sufficient servants to maintain the fine, old house.

After a year had passed, however, and he became aware of how much Redcliffe's fortune had increased—ostensibly due to an investment in a West Indies sugar plantation—he began to suspect that somehow the baronet had robbed him of his inheritance. In due course, gossip began to rise from an unknown quarter which further deepened his own suspicions. It began being bandied about from tongue to tongue that Lord

Villiers, by the time he had reached the age of two and twenty, had gambled away his fortune.

At first he had tried to put a damper on such offensive gabblemongering, and reiterated what he had told everyone from the first—that some very poor investments' over a long period of time had eradicated his father's fortune. He had never once maligned his guardian's name. So, why had such tales arisen? In his own mind, there could be only one reason—Sir Alan had set them about to defray a hard look at his own activities and subsequent phenomenal wealth.

Over the years, he had tried to discover the source of Sir Alan's wealth, but Sir Alan's influence had prevailed—every door of inquiry had been closed to him, one after the other.

How odd to think that a marriage of convenience, of all things, had led him back to Sir Alan, as well as to the creature before him, who had placed a degree of confidence in the baronet matched only by his own when he had been in his youth.

Perhaps Providence had brought him hither—not for his own sake, but for the sake of the darling beauty before him.

He posed the question uppermost in his mind. "Is Sir Alan presently residing here? I understand he has numerous properties scattered throughout England."

She shook her head. "No, but I have it on good authority that he has given his servants orders to ready his house Wednesday week. So, tell me, Mr. Swinfield, will you marry me?"

He took a deep, steadying breath. All the odd threads of his life had led him there. His common sense bid him run, but another instinct commanded him in this moment, something he could not as yet define. "Yes, Miss Cabot, I will."

The smile which suffused her face lit the room in a rosy glow. "Oh, thank you," she gushed. "You will not regret it, not for a moment, and at the end of the month you will be richer by seventy-five thousand pounds."

He stared at her. "I beg your pardon?"

She chuckled. "I know we did not discuss the figure, and I thought you might be surprised. Are you pleased? Will the sum compensate you for the stigma attached to divorce?"

"I couldn't possibly accept so much," he protested.

"My uncle was worth over half a million on the change alone. His properties . . . well, suffice it to say that I am an extremely wealthy woman—or will be, once I have been married a month. And pray don't argue with me, for I have quite made up my mind to give you the sum I have named."

Lord Villiers was so deeply struck by her generosity, and stunned by the figure mentioned, that he determined then and there to make certain the fee he would be earning for his services would be given to some charity or other. The notion that he would profit in so gross a manner from marrying and divorcing any woman offended his sense of what was noble and right. Only one question remained to be answered—should he tell her who he really was, especially since Redcliffe knew his identity?

Some small, devilish inclination prompted him against revealing himself to her. She had trusted him without knowing who he was, and the fact that she had so thoroughly rejected *Lord Villiers* strictly because of his reputation would make it an excellent and proper joke once his identity became known. Besides, everything would be drawn up legally, so that she would be protected no matter if he turned out to be John Bull himself.

Laurentia had never known anyone quite like Mr. Swinfield. He was an agreeable traveling companion, very knowledgeable on many subjects, replete with anecdotes of every kind and so even-tempered as to make the long journey to Tewkesbury seem but an easy, pleasant jaunt.

Her solicitor, Mr. Crabtree, though astonished by the odd

turn of events, did not entirely disapprove of her scheme. He was a forward-thinking man, and believed a woman should be in charge of her own future.

"And you are certain," she asked, "that there is nothing in my uncle's will which requires me to wed Villiers?"

"No. The wording is such that it was a strong suggestion only. No contracts were signed, and Villiers's response seemed somewhat vague as to his intention of seeing the marriage through."

"Indeed?" she queried, a trifle stunned.

"I said nothing at the time, believing that your uncle had discussed the matter with you and that you had agreed to his choice."

"I am surprised," she responded.

"And why is that?"

"I would have supposed Villiers would have wanted nothing more than to wed me, or any lady of fortune, for that matter."

"There is no accounting for his intentions or desires, since he is not here to explain them." For some reason he glanced for a long, penetrating moment at Mr. Swinfield.

Mr. Swinfield interjected, "Perhaps Lord Villiers had some scruples on the matter. Perhaps it was not to his liking to wed a complete stranger."

Laurentia lifted her brows and stared. "In a thousand years you could not convince me that much is true."

Mr. Swinfield surprised her by laughing. "Then I will only say I must agree with your solicitor—we are not in a way to knowing what his thoughts, motives, or desires might be."

"Any man who would waste his fortune, as Villiers purportedly did, cannot have many scruples, surely."

Her betrothed merely nodded, but did not seem convinced.

When all the documents had been signed, Laurentia bid farewell to Mr. Crabtree.

Once in the outer office, Mr. Swinfield said, "I left my

gloves within. I won't be a moment." He returned swiftly to the office and met the solicitor's serious, frowning gaze.

Villiers addressed the matter at hand. "Never fear. I have no intention of accepting the seventy-five thousand pounds. Instead, I wish to have documents drawn up to the effect that I willingly surrender the amount to Miss Cabot, to be administered by her at her discretion. She may keep the money, or use it to continue her charitable work. Will you see to it? I'll be in Tewkesbury sometime next week to sign the documents."

Mr. Crabtree shook his head. "This is a very bad business, the whole of it."

"Yes, I know. I'm helping her make the best of it."

"Just how long have you known Miss Cabot?" he inquired, bemused.

"She requested I marry her last night, she convinced me this morning, and now we are here."

"Well, it is highly unusual."

"Indeed."

"Though I will not deny I am gravely concerned that Miss Cabot will undergo the scandal of a divorce, I must say I respect your unwillingness to take even a farthing for your services in the matter. I don't know many who would have refused such a sum of money. I begin to suspect you're a very great man."

At that Villiers laughed. "Hardly. I just don't like the notion of tempting fate by accepting such a sum, or any sum. I've little doubt I would pay dearly for it."

"But what of the scandal?" he asked. "Have you considered as much?"

"I will do everything I can to divert the gossip away from Miss Cabot when the time comes."

"Well, I must say I am completely astonished by the role you mean to assume. Can you tell me a little of why you agreed to it?"

How could he explain the impulse he'd had to be party to

her scheme—not because it was a fanciful lark or because he could profit by it, but because he had certain suspicions concerning Sir Alan's interest in her. "I understood enough of her character in having spoken with her last night to comprehend she was completely determined on this course. I felt obligated, as a gentleman, to offer her my services, for if she would ask me to marry her she would certainly ask any other gentleman who appealed to her."

"And there would be some who would not be either so magnanimous or give a fig for her interests. Yet, you do."

"Yes."

"I know my question is impertinent, but may I ask, sir, are you in love with her? Such things have been known to happen."

He shook his head and smiled. "I don't think so, even though there is a great deal to admire in Miss Cabot. I believe the whole of my actions have resulted from the entire situation feeling very familiar to me, an experience from my own youth."

He nodded. "I begin to understand. Only, when do you mean to tell her that besides being mere Mr. Swinfield you are also Viscount Villiers?"

He was slightly taken aback, yet not surprised.

"How did you know?"

"I thought your signature looked familiar. I was reviewing the letter you sent, and found them identical. Only, why the disguise, or rather, this extraordinary masquerade?"

"She despises Villiers. Apparently, gossip concerning me has permeated even the wilds of the Cotswolds. Do you intend to inform her of my deception?"

"I ought to, but, perhaps like Miss Cabot, I also trust you instinctively. So, I will see you then, Wednesday next?"

Villiers nodded.

The solicitor offered his hand. Villiers shook it, approving of his firm grasp. "I was counsel for Mr. Cabot for many,

many years, and not everything I did for him was to my liking. Miss Cabot needs a friend or two at her side during the next few weeks, Just to guide her through. I would even suggest it is likely she will experience rough waters ahead."

"I want you to know that I had fully intended to reject Mr. Cabot's offer, and had arrived in Windrush to do just that. After conversing with Miss Cabot yesterday as well as this morning, I have become convinced that the wind blows ill."

Mr. Crabtree inclined his head. "It may, m'lord. It may."

With that, Villiers retrieved his gloves and quit the office.

He returned to Laurentia, who immediately begged to know if his gloves had become lost. He saw the quizzical look in her eyes and understood then that she was teasing him. He explained that her solicitor took a moment to converse privately with him, offering the opinion that she was in need of friends at this time. "I believe he was hinting that I should number among them."

"I see. Tending to my interests, was he?"

"Yes. And now, my dear, just how and when are we to be married?"

"Why, we are to fly to Gretna, tonight, of course."

He laughed at her teasing manner and, ignoring this sally, begged to know if she felt it would be easier to procure a license from a bishop or if the traditional reading of the banns would suffice.

He handed her into the carriage, and once he had seated himself beside her and wrapped the carriage rug about her legs, she responded, "Mr. Swinfield, I am most in earnest. Perhaps I should have mentioned it earlier, but I do insist we journey to Gretna Green and be married in Scotland as soon as possible. I fully intend to have a great celebration on St. Thomas Day, and must be in possession of my inheritance by then. I absolutely refuse to wait several weeks in order to gain access to my uncle's fortune. As I said before, I have a great deal to accomplish and mean to be about it immediately, and

I don't give a fig for what scandal might erupt by such an elopement as I am insisting on. Besides, there is no telling what Villiers might attempt to do were he to learn I was betrothed to someone else. A desperate man might do anything!"

Villiers was so stunned he did not know what to say. Miss Cabot had of course mentioned her desire to make some changes, but until now he had not quite understood how intent she was on them. There was only one response he could give. "Gretna it is, then."

Three

The journey to Scotland required three days, especially since in many places the roads were nearly impassable with snow. The storm which had blown through on the night Laurentia proposed to Mr. Swinfield had covered much of the northern counties, as well as her home county of Gloucestershire, with a fine layer of white powder.

By the time the parish of Gretna in Scotland had been reached, where marriages were performed by a Scottish parson since the northernmost country was unaffected by English marriage laws, Laurentia knew much of Mr. Swinfield's history. He had received his education at Eton and later Oxford University. He had been orphaned when both parents perished in a coaching accident when he had just turned sixteen. She had sympathized with him readily, having been bereft of her own parents at the age of twelve, which was how she had come to live with her Grandmother Cabot and her Uncle Percival Cabot.

The exchange of this information alone would have been sufficient to form a bond between herself and the good Mr. Swinfield, but since the journey had been as pleasant and agreeable as their first journey—from the village of Windrush to Tewkesbury—she found that by the time they were professing their vows before a kindly Reverend Smith in Gretna, she was in a fair way of thinking of Mr. Swinfield as one of the kindest friends she had ever had the pleasure of knowing. Indeed, more than once she had thought during the journey north, as well as the return trip south, that had her uncle proposed matrimony for her with Mr. Swinfield in the first place she might have actually considered the prospect.

However, even as Mr. Crabtree glanced over the marriage documents and pronounced that according to the law she would come into her inheritance on the twentieth of December—the day before St. Thomas's Day, just as she had hoped—she knew that she could never marry in earnest. She had a duty to fulfill, not to herself but to those she had grown up with in Windrush and in the general environs of Evenlode House. The fortune with which she would be entrusted on that day was already destined for many areas of Gloucestershire which she had carefully investigated since her eighteenth birthday, six years earlier.

So, even though she might cast a longing eye at Mr. Swinfield, especially now when he was kissing her gloved fingers and wishing her every happiness as mistress of her own inheritance, she set aside the glow of warmth his mere presence brought to her heart, knowing nothing could ever come of it. Her mind was set, and she would order her heart to follow the same course as her head. She had for too long a time believed in her mission to do naught else but thank Mr. Swinfield and withdraw her tingling fingers from his tender grasp.

Viscount Villiers had not known such a pleasant time in many years as he had traveling with Laurentia Cabot. Had he ordered a companion to meet his particular requirements in conversation and humor, in philosophy and general understanding, he could not have designed a better one than in Miss Cabot—that is, in Mrs. Adolphus Swinfield. Though he had desired more than once to sweep her into his arms and crush her lips beneath his own, he controlled the insensible, mad

impulses, knowing full well that in a month's time this charming Christmas season with her, this month of companionship,
must end. Even though he knew the strongest desire to hold
her to him and live the rest of his years with her, he would
never allow it, not in a millennium. Ten years ago, when his
fortune had slipped from his grasp unawares, he had promised
himself that he would never marry unless he was able to bring
to that union something substantial.

He had lived for the past decade, since having attained his
majority, by his wits and his skill as a gamester. Miss Cabot
had not been wrong in this. He was indeed a gamester, but he
was honest in his play and careful in his spending, so that
after ten years he had been able to set aside over two thousand
pounds, invested in the funds and growing daily. Until such
time, however, as that amount became ten thousand and he
was able to reopen his home in Somersetshire and live as a
gentleman ought to live, he would remain a vagabond of the
beau monde. He would continue as he had for so many years,
traveling the country from great house, to mansion, to country
manor, enjoying the annual rounds of social events peculiar to
his class and his station, saving every groat possible, and bid-
ing his time until his investments could sustain the fifth viscount, Lord Villiers, in an easy competence before the world.

If he had, in a moment of weakness, responded to Mr. Percival Cabot's letter by accepting the extraordinary offer of his
niece's hand in marriage, who could blame him? At the same
time, since he had told no one of his decision to wed Miss
Cabot, save his valet of course, there would be no untelling
once the divorce took place.

He glanced at Laurentia now, as the carriage drew through
the golden stone gates of the Evenlode Carriage House, and
wondered at the bizarre circumstance which had brought about
the unwanted marriage, anyway, a marriage which in a few
short weeks would culminate in an agreed upon divorce. He
felt as though a strong hand were weighing on his shoulder,

the hand of a force beyond him, demanding that he look and ponder a future he had refused to consider previously.

His chest tightened. Laurentia was wearing an elegant bonnet of forest green velvet, gathered all about the brim and trimmed with a narrow gold band. Over the brim lay an ostrich feather of a pure white. She turned toward him, and the fiery red of her curls and the cream of her complexion made a Christmas portrait against the green of her bonnet that further constricted his chest.

As the carriage turned into the drive leading to Evenlode, she directed his gaze to the mansion. Snow covered the entire hillside upon which the dwelling had been built. The late afternoon sun, even though dulled by winter's light, illuminated the house in a pale glow.

"Good God," he murmured. "I've never seen anything so lovely. The golden hue of the stone is magnificent indeed!"

Laurentia felt her throat tighten as she gazed upon her husband's face. He was still looking at Evenlode, in obvious admiration. She was transfixed by *him*. The *timbre of his voice* had caught her, yet again, as rich and as deep as it was, like a pool of warm water in which one wants to sink up to the chin.

After a time, she glanced out the window to the right as the carriage made its ascent along the well-protected drive to the house. In the narrow vale below, the River Wind meandered slowly to the west, toward Wales. Houses of varying degrees of wealth dotted the landscape, farms littered the valley, and alongside the river a group of children with a strong draft horse caught her attention. "Do but look!" she cried. "They've captured what must be a Yule log. Do you know, I think those are the Marycote children. You will meet them all in the coming weeks, I'm sure. Their mother is a friend of mine, a widow of some two years. A fine woman." She took in a deep breath, a feeling near to euphoria flowing in her chest.

"Why do you smile as you do?" he queried. "Laurentia, you must be the happiest female I've ever known."

"I am, of the moment. Most assuredly I am. You have no idea what my inheritance means to me, or what it will mean to our community. Mrs. Marycote will very soon be the recipient of a goodly sum of money with which to restart her wool-fulling mill."

He frowned slightly as the horses struggled up the last length of drive. "You will be giving her a large sum, then?"

"Not giving. Investing. These are hard times, as you very well know, and the northern factories have changed everything for the countryside. So many have quit Gloucestershire seeking employment elsewhere. Even the village shops have had troubles, with so many leaving as they have. And the orphans are not fed or clothed properly, and take to pilfering the merchants' cupboards. As I told you, there is much work to be done, and I intend to begin at once!"

He was concerned, wondering if she was overzealous in her desire to help those in need. This opinion, however, he kept to himself.

The ground floor of the mansion was of stone, as carefully laid as the entire structure and so smooth as to defy nature. Aubusson carpets of varying hues and patterns stretched along all the rooms and hallways that were visible from the entrance hall.

Laurentia began untying the green silk ribbons of her bonnet and lifted her gaze to the lofty staircase, down which her grandmama was being carried quite carefully by four servants whom she abused at will. "You there! On the left leg! You are out of step with your fellows! Behind me! Why do you lumber along? I feel as though I am on a boat in the middle of the ocean. Have a care! Have a care! What heedless fellows you all are."

Laurentia watched the procession descend the stairs. The

footmen were smiling in spite of her grandmother's cross words.

"Laurentia, you've come home!" she called out.

"With a husband," she responded brightly.

The elegant old woman finally came to rest at the foot of the stairs. She sat imperiously in a gold, silk-striped chair and surveyed both her granddaughter and Mr. Swinfield with a stately dignity which had been her predominate quality since ever Laurentia had known her. She wore a lovely beaded cap from beneath which gray curls peeked, a monocle dangled from a maroon silk ribbon down the front of her well-gathered, long-sleeved gown of fine gray silk, and earbobs of a ruby color adorned her ears.

Laurentia slid her bonnet from off her red curls. She settled the elegant green creation on the long, rectangular table in the center of the entrance hall and moved quickly forward to meet her grandmother.

The elderly woman was shrunken and thin, but a kind of wisdom floated about her wrinkled face and in the soft, curled fingers which found Laurentia's cheek. "Your note was rather cryptic, my dear," she said. "But I am happy to see you have returned safely. Mr. Swinfield's man has been here for some-time now, and I'm certain has all in readiness to—" She broke off suddenly as she glanced at Mr. Swinfield. "Oh! I do beg your pardon, for I see that you decided to marry Villiers, after all. Of course it is quite odd to have Swinfield's man here, but thank God you've come to your senses! Only, whatever did you do with Mr. Swinfield? Did you leave him at the Tump and Dagler?"

Laurentia chuckled. "Grandmama, whatever are you about? Allow me to present Mr. Swinfield to you, after which I believe we should have you fitted with a pair of spectacles! Villiers, indeed!" She turned and beckoned Mr. Swinfield forward. "Mr. Swinfield, I'd like you to meet my grandmother, Mrs. Cabot. Grandmama, Mr. Adolphus Swinfield."

Mrs. Cabot squinted and patted her stomach in order to locate her monocle. "But I was so certain . . ." She raised the single eyeglass to a failing blue eye and stared for a long, hard moment. Laurentia was a little surprised, since ordinarily her grandmother's vision was not so completely hopeless as this. Yet, she could plainly see that the old woman was struggling to make sense of the man before her.

"How do you do, Ma'am?" Mr. Swinfield began gently. "Laurentia has spoken of you in so many kind terms that I consider it an honor to meet you at long last, although I begin to think I may have met you before, have I not?"

Mrs. Cabot frowned and stared a little more. She blinked, opened her eyes wide, and pursed her lips. "Perhaps," she responded in her blunt voice. "So you've obliged my silly granddaughter by agreeing to this ridiculous arrangement."

Laurentia was horrified that her grandmother was speaking of the sham marriage in front of the footmen. *"Grandmama,"* she murmured with raised brows.

"Yes, yes dear," Mrs. Cabot responded. "You are quite right." She huffed and waved an imperious hand toward her servants. "Do go away, the lot of you!" As she rose to her feet, one of the footmen picked up the chair, and together they marched off down the hall toward the nether regions.

"Give me your arm, Swinfield. Ah, that is much better. I'm not so steady on my feet as I was used to be. Don't grow old, Mr. Swinfield! There's nothing but aches and pains, weak knees, and failing eyes. A little slower, if you please. Much better. I've ordered the fire built up in the drawing room in expectation of your return. We'll be comfortable there, and you may tell me all about this wretched business in Gretna! Oh, my! To think that a granddaughter of mine has actually eloped, and plans to divorce! You young people are far too flighty for me. These modern manners and forms! I am getting too old for this world, I tell you. Too old, indeed."

Laurentia laughed as she, too, walked beside her grandmother. "You will outlive us all, dearest, so you don't fool me by half by saying such a thing. Only tell me, when did Villiers arrive, and did you have much trouble in fobbing him off after he read my letter?"

"I must be losing my mind," Mrs. Cabot replied. She paused in her tracks and once more stared at Mr. Swinfield. "Villiers never arrived, it was the oddest thing! Nor has there been even the smallest piece of correspondence by his hand. I consider the whole situation quite vexing, not to mention that such conduct reflects manners of the shabbiest!"

"I don't give a fig for that," Laurentia responded, "though I daresay you are very right. However, I shall choose to be grateful his lordship failed to appear. Indeed, how could I be otherwise?"

Once settled in the drawing room, Laurentia told in vivid detail the course of the journey to Gretna Green, her disappointment that she wouldn't be married by a blacksmith, after all, her solicitor's belief all females should have sole control of their fortunes, and numerous instances of her husband's kind nature.

Mrs. Cabot turned to him abruptly. "I do like that man of yours, what's his name—Coxcomb?"

Laurentia chuckled and met Mr. Swinfield's laughing eyes. "Not Coxcomb, Grandmama!"

"What?" Mrs. Cabot cried. "Did I say that? Oh, Vill—I mean, Mr. Swinfield, I do beg your pardon. It's Coxwell, isn't it? It would seem he has quite taken over the entire house. Even the housekeeper, who has the worst temperament of any female I've seen within fifty miles of Evenlode, bows to his superior knowledge. I've never witnessed anything of the kind before. I was introduced to him when I met him in the hallway outside my niece's chambers—yours are next door, and mine are just across the hall so it was natural to see him there. He is quite refined, and has a considerable air about him."

"Indeed, I believe you are right," Mr. Swinfield said. "I

often receive compliments on his behalf, although I am convinced a great deal of his popularity is due to the fact that he knows how to get a stain out of just about every fabric imaginable."

"Well, that would explain it then, wouldn't it? Though I don't doubt you will be grateful to be back in his capable hands after making such a madcap dash to the border and back in less than a sennight."

"I will confess it, though I daresay I might give some offense to my wife by admitting as much."

"You may say whatever you like, Mr. Swinfield," Laurentia said grandly. "Because I cannot tell you how much I look forward to *my maid's* ministrations this evening."

Mrs. Cabot glanced from one visage to the next as the couple before her held one another's gaze for the longest moment. She was shocked, severely so, on more than one score, and was still reeling from the truth so plain before her that Laurentia, quite unawares, had married the very man she had been determined to jilt. So what, then, was Villiers's game?

Her gaze drifted toward the viscount, who leaned forward and gave his wife's hand a gentle squeeze. Did he hope to woo the heiress and persuade her to remain married to him? Was he such a fool as to think that his identity would forever remain unknown to the lady, or that once it was known she would ever forgive him? Beyond these rather obvious questions was a larger one—was it possible love could actually blossom in a marriage that would be dissolved in a month's time?

She knew what she wanted to do, for she had only Laurentia's happiness in mind, but before she could act she must know the truth of Villiers's intentions. She therefore turned to her niece and said, "Laurentia, my dear, would you be so good as to fetch my shawl? I left it in my chamber, and I find I've grown rather chilled."

Laurentia appeared ready to protest, but she quickly stopped herself and rose to her feet. "I can see by the hour that I must begin dressing if I am to be ready for dinner in time to please Cook. Why don't I send a servant to you with your shawl that I might place myself in my maid's care? Would that be agreeable to you?"

"Perfectly. I shall send Mr. Swinfield to you shortly."

Laurentia leaned down to place a kiss on her cheek. "I missed you, darling one," she said softly.

"And I you, my pet. The house seemed awfully big while you were gone."

"I imagine it did. Well, I'll leave you to become a little better acquainted with my husband."

When Laurentia's skirts had disappeared from the room, Villiers turned toward her. "There is something I have been pondering since I first met your granddaughter, Mrs. Cabot. How on earth did such a charming creature escape being married beforetimes?"

Mrs. Cabot leaned back in her chair. "Villiers," she stated firmly, "fetch me a sherry—a large one, if you please. We've a few details to discuss, you and I. Maybe I'll answer your question, and maybe I won't. For the present, do as I bid, for I find my head is swimming!"

"Of course, Madame," he responded seriously. He rose and fulfilled her request, handing the sherry to her and taking his own glass to a seat opposite the fine old woman.

Sipping the nut-flavored wine, Mrs. Cabot eyed him thoughtfully and consideringly for a long, long moment. Finally, she spoke, responding to his original question. "Laurentia was betrothed twice before wedding you. Ah, I see by your expression, she did not tell you."

"No, she did not."

Mrs. Cabot nodded. "The subject, undoubtedly, still wounds her. She, of course, would never admit to it, yet her silence tells me more than were she to weep and wail for a fortnight—although I do recall hearing muffled sobs from behind her bedchamber door some few years past. She never wept openly.

She is a very private person in that regard. This you must know about her if you intend for the marriage to last."

"I intend no such thing," he stated, a sudden frown splitting his brows.

"I am confused, then, for I can comprehend no other reason for your having wedded her in the first place." When a maid approached, she fell silent on the subject, permitting the servant to carefully drape a shawl about her shoulders.

When she was gone, Villiers leaned forward, laying his forearms across his knees and holding his sherry with both hands clasped together. "Since you know my identity, I can only presume you also know the vile extent of my reputation."

"I don't pay a great deal of heed to gossip," she replied, her eyes piercing and shrewd. "I prefer to take a man's measure when I meet him. Besides, there were as many reports of your good character as their were rumors of your having lost your fortune at the gaming tables."

"But I did no such thing," he stated firmly, meeting her narrowed eyes directly. "Rumors surfaced to that effect, but only several years after my fortune vanished quite suddenly and unexpectedly. I don't know how the rumors began, though for the past few years I have held certain suspicions. These tales you've heard are false—entirely so."

"Then what happened to your fortune, if you did not spend it in the East End Hells?" she inquired bluntly.

"That can only be a matter of conjecture on my part. Will you promise to keep your peace if I tell you something of which only a scant few have knowledge?"

She nodded gravely.

"My guardian, a fortnight after I had attained my majority, informed me that the numerous investments to which I had agreed over the years had become insolvent, and that the whole of my inheritance, most unfortuitously, had vanished because of that. He was very sorry, even deeply and humbly apologetic. I was devastated at the time, but as the years wore on, and I gained a little Town Bronze and a bit of knowledge of how investments and guardianships were supposed to function, I began to wonder at just how the Villiers's fortune could have disappeared as it did. Another circumstance made me question the honesty of my guardian, since his fortunes had multiplied immensely during those intervening years."

"What you are saying is that you suspect your guardian of having cheated you out of your entire inheritance," she stated, obviously horrified.

He nodded. "Yes, but I have no proof. You asked what possessed me to agree to your granddaughter's schemes, and I must respond by telling you that it is because of my guardian. It would seem he has expressed a great deal of interest in Laurentia, that he has asked for her hand in marriage more than once in the past several years. If what I believe of him is true, I fear for her. And since I learned he lives in the vicinity of Windrush, I thought perchance I might be able to discover for myself what happened to my own fortune and what his intentions toward your granddaughter truly are."

Mrs. Cabot, who had finished her sherry, now settled the small crystal glass on the kidney-shaped table at her elbow. Her eyes were wide with shock. She leaned heavily back into her chair. "I always knew there was something wrong with that man. But Laurentia is of such a sweet, trusting nature that she would never divine the worst in him, as I believe I have."

"You know, then, to whom I am referring."

"Sir Alan Redcliffe," she murmured, her lips drooping into a frown. "He was my son's bosom beau, and to my knowledge his partner in many business transactions. I remember when Redcliffe's fortune began to exceed all expectations, amazingly so. It was over ten years ago. That was when Redcliffe began construction on his house." She snorted. "Not a house, precisely. More like a gothic castle. You have seen it, haven't you? Windstone Manor? Even the name is an impertinence!"

He shook his head.

"Have Laurentia take you to view the monstrosity. He says it is built in the style of the picturesque so popular today. I think it a complete disgrace. When I asked him how he had been able to afford such an edifice, one of a number of houses he owns throughout the island, he said that an investment in the West Indies, a sugar or tobacco plantation—employing black slaves, no doubt—had proved enormously profitable."

Villiers stared at her. "He said as much? Do you recall the details? The name perhaps of the plantation?"

"No. I'm sorry, I do not. It was a long time ago."

"Sir Alan told me the plantation had failed—a blight had wiped out the crops. I remember it most specifically, the day he spoke of all the investments which had failed, thereby reducing me to a state of penury—a West Indies plantation had been the prime cause of my loss of fortune."

Mrs. Cabot shook her head again. "That must have been a lie, for according to Redcliffe it did not fail. My son also invested that year in the plantation, and earned quite an increase to his own fortune. I remember it as clearly as I recall the conversation. He was quite *aux anges,* and said he had made the investment a year prior, had earned a substantial profit, and had just formed a partnership with Sir Alan that would double his own fortune in just two or three years. He was content for at least a sennight. I recall it all quite vividly."

"What years did these investments cover?"

She blinked several times. "The first year was eighteen oh three, I think."

Villiers fell silent, the gravity of the situation striking him deeply. Was it possible that after all these years he had stumbled into the very place that would give him the answers he had been seeking since times out of mind? Part of him felt dizzy with exhilaration—he might at last be able to prove his suspicions concerning Sir Alan's guardianship of his fortune. On the other hand, some heaviness within his chest sent a warning that he was not involved with just his own past but with Laurentia's future, as well.

Mrs. Cabot leaned forward and covered one of his hands with her own. "I refuse to permit you to be overset on this your first night in your bridal home. Yes, yes, I know the marriage is naught but a masquerade, but for this time, this month, it is a very real thing. I can see that you have already formed a fondness for my granddaughter. For her sake, then, shake off this brown study into which you've fallen. I daresay Coxcomb is awaiting you."

"Coxwell," he corrected her gently.

Mrs. Cabot chuckled. "I was just funning. Go on, then."

Once dressed for dinner, Villiers knocked on the door which adjoined his chamber to his wife's on impulse, thinking he might escort her to the dining room. He heard a hushed command excusing her maid, a trill of feminine giggles, a closing of the door to the hall, and finally Laurentia's voice beckoning him to enter. A new bride was always the object of much curiosity, and her new husband of much speculation.

Opening the door, he found Laurentia standing near her looking glass. He caught his breath, for she was absolutely lovely in a gown of white silk adorned with gold tassels. Her hair had been properly dressed high on her head and threaded with a gold ribbon. Her curls cascaded everywhere, with an exquisite fringe across her forehead drawing attention to her lovely green eyes.

"Is your room to your liking?" she asked.

"Very much so. Everything is of the first elegance."

Her expression changed from one of delight to that of sweetness, and perhaps a little shyness. "You deserve nothing less for having joined me in this completely madcap adventure."

He crossed the chamber and took up her hands in his own. He kissed the backs of them, the lace of her gloves tingling his lips. Nothing but devotion and admiration was in his mind and heart in that moment, except perhaps a little warm gratitude. "I must confess I am overcome, Laurentia. Everything about you is beyond wonderful, and I mean that most sincerely. I consider it an honor to be of service to you."

Laurentia lost all sense of where she was. Her heart was trembling as she gazed into Mr. Swinfield's eyes, just as it had a hundred times or so since having met him a sennight past. She was still amazed at how she felt when she was near him. She could think of only one thing, of the moment—what it had been like to be kissed by him, beneath the mistletoe, the night she met him.

The truth stunned her as the sentiments of her heart slipped into her mind. She realized she wanted him to kiss her again, quite desperately. "Mr. Swinfield," she whispered, "would you—?" She couldn't bring the words to life. She felt horridly brazen at the thought of requesting a kiss. Besides, whatever was she thinking? She couldn't go about kissing her husband, not by half, not when she intended to divorce him in just a few more weeks.

Oh, but she did so want to!

Villiers knew precisely what his bride was thinking, and the knowledge that she was longing to be kissed worked in him like a kind of madness. He wanted to oblige her, more than was good for either of them. She slid a hand from his grasp and laid her fingers gently on the smooth superfine of his black coat, quite near his heart on the left side. The invitation was gentle, elegant, and unambiguous. Whatever was he going to do?

Four

Mrs. Cabot watched her granddaughter and her grandson-in-law carefully through dinner. They seemed to be sharing some kind of joke, for he would catch her eye and she couldn't restrain a smile, and then, a few moments later, her gaze would attach to his, and he'd emit a chuckle or two. She couldn't help but wonder what the substance of their private amusement had been. Even more so, the very nature of their intimate exchange was prompting all sorts of notions to enter her own head.

For one thing, she began to consider the possibility of having the old sleigh polished with wax, the leather seats rubbed and softened, and the silver bells attached to that beautiful Spanish harness her husband had given her on their fifth wedding anniversary. She could remember having taken Laurentia on sleigh rides with her husband, but that had been many, many years ago when Laurentia had been but a child. When her husband passed away, she had refused to ride in the sleigh, for the experience had evoked far too many tender remembrances to be in the least degree comfortable for her.

But now, well, she was beginning to catch a vision that so appealed to the latent romance of her soul that—unless the poor sleigh had been eaten by worms—she rather thought it was time to resurrect the old beast. When Villiers lifted a cup to Laurentia and she burst out into a trill of laughter, Mrs. Cabot was sure of it. Whatever were the pair laughing about?

Later, in the drawing room, Villiers guided his bride to the pianoforte. "Your grandmama has boasted of your abilities far too much to have you deny me a song or two, unless of course you are greatly fatigued from the journey."

She tossed her curls. "How could I be fatigued when I have laughed through dinner?" He watched her cheeks turn a delightful rose, and he smiled in response.

"How could you, indeed?"

Laurentia giggled again, and once more Villiers was caught up in the absurd but quite endearing encounter in her chambers before dinner. . . .

He had succumbed to his own desire to oblige his wife by kissing her. He had leaned toward her, quite purposefully, and she had seemed most hopeful.

However, at the very moment his lips might have touched hers, her knees had buckled. Though he tried to support her, she slipped from his grasp and slid to the floor, whereupon she promptly fell into a fit of the giggles.

"Of all the absurdities!" she had cried, over and over.

He had been a little embarrassed at first, then charmed, utterly and completely, for her laughter, which soon became a trill, filled her bedchamber. She sat on the floor, her white silk gown surrounding her like drifts of snow, her hands covering her face. She did not look up at him, but occasionally wiped at her eyes.

Eventually, he had lifted her to her feet, but she had been unable to do more than blush and apologize for her ridiculously weak knees that couldn't even support her to enjoy a kiss, all the while trilling her laughter until he, too, was smiling and laughing.

In the end, he was grateful for the silly incident, for it had prevented him from kissing her, and God knew he didn't need to be kissing this adorable, charming creature!

He how had to admit, though, as he settled Laurentia in a chair before the pianoforte and as she began removing her gloves, that he was in considerable danger once more of throwing caution to the wind and taking her up in his arms as he had the first day he met her. He could only be grateful, therefore, that Mrs. Cabot was present, for he rather suspected that she, alone, was preventing a second attempt.

Laurentia opened her book of music and, after searching through the pieces, settled on a familiar Mozart sonata. Villiers drew forward a chair to watch her fingers ply the ivory keys. She soon became lost in the intricate piece, playing with both skill and artistry. He was again struck by the gem she was—a perfect emerald, cut to perfection, glimmering great beauty from every aspect.

He wondered at her grandmother's revelation that she had been engaged twice before, or nearly so. Why had the romances fallen off? Surely not for any fault of Laurentia's!

The longer he stayed within her sphere the more one mystery after another arose. Where would he find the answers?

Mozart was followed by several traditional Christmas carols—"Silent Night," "O Christmas Tree," and one that reminded him of the night he met her, "Here We Go a Wassailing." Her voice was pure but not always directly on pitch, a circumstance which made him smile. His emerald, it would seem, was in possession of a flaw, after all.

She rose at last from the fine rosewood instrument when the clock struck nine. She stretched out her fingers and shook her hands gently, then lifted a hand to her lips and yawned.

Country hours again!

He gathered up her gloves and handed them to her. "Perhaps we ought to retire." She agreed readily.

Mrs. Cabot declined to be escorted upstairs, saying that she had some minor business to attend to with the housekeeper but would look forward to seeing them both in the morning. To Laurentia she said, "I'm glad you've come home, dearest."

"As am I, Grandmama," she responded, leaning down and kissing her cheek, which seemed to be a sweet habit with her.

To Villiers, when he bowed over her hand, Mrs. Cabot whispered, "I am wishful you should remain longer than a month, but if you indeed cannot, bless you, Villiers, for saving my granddaughter's inheritance."

"My pleasure, Ma'am," he responded sincerely.

When he was mounting the stairs beside Laurentia, she said, "I am all agog to know what Grandmama whispered in your ear." She glanced at him and tweaked his arm. "You must tell me, for it is not at all like her to tell secrets, especially not in the presence of others."

Villiers laughed and sought about in his mind to discover some whisker he could tell her. He did not have far to reach, and the nature of it was such that he could not resist saying, "Only that she wishes I would stay forever."

"What a rapper!" she cried. "She would never say such a thing to you, not when she has known you but a day."

"Why not?" he countered readily. "You knew me but a handful of minutes and asked me to marry you."

"Oh, that was very sly of you, and now I do not know whether to believe you or not. Does she really wish you to stay?"

Was there a gleam of hope in her eye? Yet what would that matter? He could never stay. He had nothing to bring to this lovely heiress, with her eyes like emeralds and her smile like heaven, except a ramshackle estate in Somersetshire. "In truth, I cannot say for certain, since she seems to enjoy teasing me."

Laurentia chuckled. "She does at that, Mr. Swinfield, and why shouldn't she, for you are very much the gentleman and never seem in the least overset by anything she might say. You have a great deal of countenance and restraint. I believe she admires you very much, as do I."

He warmed toward her, quite deeply, yet again. Faith, she had but to flatter him a little and his soul set to burning, longing for much more from her than a month's sojourn as her husband. "I wish you will not call me Mr. Swinfield," he said at last, unwilling to address even the smallest ruminations of his heart, "not when we have become such fast friends."

"Adolphus, then?" she queried. "It is quite an unusual name. One never hears of it."

"I was named for my grandfather, my mother's father. I never knew him, but apparently he was a clever man and a kind father, traits my mother wished for in me. However, since I share two other Christian names, I beg you will choose between Thomas or Michael."

"Oh, let it be Thomas!" she cried. "For I once had a most excellent friend named Thomas—not a real friend, just someone imaginary with whom I shared my most secret thoughts. Would you mind that? I know it must sound quite silly, and very childish, but as you've already seen this is a rather large house, and I had to fill it with someone who would listen to my youthful ramblings."

"I shall be your Thomas, then," he stated, reaching the top step.

She fell silent as he walked her to her door, her arm still wrapped about his in the nicest way. "Well, I shall say good night to you then, Thomas, and Merry Christmas. I am convinced this shall be the finest Michaelmas of them all with you here. How shall I ever repay you for accepting the terms of this marriage? How can I ever convince you how much this means to me?"

"I am convinced." He leaned forward and placed a kiss on her forehead. He longed to drop to her lips and taste of her sweet innocence, but he refused to succumb to the temptation. He felt certain it would be all too easy to make her love him—given her sense of loyalty, her gratitude for his part in the charade, and her trusting disposition.

"Goodnight, then," she said with a smile.

"Goodnight."

When she passed into her room and the door closed behind her, Villiers stared at the fine-grained wood panels for some time. A question rose to mind which he was certain would soon begin to plague him. What would happen to that untried, innocent trust once she learned of his true identity? Would she ever forgive him for being the infamous Lord Villiers?

He turned abruptly and made his way to his own bedchamber. Whatever the answer to that question might be, he had no desire to know. Entering his room and closing the door quietly behind him, he recalled that earlier he had instructed his valet to learn what he could from the staff concerning anything they might know about Sir Alan Redcliffe.

When Coxwell began to undress him, he queried, "Did you learn anything of Redcliffe?"

"Yes. He is not due to return to Windrush for another fortnight."

"Excellent. As far as I know, he is the only personage Laurentia has mentioned to me, of which there have been dozens, who would know me. What of Quince?"

"He is gone to Redcliffe's house. The particulars of his business are unknown at this time."

"Do your best to discover what they might be."

"Of course, m'lor—that is, of course, sir."

Laurentia moved to the center of her bedchamber and slowly drew off her lace gloves once more. She tossed them one after another onto the forest green, velvet counterpane which covered her bed. How pretty they looked, like little mounds of snow against a bed of pine needles. She felt oddly, yet wondrously, lost. She tried to force her mind to one spot, that she might consider what ought to be done about her growing affection for Thomas Swinfield. Instead, however, her mind seemed as fluid as a melody that went on and on without end, refusing to let the music to stop, refusing to allow the necessary work of setting her heart against Mr. Swinfield to begin.

She remained, therefore, standing in the middle of her bedchamber for a long, long time, sighing and sighing once more. Everything she had believed about her future seemed to be shifting beneath her feet, like sand before a strong wind. The moment her uncle's will had been read to her, of which she had presumed she would be the sole beneficiary, she had been living as one caught in a whirlwind. From the time she could remember, she had known she would one day inherit his fortune and had planned accordingly, dreaming of how she would conduct her life and how she would allocate every tuppence of his accumulated wealth. When she learned that her uncle had arranged a marriage between herself and Lord Villiers—who she soon learned was a hardened gamester she must wed a month before coming into her inheritance—she had been beside herself with the severest anxiety. Villiers's reputation had not been her sole concern in the situation. Once a man entered her future, what control would she then have over her fortune?

None, was the singular response.

When she had received word, through Sir Alan Redcliffe's kind counsel, of Villiers's reputation, she had been utterly horrified, especially since by that time he was known to be en route to Gloucestershire in order to marry her. Her arrival at the inn, and her subsequent good fortune in finding so estimable a gentleman as Mr. Adolphus Thomas Michael Swinfield willing to help her, was nothing short of a miracle. But then, the Christmas season had always been a time of miracles for her, ever since she could remember.

She crossed her chamber and gave a strong tug on the bellpull, summoning her maid. Afterward, she moved to the windows which overlooked the hill behind the mansion. In the dark of night, the beech grove, shrouded as it was in snow, appeared only as an inky silhouette against a star-studded, crisp, wintry sky.

She drew the velvet curtains about her, as she had been wont to do as a child, so that not even the smallest ray of candlelight could intrude to disturb her view of the heavens.

Her heart began to swell with wonder. The stars twinkled all over the sky. She had always thought of them as making little jokes for her benefit and laughing along with her. They were her friends, just as the *Thomas* of her childhood was her friend, and as now Thomas Swinfield was her friend. She drew in a deep breath. He was changing her future. She could feel it as surely as she could feel the soft velvet against her curled, gloveless fingertips.

She knew that he had changed everything for her, because now she would never be required to marry in order to possess her inheritance. Yet, some instinct warned her that a man who could make her knees buckle merely by leaning toward her as though he meant to kiss her was a man who could change everything in other ways, as well!

Tears suddenly stung her eyes. She felt a choice swoop toward her, like a gust of wind topping the hill and swiftly riding the currents toward the river below. She squeezed her eyes shut. She did not want to make another choice. She had made enough in the past sennight, of running from Villiers and of taking Swinfield to husband, of having him sign a document promising to divorce her in a month, of fleeing to Gretna Green, of all places! She opened her eyes. No, she did not wish to make any more choices, not now, not tonight, not with all these lovely stars funning and twinkling and willing to make her laugh.

Perhaps she was unable to make a choice, but she could make a decision, and so she resolved, not for the first time, to keep herself somewhat distant from Mr. Swinfield, from *Thomas*. He would understand. She had seen the same indecision in his own eye, the reluctance, just before he had leaned forward in an attempt to kiss her. He, too, showed every disinclination for the marriage to continue.

Oh, but what would it be like to have a true marriage with someone like Thomas?

When her maid scratched on the door, she heaved a sigh of relief. At least with Emmy present, she would not be alone with her thoughts. And if Emmy stayed long enough, she would be so tired that she would fall asleep without once thinking of how nice it would be have Thomas Swinfield for a husband in earnest.

"Come," she called out brightly.

Emmy entered on a quick step. She was breathing hard, and indeed she had arrived quickly from the nether regions, but there was a smile on her cherry red lips. "I ran the entire way, Miss, I did. Ye must tell me everything about the new master. 'e is that 'andsome, 'e is. Wat a lucky girl ye are, after all! But then, Christmas always were yer luckiest time of year, weren't it?"

Laurentia nodded. "Indeed, it always has been." She thought of Thomas, and of her strange marriage. A chill suddenly drove through her. Would her luck hold, or had she tempted fate sorely by whisking Thomas off to Gretna, with hardly a by-your-leave, to wed him?

The next day the sun rose once more over the wintry countryside. Many of the lanes were already running with snow-melt, though scattered patches of icy snow were held immobile by the shade of overhanging branches. Laurentia was bundled up warmly in a thick pelisse of black wool trimmed in red. On her lap was an enormous muff of a matching wool, stuffed with more feathers than could be found in three plump pillows. Her booted feet rested on several of the bricks which were kept warmed in constant readiness on Cook's hearth exclusively for the calling of carriages.

Beside her, Mr. Swinfield, that is, *Thomas,* appeared positively splendid in his many-caped greatcoat of a fine gray Merino, glossy beaver hat, moderate shirt-points held rigid by a white neckcloth—the latter arranged to perfection by Coxwell, no doubt—and black pantaloons. His gloves were of a fine York tan, and his Hessians, dangling with gold tassels, were nearly as shiny as his hat, a mark which she had long since come to understand was the true sign of a superior valet.

"So, what you are saying, Laurentia, is that you believe the manager of the orphanage has been pilfering the funds allocated to the children since times out of mind."

"How else could one possibly explain the destitution of the place? You will see what I mean once we arrive. My uncle, though clutchfisted to a fault, had once told me of the sums the orphanage had use of for coal, clothing, food, and bedding for the children. Yet, all the orphans go about in rags, they are thin as rails, to the last of them, and I doubt, sincerely, that there is even a chunk of coal to heat them through the worst part of the winter. We have lost more children every January and February than you can imagine, but whenever I approached my uncle on the subject, he told me to mind my own affairs and to leave God to care for the orphans.

"Well, I can't tell you how difficult that was for me to hear when I was convinced a small donation, certainly from the vantage of his bulging pocketbook, would have helped God enormously in saving the lives of these poor little ones, regardless of who was to blame. Of course, I could never have suggested to him that I suspected mismanagement on the part of Mr. Frome, who oversees the orphanage."

Thomas appeared to turn this over in his mind and finally said, "I don't like to mention it, but the portrait you have painted of your uncle over the past sennight is not an entirely pleasing one."

"My uncle, God rest his soul, was a coldhearted miser who cared nothing for me, nor for anyone else, during his lifetime, including his own mother. He wrested from his tenant farmers more rent than any of them could afford, and never once gave me a present, even when I was a child, not even during Yuletide or on my birthday. What do you say to that?"

"First, that I cannot imagine how you could smile through such an unhappy speech, and secondly, how was it possible in the face of such indifference you developed a heart so large and grand as it is?"

"That is a lovely compliment. Ah, we are nearing the orphanage. You will note that the sky is completely clear of even the smallest wisp of coal smoke."

"So it is."

Ten minutes later, Mr. Frome was greeting them in the icy foyer of the orphanage. His nose was thin and pink-tipped, and he wore a muffler about his neck, mittens on his hands, and a thick woolen coat over trousers of the same fabric. He was congested as he spoke, sniffling at the same time. "Had I known you were arriving, Miss, er—"

"Mrs. Swinfield," Laurentia offered coolly. "May I present my husband, Mr. Swinfield?"

"Very pleased to meet you, sir," he said, clearly miserable in his suffering as he offered a polite bow. He turned to Laurentia and bowed again, "And my best wishes for your every happiness." With a sneeze he turned and bowed once more to Thomas. "And my congratulations. I'm sure you will be very happy. There is not a kinder soul in the whole of the vale than your lovely wife."

Laurentia was a little taken aback by this speech, and would almost have pitied Mr. Frome had she not suspected he had been for years robbing the orphanage of its funds.

"As I was saying earlier," Mr. Frome continued, "had I known you would be visiting I should have had some of the children present to greet you in song, though I must confess at present we have something of a fever going about, so perhaps your unannounced visit was in this way fortuitous." He weaved slightly on his feet and blinked ominously several times.

Laurentia laid her hand impulsively on Mr. Frome's arm and steadied him. "Sir! You do not look in the least well. Why on earth are you not in your sickbed?"

"Who would look after things, Ma'am?" His expression was stoney, she thought. She didn't understand him at all.

"Well, I am sorry for your illness. As it happens, I have come on a matter of business. Are you well enough to answer a few questions for me?"

He nodded. "I daresay you will wish to review the accounts as your uncle was used to do."

Laurentia blinked. She didn't know her uncle had done so. He was on the board of regents for the facility, but she had been little aware of his activities. "Why, yes, I would," she stated, hoping she sounded as though she wasn't taken entirely unawares by his comment. "That is one of the reasons I've come."

"Very good, Ma'am. If you will both follow me."

Mr. Frome was very thin, and his shuffling gait brought the worst sort of presentiment coursing through Laurentia's already breaking heart.

Once within his office, however, he immediately withdrew two black ledgers. "One for October and the other November. You will want to take them with you, of course. The various tradesmen's receipts are in an envelope in the back of each book."

Laurentia took up the first volume and seated herself in a chair near Mr. Frome's spartan desk. She perused the first week's expenditures, which were oddly low, and lifting her face to him said, "This can't possibly be right, Mr. Frome. I wish to tell you quite plainly that I have for some time questioned your management here, and now I've seen the figures. Being a person acquainted with the cost of running a house of my own, I don't hesitate to tell you I see a grievous disparagement between what would be reasonable for a facility such as this and the figures you have listed here."

"Perhaps you will wish to do as your uncle did," he suggested, his expression dull-eyed. "Whenever he felt a figure was inappropriate, he deducted the sum from the subsequent month."

Laurentia tried to make sense of this. "I'm afraid I don't quite understand what you are trying to tell me. However, there is a question I wish to pose to you. I hope you will forgive me for being blunt, but have you perchance been stealing from the orphans by way of cheating them of sufficient food and coal?"

Mr. Frome paled, even the cold pink of his nose turning a chalky white. In a whisper, he responded, "Of all the cruelties to speak to me, after these many years of . . . of—"

He was trembling, and began weaving once more on his feet.

Thomas rose suddenly. "Here now, Mr. Frome, please seat yourself! I can see that Mrs. Swinfield has given you a shock. Yes, that's it. Do sit down and compose yourself."

Laurentia scooted forward to the edge of her chair. "Please, tell me the truth, Mr. Frome. I promise I shall not prosecute, but don't you think it would be best if we began on a basis of complete honesty?"

Mr. Frome blew his nose soundly into a kerchief, then replaced the rumpled ball in the pocket of his coat. He was breathing with some effort. "I have never stolen anything in my life. I grew up in this orphanage from the age of three, but during a time when there was plenty of food and coal for all. Eventually, I rose to oversee the facility myself. We hardly had any children die in those days. But good Mr. Cabot, your grandfather, was the prominent trustee at the time. With his passing things soon changed, and not for the better, for his son, your uncle, took the helm. I can understand that you might believe that I was at fault. After all, I am in charge. But I can do little more than what the trustees allocate to me, and the only member of the board who ever addressed me was your uncle."

Laurentia stared at the figures in front of her, not wanting to believe what she was hearing. Though Mr. Frome had only implied the truth, she knew enough of her uncle to comprehend the rest. "He systematically cut the funds," she whispered, almost to herself. After a long moment, she lifted her gaze to him.

"I never had control of a tuppence. Mr. Cabot paid the tradesmen's bills himself, as well as the staff wages. You will of course wish to speak with the tradesmen, to ascertain the validity of the enclosed receipts."

Laurentia slowly closed the book and sighed heavily. "I will need do no such thing. I wish to apologize for my wrongful accusations."

"Of course you loved your uncle, and I'm certain—"

"Oh, but I did not," she stated firmly. "Yes, I know it is hardly seemly to say as much, since he is no longer with us, but you cannot imagine the chagrin I have experienced over the years at knowing how severely his miserly ways affected our entire community. I just never supposed that he would have gone so far . . . as to . . ." She simply couldn't complete her thought, for it was too wicked, too vile to pass her lips. Her throat grew very tight as she strove to regain her own composure.

Finally, she continued. "I wish to assure you that I shall be tending to the requirements of your facility this very day— proper bedding, food, clothes. You will no longer watch the children perish due to failing health or a lack of food or proper winter heating, I promise you that much. As for requiring to look at the books, I expect I shall have to do just that, at least for a time, until I can see for myself exactly what the proper maintenance of the orphanage will be. Oh, and I shall send for my physician in Tewkesbury to come at once and see what can be done about the fever you mentioned earlier."

Overcome, Mr. Frome blinked and strove to speak, but his lips were trembling. When he could order his vocal chords to respond, he said, "I have been *praying* for this day to come. I swear it is so."

Laurentia rose to her feet. "May I take these ledgers with me? And I would presume then that the rest are presently at Evenlode House?"

"Of course you may take these, and as far as I know the volumes for the past ten years have been kept at your home."

Laurentia extended her hand to him. "Thank you for your time. Expect a number of deliveries to begin arriving this afternoon."

He was so moved that he rounded the desk and clasped her extended hand in both of his. "You are giving us our Christmas miracle, Mrs. Swinfield. I shall be forever in your debt, so long as I live. If there is anything I can ever do to repay you for this great kindness, you have but to summon me and I shall come at once."

Laurentia smiled falteringly and spoke softly, "I only wish I could have done something years ago. But my uncle was a hard man."

Mr. Frome nodded. "No one will ever blame you. The fault will always lie solely at his door."

Five

By the time all the arrangements had been made for the orphanage, the hour had advanced nearly to five o'clock, which was the dinner hour for Evenlode. Laurentia hurried up the staircase, her hand on Thomas's arm as together they mounted the many steps leading to the first floor.

At her door, he prevented her from entering her chamber. "One moment, please, Laurentia," he whispered.

She turned toward him and found him but a breath away. He looked deeply into her eyes. "You were magnificent today, an avenging angel. I've never seen so many shopkeepers scurrying about in that fashion before."

Laurentia felt sheepish. "I was so angry, you see. I know I was barking one order after another, but I kept thinking about my wretched uncle and all those starving children! I became furious."

"You certainly did," he agreed with a smile. "At times your cheeks were nearly the color of your hair."

She stared into blue eyes lit with humor and not a little admiration. She thought certainly there was something she ought to say in this moment, but she became utterly bereft of speech, even though her lips parted quite strangely. The sole response which issued from her throat was a thready, "Oh."

Villiers felt himself slide into her eyes, a long fluid motion which robbed him of speech. He was, for this moment, completely lost, just as he had been lost several times before during the course of the day as he witnessed the generosity of his wife's heart. He had spoken truly when he called her an avenging angel, for she was making right a terrible wrong.

Her last act involved sending a stableboy, with the perMission of the landlord of the Tump and Dagler Inn, to her physician, Dr. Ignatious Ward of Tewkesbury, summoning him to treat a rampant fever at the Windrush Orphanage. Villiers had been wholly at her service, waiting on her the entire day so that she could be free to accomplish one of what he came to understand were many missions she meant to complete as soon as she was in possession of her inheritance.

He had found himself moved beyond words, perhaps not more so than because she stood in stark contrast to most of the ladies of quality with whom he was acquainted. Such zeal was as unusual as it was remarkable, and he could think of no one, male or female, who equaled her passion for initiating change.

With all these thoughts moving swiftly about in his head, he finally said, "whatever your uncle's faults might have been, I am fully persuaded your having inherited his fortune will be a form of justice such as this vale has never before witnessed."

"But he wished for Villiers to inherit his fortune," she said darkly.

"Ah, Villiers, again." Something within his heart sank. Her opinion of *his lordship* came forward to nip at him. He wished more than anything that his unfortunate reputation had not preceded him, for then . . . but what was he thinking, that if she learned of his identity, she then might regard him in a hopeful light? To what end?

Still, as he looked into her eyes, at the swell of interest he found reflected there, he couldn't help but wish that he had met her under more propitious circumstances. He knew only one thing for certain—he wished to kiss her more than anything on earth at the moment, and he knew with equal certainty she wished for it, as well.

Only with the strongest effort of his will was he able to tear his gaze from her and to remind himself how utterly hopeless forming any sort of attachment to her would be. He drew back and smiled, saying that when she was ready for dinner he would be happy to escort her to the dining room.

She sighed, the tension broken. Her smile broadened, though, and did she seem to stumble a little as she turned back to her door? Oh, Lord, he had never made a lady's knees weaken so before, and the thought of it made him march determinedly toward his bedchamber, where he meant to give himself a strong shake and forget all the wishful hoping which had been attacking him in the past few minutes.

Laurentia closed the door on the hallway and, with her maid busy laying out her apparel, she leaned against the door and squeezed her eyes shut. She felt wondrously dizzy—and her *knees!* Her knees were all weak and wobbly again.

Had any man ever made her feel thusly? No, not even the two handsome young men with whom she had tumbled in love so many years past. She had been betrothed to a Mr. Dursley some four years past, and more recently to a Mr. Cameron. She wondered for the first time at the depth of love she had felt for either young man. She had thought she had loved, and been loved. Her joy had certainly known no bounds with both her suitors. However, this knee-trembling, head-dizzying experience she was undergoing merely in the presence of her husband . . . ! Oh, *her husband.* How fine the words sounded, even reverberating silently in her head.

She realized with a start how very much she had been wishing for the precise thing she knew she could never have—a husband, a mate, a companion with whom to share her days, with whom to have a passel of children—certainly more than one, so that the halls of Evenlode would be a happy kingdom, instead of the lonely island on which she had grown up. A husband, a companion, a friend. Could Mr. Swinfield actually be these things to her, were she circumstanced differently? She opened her eyes and wondered.

"Miss? Are ye feeling well?" Emmy called to her.

"Yes," she responded, turning to enter her bedchamber more fully. "I am quite well. That is, I have a certain dilemma teasing me a little, but nothing to signify."

No, nothing to signify, she thought dismally. She couldn't have a husband, a companion, a friend, not if she wished to remain mistress of her fortune and to care for those her uncle had injured so desperately during his lifetime.

Emmy smiled. "The whole house is talking of naught else but yer visit to the orphanage today, and the village later. Oh, Miss, ye've been an angel of mercy to them poor orphans."

Laurentia shrugged her shoulders. "I only did what was right, Emmy. You would have done the same."

Emmy's eyes filled with the light of happy reflection. "I don't know as it would 'ave been the first thing I might a done wi' a fortune of me own. I think I woulda purchased a curricle and pair, black 'orses, matched to a shade, and a red bonnet fer meself, and I would a driven me carriage all about the countryside. Mebbe then I woulda given someat to the orphans. Yes, I would a, but mayhap not as ye've done. Say wat ye like, Miss,"—she giggled and blushed—"I mean, *Madame*—I do be fergetten yer a married woman now—but as I were sayin', wat ye did today was saintly, and naught else but that!"

"Emmy, you've lost your mind," she returned, "for I promise you I am no saint. And now I must dress, and quickly, or Cook will bite my nose off the next time I see her. Oh. What is that?" She crossed the room quickly to retrieve a missive leaning up against the looking glass on her dressing table.

"I forgot to tell ye. Mrs. Cabot's maid brought it in earlier."

She quickly broke the seal and read her grandmother's Missive, the sum of which shocked her.

Dearest Laurentia,

I have a surprise for you and your new husband. Yes, I know, all seems to be settled toward a separation later on, but for the present I thought it might be pleasurable if you and Mr. Swinfield dined alone in the music room. All is arranged, so don't attempt to dissuade me from this course. The staff has gone to a great deal of trouble on your behalf.

Yours affectionately,
Grandmother Cabot.

Laurentia immediately turned to her maid, who was studiously ignoring her. "You knew of this. Oh, Emmy tell me what is going forward, for I don't think it a good notion by half!"

Emmy turned shocked eyes upon her. "How can ye say so when ye've just gotten buckled, as it were?"

There was no answer that would be in the least suitable to such a question. She could not tell Emmy that she would be divorcing Mr. Swinfield in less than a month and that the marriage was a sham, for she had no wish for the staff or anyone else to know of her arrangement with Thomas until he could leave Windrush. She felt her heartbeat quicken in something close to fear as a more complete awareness swept over her of what she had done to Mr. Swinfield, of what awaited them both once it became known she meant to divorce him.

She had come to respect Thomas Swinfield and to hold him in a rather high degree of affection, so that the very notion of the scandal which would surely descend upon him once the marriage was dissolved made her feel very ill, indeed. She sat down on the chair before her dressing table and folded the letter up into a tidy square. What had she been thinking, to embroil a complete stranger in her problems? In order to obtain a divorce, she would have to prove that Thomas had treated her badly in the brief course of their marriage. She would have to slander his already sullied reputation.

She dropped her head in her hands. What a terrible flaw to possess—to be a person who never quite thought things through—but then, she hadn't expected to become so attached to her husband in such a short space of time. After all, he had agreed to the proposition, and once it was over he would be in possession of seventy-five thousand pounds.

She lifted her head abruptly and stared at herself in the looking glass. What a fool she was being. She was fairly handing him a fortune for his month of service. What did he care for his reputation, with so much money due to be placed in his hands?

Somehow this thought was more lowering to her than all the rest. She could only suppose that Thomas's sweetness and tenderness to her was because he meant to play his part to perfection. After all, he was being paid handsomely to do so.

Perhaps, then, he didn't have the smallest amount of feeling for her. His many kindnesses toward her, and his compliments, were all part of the masquerade as a husband for hire.

"Will this do fer the evening, Madame?" Emmy asked, drawing her attention toward the door of the wardrobe.

Laurentia turned around and saw that her maid was holding up a lilac silk gown trimmed with Brussels lace. "Yes, of course," she responded flatly.

"Whatever is the matter?" Emmy cried. "Ye've grown quite pale, almost white as chalk."

"I—that is, everything is so new. I find I'm all at sea just thinking about being a wife, having a husband, that sort of thing."

"Well, it did happen so very fast. It is no wonder yer overset. Just rest fer a minute. Do ye wish fer a little sherry, or perhaps a cup of chocolate?"

"No, thank you." Her gaze rested on the lilac silk. She

thought of the special evening to come, arranged entirely by her grandmother, undoubtedly to support the ruse for the benefit of the household. She knew her grandmother wouldn't want anyone knowing of the impending divorce.

Sighing deeply, she felt there was nothing to do but play her part in the charade with as much effort as both her husband and her grandmother apparently felt was necessary. She therefore addressed her maid. "Emmy, I think I would prefer to wear the gold silk, the one trimmed with white lace."

"Oh, Madame," Emmy gushed. "Yes, that would be a better choice. And ye'll see why the moment ye go to the music room."

At that, Laurentia laughed, for she had not told her maid of the contents of the letter. "Then you do know all about my grandmother's surprise."

"Aye, Madame, that I do, since it were I which gave her the notion in the first place. I 'eard tell of her own bridal dinner, as it were, so many years ago. T'were in the music room with Mr. Cabot. I wish I'd known the old gentleman. Cook still speaks of 'im wi' great respect and fondness."

"I was too young to remember him well, only vague memories of playing at his knee. I do recall his smile, though, which was really something from heaven, the one in his portrait."

"In the music room?"

"Yes, the very one, come to think of it!"

A half hour later, Laurentia permitted her husband to lead her into the music room. She had been prepared for a little Christmas festivity, but she was completely unprepared for the sight which greeted her eyes. "Oh, my," she murmured, letting her hand fall from Thomas's arm. "Why, the servants must have been busy the entire day!"

There wasn't a level space in the chamber that remained uncovered by exquisite greens. Two score candles must have been placed and lit among the trailing fir branches and yew sprigs. From the chandelier, swaths of tulle and gold and white silk billowed to the fine instruments collected in a triangle on the floor below—an old-fashioned harpsichord, a pianoforte, and a gilt-trimmed harp. A small table had been arranged by the fire which glowed quite fiercely and beautifully with a half-dozen blazing logs. Scattered about the evergreens were Mrs. Cabot's special collection of music boxes.

Laurentia surveyed the chamber with a strange sense that she had entered a dream. *Thomas.* She could just see her friend from childhood calling to her from behind the tulle, laughing at her and crooking his finger with an invitation to follow after him. *Your uncle will not like that you removed all the apples from the cellar and took them to the neighbors.* Her uncle had followed her into the music room. How angry he had been, redfaced, screaming angry. She had never made such a mistake again. She had never taken all of anything again and given it away. From then on she'd only taken portions, daily, endlessly, in hopes that not everyone would move away from the vale, as so many of her friends had.

Her uncle had been such a terrible spectre in her life. She moved forward and wound up the nearest music box. The tune was lovely, German perhaps, yet neither she nor her grand-mother knew the name of the song.

Her grandmother had been unable to curb her son's dreadful disposition, though she had tried frequently to do so. Once, conversing with her granddaughter on the subject, Mrs. Cabot had sighed mournfully. "I can only trust that one day he will repent of his terrible conduct. At least I hope so." But he hadn't. One day, he simply sickened and died.

She glanced toward Mr. Swinfield, *Thomas,* and saw that he was watching her with a quizzical light in his eye. He drew close. "Whatever is the matter? I don't think I've seen you so blue-deviled as tonight. Have I offended you in some manner?"

"No," she replied quickly. "How could you have?"

"But I must have. How else can I account for your grimness and your silence?"

"Am I grim in this moment? Yes, I suppose I am. I was thinking of my uncle."

At that, she watched him visibly relax. "I wish you would not, then, for I know that your grandmother would be gravely disappointed were her extraordinary efforts this evening to be entirely wasted because you've been dwelling on your uncle's unfortunate conduct."

Laurentia could not tell him all of her thoughts, though she wanted to—say that something within her had been spoiled because of her uncle. Besides, she still couldn't help but wonder if he was merely acting the part of her husband, with his many kindnesses, because she had hired him to do so.

As she looked up at him, however, many of these doubts were laid to rest. There was something in his eyes, in the cast of his shoulders, in his bearing, that commanded respect and trust. She had felt it implicitly that first night at the Tump and Dagler. She would therefore trust in her instincts, at least for now, unless some action of his in the future should bear witness against him.

She therefore ordered her thoughts and concentrated instead on how handsome her husband was, how very fine he always appeared, immaculately groomed, down to his well-rubbed leather shoes.

The butler arrived. "If it pleases you, Madame, dinner is ready to be served."

At that she blinked, and her stomach rumbled. "Goodness!" she cried. "I have just realized we haven't eaten since quite early today, perhaps noon, and now it is past five. Mr. Swinfield, you must be quite peckish."

Thomas smiled and chuckled. "Yes, as it happens, I am."

Laurentia nodded to the butler, and Thomas seated her quite skillfully at the table. When he took up his place, the first course was served—a fine ham, cod in a lemon sauce, and roast partridges. A salad accompanied the course. Thomas smiled warmly upon her and began recounting more fascinating anecdotes of tonish life. As was usual, he had many stories to relate which kept her vastly amused, especially the many tales of Lady Caroline Lamb and her infatuation with Lord Byron.

"Did she really dress up as a page?"

"Indeed. I saw her, for I happened to be leaving a ball just as Byron was arriving, and she approached him. Her voice is quite distinctive, and there were many personages coming and going, so of course her adventure soon became known."

"How very shocking, but how delightful! I mean, I truly admire such spirit. Clearly she was besotted with the poet, but at least she did not sit resignedly by and do nothing to advance herself with him."

"She was married," he whispered, a teasing light in his eye.

"Oh!" Laurentia cried. She felt her cheeks grow exceedingly warm.

"Now I have shocked you. Perhaps I shouldn't have related such a daring story."

"Nonsense. I'm glad you did. I've been kept such an innocent all these years. I wish to know better the ways of the world. Then I might have some understanding of why things happen as they do." She was thinking of the two young men she had once loved and to whom she had been secretly betrothed—one who had deserted her, and the other who had betrayed her. She felt certain she had been at fault, somehow, yet she knew she had not had enough experience to know precisely in what way.

She wanted to know more, to know everything about life among the *beau monde*. When she asked if it was indeed true that young ladies sometimes slept until noon, his answer charmed her. "Only if the night before such a young lady has had a proper evening of attending at least two soirees and two balls, and of dancing until either the gray of dawn could be seen in the sky or her slippers had worn completely through. Did you not have even one season?"

Laurentia shook her head. "No, my uncle would not permit it."

"Then, not even a brief summer sojourn in Bath?"

She smiled. "Never. Though I have longed to go to Bath, if to do nothing more than to partake of the waters."

"Well, the waters are one thing, but I am persuaded you would enjoy immensely the Upper Rooms. Some say the balls are inordinately stuffy, but I believe the company to be found at the assembly rooms are as fine as in London. I only wish you had had at least one London season. Knowing your liveliness as I do, I am certain you would have cut a dash among the *haut ton.*"

She sighed. "I know I would have. I mean, I don't think I would have cut a dash, precisely, but I should have enjoyed nothing so much as meeting hundreds of people I had never met before."

He eyed her softly for a moment as he picked up his glass of Madeira. "You must have had numerous beaux, however, even in so rustic a place as Windrush."

"A few," she confessed with a faint sigh. "I was betrothed when I was twenty, though quite without my uncle's knowledge. Thomas, your lips have parted, and I can see the quite impertinent question forming on your tongue."

"I won't ask it if you do not wish me to."

She giggled, but glanced at the footman who was refilling Thomas's glass with Madeira. "A tale for another time, I suppose."

He took up her hint and told her of a journey north he had made once to see Hadrian's Wall. She listened attentively as the second course was served, consisting of lobster, a stuffed pike, goose with currant sauce, boiled potatoes, and cabbage.

Nuts, slices of oranges and apples, and a plum pudding completed the meal.

Once the fine repast had been thoroughly enjoyed and the dishes and covers cleared away, Laurentia felt compelled to elucidate her previous loves, though she wasn't certain why. Perhaps she simply wanted to talk about her disappointments, which she had never done before. She wanted to voice the thoughts aloud, and to see what Thomas, who always seemed to have a sensible answer, would think of her young men.

"I never really understood why James jilted me," she began, drawing close to the fire. Thomas took up a seat in a black-lacquer Empire chair opposite her. "He seemed completely enamored one day, then the next was gone with nary a word, either written or spoken, to ease the many questions which have haunted me for years. Yes, you may well stare. I have long since decided, however, that he simply did not have the courage to face me, to confess that his heart was not sufficiently engaged to beg permission of my uncle for my hand in marriage."

"My poor dear," Thomas said quietly, his expression sympathetic. "You must have been utterly heartbroken."

"I was," she stated honestly, "for I thought the world of James. I still do, although I've always wondered what became of him and whether he was happy in his choices. I suppose by now he must be well-married with several sons to bear his name—"

"Or daughters to spoil terribly. You mentioned a second young man?"

"Oh, dear. Memories of him are more of a trial, for he drifted in and out of my life only this past twelve-month. I tumbled madly in love with a cousin of our local squire. He was very near to thirty, and quite handsome. He was heir to a tidy property in Wiltshire. I met him Christmas last at a ball at the squire's house. We were secretly betrothed but weeks later."

"What was his name, this vile fellow who used you so ill?"

"Matthew Cameron, but to own the truth he did not leave me. Instead, I asked him to go. We could not agree on something quite vital to me, and the betrothal was ended very nearly as soon as it was begun. But never mind that. It is a subject I have given very little thought to in recent months."

Thomas nodded as though understanding she did not wish to be questioned on the subject of Mr. Cameron. She still felt uneasy when she thought of him. As she had said before, memories of him were a little recent to be contemplated with complete equanimity.

Thomas was silent apace. Then with a smile he queried, "Your name is quite beautiful and unusual. *Laurentia*. Is it a family name?"

She smiled and nodded. "I was named after my father—*Laurence*. I have always been inordinately proud to be called Laurentia, because though I was a girl and his firstborn child, he still allowed me to carry his name."

"He chose well, even if he had had a dozen sons to follow after you."

"How you do flatter me, Mr. Swinfield," she responded lightly, warmed by his compliment.

"Do you have a middle name, or perhaps two middle names, as I do?"

She ought to have known that question would one day arise, but she was unprepared for it. Her middle name was a source of some consternation for her, since whenever she spoke it aloud laughter quickly followed. She turned to stare into the fire. "I do, but I shan't tell you. It is too absurd by half."

She stole a glance at Thomas and saw that his lips were parted as though he wished to pose the question again, yet he hesitated. "I see," he murmured. "And I thought Adolphus absurd."

At that she could only giggle. "Perhaps I shall tell you one day, but not today, if you please."

"Very well," he said, not unkindly. After another pause he changed the subject. "I have business in Tewkesbury tomorrow. May I have your permission to commandeer the traveling chariot?"

Laurentia turned to him abruptly. "Oh, Thomas!" she cried. "You must never feel you have to ask my permission for anything during this month. Please, I beg of you. You are giving up quite enough without having to be reduced to that. We have several carriages you may command at any time—a well-fitted barouche and two traveling carriages, a curricle, and a smaller gig which I am wont to use during the summer just to tool about the countryside and pay the usual visits. All of them are yours to use at will."

"Thank you," he said. "Our situation at best is awkward."

"Yes," she agreed. "I suppose it is."

She fell silent at that, and turned her gaze once more to the fire. From the corner of her eye, she watched Thomas rise from his chair. He lifted the largest of the boxes on the mantel and carefully wound the music mechanism. When a tune started, which happened to be a waltz, he bowed formally before her. "Will you do me the honor of this dance?"

Six

Laurentia was both delighted and surprised by his request. "You wish to dance with me? Here? But we haven't an orchestra."

He smiled warmly. "I think these music boxes will suffice if you will allow me to guide you about the room."

As always, her' heart quivered as she met his amused gaze. His blue eyes were wonderfully kind and encouraging, and she couldn't help but comply with his playful request. "Yes, if you please, sir," she responded grandly, dropping into a full, court curtsy. "Nothing could be more to my liking, for I dearly love a waltz."

He bowed equally as formally in return. When she rose, he slid his arm about her waist and settled her hand neatly in his own. Pressing her waist slightly by way of guidance, he led her into a whirl about the music room, turning in swift circles to the delicate tones emanating from the music box.

Laurentia gave herself to the dance, which seemed oddly childlike in nature because the sound of the music box was so very high-pitched. She couldn't help but laugh, therefore, especially since the pace was so brisk.

How lovely it was to dance, to let the worries of her life and the sadness of her past leave through the bottom of her slippers as she followed Thomas's lead and swirled through the chamber on quick feet. The pace of the music box was far too fast to be entirely comfortable, but it did have the advantage of setting them both to huffing and laughing after three minutes. Fortunately, the mechanism quit before she dropped to a faint.

Thomas was not finished, however, and wound another box. The music was more suitable to a country dance, which he quickly engaged her in, at least as much as was possible without other dancers to complete the steps. Even so, the experience proved to be the exact balm she needed to relieve the difficult experiences of the day—of discovering the truth about her uncle's abuse of the orphanage's finances, of making so many arrangements during the afternoon, and of having to accept that Thomas was a completely transient part of her life, just like her two former beaux.

The music box finished, and Thomas wound another. A second waltz followed, much slower this time, which seemed to be a far better tempo for a true enjoyment of the dance. He rewound this box several times in a row. The last time it quit playing, he said, "Let's dance a little without the music. I'm enjoying escorting you about the floor prodigiously. You are a delightful partner, light on your feet and so quick to respond to even the smallest pressure of my hand."

"You are being too kind, I'm sure," she returned. "Though I daresay my dancing master would be pleased to hear that his lessons had not been proffered in vain."

"You may tell me that the credit is due to your teacher, but I am convinced otherwise. I've had a great deal of experience in a ballroom. Without fail every young lady I know boasts of having had an excellent master, but I promise you, the *application* of that knowledge varies exceedingly. I have permanently bruised feet in proof of it."

"You poor creature," she cooed sympathetically, but not without an ironic smile.

"Yes, I have suffered a great deal, haven't I?"

She giggled.

He smiled again, his expression once more amused and inviting. After several more turns about the chamber, he drew her to a stop. He did not release her immediately, and for some reason she was entirely disinclined to insist he do so. She was tingling from head to toe, and knew a marvelous sensation that all would be well. In the distance, she could hear church bells chiming softly down the vale.

"You are too beautiful for words," he murmured, his gaze drifting from one feature to another.

Her knees began to wobble alarmingly—again! He must have sensed as much, for he suddenly drew her very close—just to support her, mind!

She did not even try to resist. After all, why should she? He was her husband, as her grandmother had said, *for this time*. Besides, he was leaning toward her in the most hopeful way.

She sighed deeply and raised her face to him, and then his lips were on hers as they had been the first evening they met. Only this time, there was no mistletoe above her to justify the occasion.

She melted against him, realizing that she was giving herself over to something she had been longing for since he had first placed his lips on hers so many days ago. She parted her lips, and he began the softest, gentlest search of her mouth. What a tender man he was, even in his kissing. Desire sparkled over her in a sensual, rippling flow, like an endearing melody from one of her grandmother's best music boxes. He was so different from anyone she had ever known, magical, as though she had somehow summoned him from her deepest, sweetest dreams. Was he truly here with her now? Or was he a phantom who would vanish without warning?

She feared suddenly that he would simply disappear, that he wasn't real, that she had made him up. She slid an arm about his shoulders and clung to him, feeling the hard muscles of his back and arms and reassuring herself that yes, Thomas was very real. Too real. Too wonderful and gentle and kind and real.

And he would be leaving . . . one day.

Oh, but she didn't want to think about that. Not yet. She wanted the moment to go on forever. She wanted him to be her true husband, to end the masquerade and to take her to wife.

His kiss became suddenly wild and passionate, as though he knew her thoughts and the wishes of her heart. His hand drifted over her back. He caressed her and whispered in her ear, "I have been longing to hold you in my arms since that first night. Laurentia, tell me you've been longing for the same."

"Yes," she murmured, kissing his cheek in return. "Oh, yes, only . . ." She could not finish the thought, for to do so would destroy the moment.

"Yes, I know," he whispered in complete understanding.

He turned slightly, molding himself to her, and his lips were on hers again, crushing her mouth. Desire writhed over her, a living, breathing fire that spoke of the future and unfulfilled yearnings.

She drew back from him, suddenly frightened. "Please, Thomas, this can't be. I can't be feeling these things for you, not now. You will tear my heart out when you leave if I permit you to continue kissing me like this." She clutched his arms, and tears stung her eyes.

"I don't want to hurt you," he said in a hoarse whisper. "I am beginning to think our arrangement was one of madness. I should have refused you, for as each day passes I find I am wanting more from you, yet I have nothing to offer."

"I don't know what you mean," she responded.

"I fear I am becoming attached to you, but were my affections to deepen, were yours to grow as well, I could bring nothing to our union. I have so little, you see."

She had never asked him about his circumstances. She

wasn't certain she wanted to know, now, but she felt the subject could hardly be avoided. "Are you saying you are otherwise penniless?"

He nodded, his expression pained. "Nearly so. Not that it matters."

She released him and let her arms fall to her sides. "Then you must have been exceedingly grateful when you learned of the amount I intended to fix upon you once our month together was over."

"Don't say that—ever!" he cried, stricken. "What man who would call himself a gentleman could ever be content earning money in such a way?"

She released a deep sigh, her heart relieved beyond words. Here was the answer she had sought, that Thomas was not in the least happy about earning his keep as her husband. She smiled and touched his cheek with her gloved hand. "You are saving me," she said, "by posing as my husband, and for that I will be grateful the rest of my life. I want you to have the money, very much so. Indeed, if anything, I have begun to feel horrible that very soon your reputation will suffer because we must divorce."

"Please don't ever concern yourself about me or my reputation. I am truly happy to be of service to you in this way, more so every day."

The large grandfather clock in the entrance hall suddenly announced the hour.

Laurentia listened, and when the last chime had echoed through the house she murmured, "It is late."

"Yes." He nodded, a smile beginning at the corners of his mouth. "Nine o'clock."

"You are laughing at me again. Will my country hours never cease to amuse you?"

"Not the hours," he argued. "You. You amuse me. You please me, and amuse me, you touch my heart with your innocence, you make me want to strive toward impossible goals because of your generosity. Oh, the devil-take-it! I wish to God I hadn't signed those ridiculous documents. I wish I'd never met you, do you understand?"

Her heart crumpled. "Yes," she whispered. "I do understand, for I am beginning to regret the whole thing, as well."

He ground his teeth together, bowed, and was gone.

She listened to the direction of his footsteps, which shambled off toward the library and her uncle's office. She rang for the butler, and when he arrived she bid him send brandy and a snifter to the library for Mr. Swinfield.

"Very good, Madame."

"And will you send Emmy to my bedchamber?"

"Of course, Madame."

An hour later, Laurentia fell asleep, pretending that Thomas meant to come to her and to make her his wife. Her dreams tumbled her heart about further as Thomas invaded one image after another.

When she awoke, a general sadness clung to her, amplified by the knowledge that he would be gone for the day to Tewkesbury.

How strange to think that her pretend marriage had brought her so much odd misery.

By nuncheon, however, her spirits began to renew themselves as thoughtful gifts arrived, sent to her from the many merchants in town, in appreciation for her efforts on behalf of the orphanage. As she opened the packages, she was reminded of why she had chosen this desperate path in the first place, a circumstance which had the beneficial effect of forcing her attention away from the hopelessness of her marriage and toward the numerous pressing duties which were demanding her attention. Not least of these was a call she meant to pay on Mrs. Marycote regarding her wool-dying mill.

She was just donning her pelisse and bonnet when she received an unexpected missive from Sir Alan Redcliffe saying that he had arrived to enjoy Michaelmas in Windrush a little earlier than previously planned and would call on her tomorrow, at one, to express his hopes that her marriage would be a long and prosperous one.

She felt nervous suddenly. Sir Alan had pressed his suit most strongly a sennight before her uncle died. She had refused him with gentle firmness, but he had given her the distinct impression—smiling all the while, of course—that he would not cease his efforts to win her to his way of thinking. She had been a little shocked by the look in his eye, one of complete determination. In truth, he had frightened her a little. She could only wonder now what he would think of her sudden and unexpected marriage.

A half hour later, Laurentia was seated in Mrs. Marycote's parlor, holding a cup of tea in her hand and cradling the companion saucer on her lap. Her friend had greeted her warmly, begging her to sit beside her on the sofa, and congratulated her on her marriage. After this Laurentia had begun leading the conversation in the direction of the fulling mill.

However, within a few minutes, Mrs. Marycote had taken the discourse firmly in hand by bringing forward the subject of her uncle's business interests. Laurentia found herself rather astonished when Mrs. Marycote informed her that her uncle and Sir Alan had had several joint business interests, and that for years there had been rumors up and down the vale that Mr. Cabot had committed some great wrong involving a plantation in the West Indies.

"I do not generally give a great deal of credence to rumors," the handsome widow said. "However, they were repeated so often, and from an odd number of quarters, that both my husband and myself came to believe there must have been some truth to them. I don't feel I ought to say more, for we are speaking of rumors, and who among us has not been harmed at one time or another by the injustice of a false one? I would only suggest that you take great care in reviewing your uncle's papers. Was I wrong to have said anything to you?"

"On no account!" Laurentia cried. "Though I must say after what I learned at the orphanage yesterday little would surprise me. But what is the nature of this supposed *wrong?"*

"I don't know," Mrs. Marycote admitted.

Laurentia could not imagine in what way her uncle's ownership of a plantation might have resulted in a perfidious act. However, until recently, she would never have believed that her uncle would have been starving orphans in order to swell his own purse! She began to think there was nothing he would not have done to gather another groat into his proverbial warehouse.

"I never heard mention of a plantation," she said at last, frowning, "but my uncle never concerned me much in his affairs. I will heed what you have told me, however, and will begin searching immediately for some reference to a business of that nature. I vow I have never been so at sixes and sevens before. Everything seems to be changing so quickly, and at every turn I learn another startling facet of my uncle's affairs." She took a long sip of tea before turning once more to her friend. "I hope you don't mind if we address a quite different matter."

"No, not in the least. I only hope I haven't overset you."

"I am becoming more accustomed daily to having my world overturned," she responded lightly. "But let me suggest something to you which I have been pondering for a number of weeks with regard to your wool-making mill. The reason I came to you today, at least one of the reasons, was that I have an interesting proposition for you concerning the reopening of the mill. How would you feel . . . that is, I have for a long time hoped . . . that one day I might be able to become partners with you, and that very soon we shall see an increase once more in the wool-dying industry around Windrush, beginning with your mill. Are you at all interested?" Her heart was beating with rapid excitement as she waited to hear her friend's response.

Mrs. Marycote tilted her head. "But Mrs. Swinfield, are you not aware that presently *you* own the mill? Your uncle held the mortgage on it, and foreclosed the very week of my husband's death."

Laurentia was so shocked that she dropped her tea cup onto the saucer and splashed tea on her light blue, silk pelisse.

"Oh, my dear!" Mrs. Marycote cried. "How will you ever get tea out of silk?"

"I—I don't know, though I daresay Mr. Coxcomb will know what to do."

"Mr. *Coxcomb?*" she cried.

Laurentia burst out laughing. "No, no! I mean Mr. Coxwell, of course."

"Ah. Mr. Swinfield's valet. *His* reputation has most certainly flown about the vale, as if on wings. Your housekeeper, Mrs. Bourton, is quite *aux anges* with the fellow, if I don't much mistake the matter."

"She does sing his praises, and with such a glow in her eyes as has made me wonder if she does not view him in something of an amorous light."

"I believe you may be right, but I can see that I have overset you—again. Indeed, I never meant to do so, but I had thought you knew about the mill."

Laurentia shook her head as she dabbed at the spilt tea with her linen. "You were always such a good friend to me, and for some time now I have been thinking of helping you financially to reopen your mill, for in my mind it always will be your mill." She lifted her gaze to her friend. "You cannot know how distressed I am to learn this news, that my uncle behaved so badly toward your family. I—I mean to return it to you—at once!"

"Mrs. Swinfield," her hostess began gently with a sympathetic expression in her eye, "may I offer you a bit of advice from a woman who knows what it is to carry on after someone very close passes away?"

"Oh, yes, please."

Mrs. Marycote smiled softly. "Slow down just a bit. I can see that you've a good heart, and you mean well, but the world will march forward with nary a misstep until you are ready to proceed, fully informed and with a more peaceful heart."

The very thought of having to wait to continue her charitable efforts caused her whole heart to squish up into a knot. "Your advice is undoubtedly sound, but you've no idea how painful it has been for me all these years to watch the suffering in Windrush—the disappearance of cottage industries, the death of the orphans every winter, the obvious poverty of the farmers hereabouts. I vowed one day that I would do all I could to eradicate the ills which have plagued our vale. Now, having come to an understanding of how nearly involved my uncle was as a cause of so much evil, I can't tell you the urgency I feel in my heart to right these wrongs. You can have no idea!"

"You forget," Mrs. Marycote said. "I do have an idea, a very clear one, for I have been your friend for years. I do know your heart and the sweet nobility of your intentions, but I beg you to pause and ponder all of your uncle's deeds before proceeding. Indeed, I urge you most strongly to do so."

Laurentia drew in a deep, steadying breath. "Very well," she said at last. "I promise I will consider what you've said."

"Please try," she stated emphatically. "For I feel you are just beginning to learn the truth about a great many things. I say this not so much based on specific knowledge as on a general comprehension of Mr. Cabot's character."

Laurentia thought of Mr. Frome's ill-health, and the icy cold halls of the orphanage. She could do but little else than nod in agreement.

Mrs. Marycote continued. "As for the mill, I truly have no interest in having it restored to us. From what I have read in

The Times over the past several years, our society is on the verge of a great many changes, industrially I mean. The factories to the north are truly a marvel, and even if Mr. Cabot had not taken the mill I am persuaded that such means of processing wool will not remain viable for long."

"But . . . I thought. Have you enough to live on, to . . . ?" She broke off, feeling her cheeks darken with color.

Mrs. Marycote swept her into a warm embrace. "You are a dear child! But you mustn't be concerned for me. I shall tell you something in the strictest confidence, something I have revealed to no one, but which I hope will give you some relief. I have for several years now been the mistress of my own fortune, left to me by a distant relative. You may recall my numerous visits to a cousin in Surrey?" Laurentia nodded. "I don't speak of it because I don't wish for my life here to change, but I am presently a woman of some means. So, now I hope you will not feel a degree of sympathy for me entirely unwarranted."

"Oh, Mrs. Marycote, is this indeed true?"

Her hostess smiled. "Very much so."

"I am so happy for you—beyond words—for I know what a wonderful gift independence is! It is a state I would wish for every woman. You do relieve my mind!"

"Excellent. Then, let me prepare you another cup of tea and perhaps we can speak of other more significant matters—your new husband, for instance? Tell me of Mr. Swinfield. I hear he is quite the gentleman."

Laurentia knew she could not reveal the truth of her sham marriage, even to her dear friend. However, she did not have the least difficulty enumerating her husband's many fine qualities, which brought the conversation into the sunshine for many minutes to come. After she had given at least three examples of Thomas's innate kindness and further extolled his abilities as a dance partner, she extended an invitation to the St. Thomas's Day celebration. Only when Mrs. Marycote had promised to attend, only then did she take her leave—with a much lighter heart than she had first expected, yet an even darker opinion of her uncle's character.

"This will clear the matter entirely, then?" Lord Villiers queried, lifting his gaze from the document.

"Yes, precisely," Mr. Crabtree said. "The decision as to what to do with the seventy-five thousand pounds will be entirely in Mrs. Swinfield's hands. She may reclaim it or give it to a philanthropic endeavor of her choice."

Villiers finished signing the formally written document and returned it to Mr. Crabtree.

He shook his head wonderingly. "I believe you are one of the few men I've had the privilege of knowing who would have acted as nobly in this circumstance. Your actions do you great honor, especially in these times when so few seem to value nobility of purpose or action."

"Thank you, but I doubt that very many men would care to have earned a fortune by disgracing a lady—as our forthcoming divorce will undoubtedly do."

"As to that," he returned, "how many gentlemen are given the opportunity to know just what they would do?" He set aside the document, then opened the side drawer of his desk and withdrew a small sheet of paper which had been folded thrice and sealed with maroon wax. "Before you leave, I wonder if I might discuss a certain matter with you."

"Yes, of course," Villiers said with a smile. Mr. Crabtree was an intelligent, thoughtful man whom he admired very much.

"Several years ago, I performed a transfer of funds to a Mr. James Dursley of Bath, on behalf of a client who must remain nameless. I did not question the transaction at the time, only until recently when Miss Cabot, that is, Mrs. Swinfield, came to see me a fortnight past about Mr. Cabot's will. For some reason, she mentioned Mr. Dursley to me, quite without any former reference to him. She asked if I knew of such a gentleman, and possibly a place of residence to which she could direct her correspondence.

"Certain suspicions concerning the former transfer of funds to Mr. Dursley leapt to mind, and for that reason I told her a half-truth to the effect that I was unacquainted with the man—for indeed I had never met him. However, as I noted the look of disappointment on her face I became convinced that some mischief had occurred which I did not wish to discuss with Mrs. Swinfield. I have since wondered if you were aware of Mrs. Swinfield's relationship to Mr. Dursley."

Lord Villiers leaned back in his chair and eyed Mr. Crabtree narrowly. "She was, at one time, secretly betrothed to him."

Mr. Crabtree nodded. "I thought as much. Indeed, I feared as much."

Villiers pondered these cryptic remarks. He drew his own conclusion. "Are you suggesting Mr. Cabot interfered by offering a sum of money to be rid of the young man? But I thought he knew nothing of Mr. Dursley's interest. At least, that was my wife's belief."

"Mr. Cabot? No, no, you mistake the matter. He was not involved at all, at least not to my knowledge. I refer to someone else, another man who has an interest in Mrs. Swinfield's affairs."

Lord Villiers felt uneasy suddenly. He had no doubt whatsoever to whom Mr. Crabtree was referring. He felt the connection in his bones. "I understand you," he responded gravely. "The man to whom you refer I have suspected of crimes you would not imagine, but which I hope one day to prove."

"I see," Mr. Crabtree murmured solemnly. He then extended the paper to him. "Although I can't say whether the information I now give you will aid you at all in your own purposes, I believe it may afford you an opportunity to discover some of the truth concerning Mrs. Swinfield's past, something about which I believe she should be fully informed. Contained within is an address in Bath. If you are so inclined to pay Mr. Dursley a visit, I daresay he might be able to elucidate that which I cannot say, since I originally represented the transaction on behalf of a client. You will forgive me if I am unable to say more."

"Of course. I am in your debt, sir." Tucking the address into the inside pocket of his greatcoat, he thanked Mr. Crabtree for his assistance and soon afterward returned to his carriage. Once within, he paused, considering what he ought to do next. If he left now, he could be in Bath by midnight. Laurentia would understand if he was detained a day or so.

On the other hand . . .

Once within the carriage, he ordered the postilion to begin the return journey to Windrush.

"Dearest . . ." Thomas's deep, resonant voice floated over her.

Laurentia was enjoying the nicest dream. She knew she was dreaming, for she was walking out of doors, beneath the moonlight, and it was full summer. But of course it was not summer. It was winter.

"Laurentia, my darling . . ."

Oh, it was a dream, for Thomas was walking beside her, holding her hand and smiling down into her face. The beechwood, fully-leafed, was quickly approaching.

"I wish you to be my wife."

"Oh yes, Thomas. I would like that above all things."

"My beautiful one, whom I am coming to adore more every day—will you wake up, now?"

"I really don't want to, Thomas. Kiss me, instead."

She turned her face toward him and he gathered her up swiftly in his arms. He was kissing her, only she couldn't feel his lips against hers. Instead, she felt a soft pressure on her cheek. . . .

Laurentia opened her eyes. Her other cheek was pressed against a stack of papers, and all but one of the candles had guttered. Someone was with her! Someone *had* kissed her cheek!

A dart of fear coursed through her, and she sat up abruptly. A man was beside her, in the shadows—Thomas. Thank heavens! "Oh, Thomas, you've given me such a fright! Wh—when did you return?"

"Just now."

She glanced around her uncle's office, feeling entirely disoriented. "What is the hour?"

"Past midnight."

"Oh, dear. I must have fallen asleep." She remembered her dream suddenly, and she looked up at Thomas, her lips parting. "Did you kiss my cheek just now?"

He nodded. "I felt I had to do something when you had just asked me to kiss you, but it was rather awkward, since you were slumped over the desk."

She giggled, her head still swimming with the summery memory of the dream, of the feel of Thomas's hand in her own, the scent of ferns rich in the air and the beauty of the thick beechwood so close at hand. He had asked her to marry him, and she had accepted of his hand.

"I can see that sleep is still curling about in your brain. However, I wish to know if you are awake enough to converse, for I have something I wish to ask you."

Laurentia nodded, even though her thoughts were hazy.

He smiled and gently pushed an errant curl away from her cheek. "How would you like to accompany me to Bath next week?"

She wasn't certain precisely what he had said. She was still caught up in the sweet ambience of the dream.

Bath?

Suddenly, she was very shocked. He wanted to see her bathe? She had grown up in a cloistered circumstance. Still, was that what married people did? She felt herself blush to the roots of her hair. "I—I don't think that would be at all acceptable, given that we are not truly married," she responded haltingly.

He chuckled softly and seated himself on the edge of the desk. Looking down at her with an affectionate expression, he covered her hand with his own. "Surely you are being far too nice in your principles, though I promise you I would maintain a proper distance the entire time."

Her heart was racing. "The only distance I would consider proper would be if you were not in the same room."

His brow grew furrowed. "Laurentia, I never thought to embarrass you so thoroughly by making such a suggestion. Let me assure you that we would continue to inhabit separate rooms, of course, just as we do now."

"You are making no sense," she stated firmly. "But I will tell you again, I don't think it at all proper that you be present while I'm taking my bath."

His mouth fell open, and she realized she must have somehow misunderstood him. He let out a roar of laughter. "Oh, my dear!" he cried after a moment, wiping his eyes. "You truly did misunderstand me. I was suggesting we take a trip to Bath, to the city of Bath."

She covered her mouth with both hands, as a child might. "Oh, Thomas," she murmured, her cheeks warming up more hotly still. "How stupid of me. I believe I am yet half asleep. And to think I thought you had asked to see me bathe. I was never more shocked!"

She hid her eyes and tried desperately to force some of the color away from her burning features. Unfortunately, Thomas dropped to his knees beside her and slid his hand along her arm. "I wish like anything you hadn't made such an error, for now I cannot seem to get the image out of my head."

She peeked between her fingers and saw that he was quite in earnest, then let her hands fall away. Her cheeks began to cool as her heart warmed up. Why was it she wasn't in the least embarrassed now, when he was making pretty love to her with such suggestive words?

"Then you must forget that I said anything of the kind," she murmured, covering his hand with her own. "I missed you today."

"I missed you, as well."

He kissed her fingers, and she leaned her head against his. After a moment, he begged to escort her to her bedchamber. She rose and settled the snuffer over the last flickering flame. A branch of candles in the adjoining library showed the way.

He offered her his arm, and she gladly accepted it.

"Were you reviewing your uncle's papers?" he asked, escorting her carefully from the darkened chamber.

"Yes. I had some greatly disturbing news from the widow Marycote today. It would seem my uncle dispossessed her of the mill a week after her husband died."

He glanced down at her, obviously shocked. "I'm terribly sorry to hear of it. You must have been deeply distressed."

"I was never so mortified. Yes, I know none of my uncle's doings are in any way connected to me, but to discover that I own the mill—I feel tainted by the knowledge."

He gave her arm a gentle squeeze. "You shouldn't, but I can certainly comprehend your feelings."

She wondered whether or not she should tell him the rest of Mrs. Marycote's revelations, especially concerning the mysterious plantation. However, an entire afternoon and evening spent in her uncle's office had failed to produce even a hint of such a place, so that she found herself reluctant to say anything.

After a moment, she said, "Mrs. Marycote gave me some advice that I feel compelled to consider. She thought it would be wise if I did not hurry into all the good deeds I have in mind, since I might not understand all that my uncle's fortune entails."

"I perceive Mrs. Marycote is a woman of sense."

"Yes, she is, and I do mean to attend to her advice, although there is at least one more task I must perform—the poorhouse is in dreadful condition, and I mean to see repairs on the building begun tomorrow. There can be little harm in that, don't you agree?"

She looked up at him and had all the pleasure of seeing him smile as he said, "There can be no harm at all, I'm sure."

She felt infinitely relieved. "I'm so happy to hear you say so. I feel utterly bewildered by all that I've learned of my uncle, and very sad as well."

"Then tell me you will come to Bath with me. At least for a few days you will be free of so many distressing associations."

"I should like it above all things," she responded decisively. "When do we leave?"

"In a few days, once I've been able to make the necessary arrangements."

Seven

On the following morning, Laurentia was seated in an empire chair in the drawing room looking up at Sir Alan Redcliffe. She wondered how she could ever have been frightened by the prospect of telling him the news of her marriage, for, once told, he seemed to comprehend her dilemma perfectly.

"Swinfield," he murmured. "The name is familiar, but the face is lost to me. Ah, well. I daresay I shall meet him soon enough." He stood with a booted foot on the hearth, a poker in hand, and every now and then worked at the logs in order to keep the fire burning at a golden blaze.

She had explained her hapless elopement quite haltingly at first, for who would not have been shocked by her admission that not only had she tied the connubial knot in Gretna Green, but that she also meant to divorce her husband as soon as she had been wed a month. Yes, he had lifted a brow slightly at this point in her history, but when she further elucidated her actions by explaining that one month of marriage was her uncle's requirement as stated in his will in order for her to receive her inheritance, his brow fell to its normal, relaxed height. He began to smile and nod with a great deal of understanding when she told him of her wish to be in complete charge of her fortune, that she had a great many plans to fulfill which had been brewing in her heart since she was a child, and that only her strong belief that a husband would forbid such worthy endeavors had forced her decision to remain a spinster the rest of her days.

As she watched him now, his eyes lit with warm rays of good humor, especially smiling down upon her as he was, she remembered again why it was she had always confided in Sir Alan. His entire demeanor never judgmental, evoked confidence and trust. She continued, "So you see why I felt compelled to lay my proposals before Mr. Swinfield. How could I possibly marry a man such as Villiers, for I had by then become convinced that he would never agree to divorce me after a month. I am utterly persuaded he meant to have my fortune, just as you have said."

"The entire arrangement is singular, to be sure, my dear, but I can see the logic of your choices. I commend you completely for your clever management of a ticklish situation. Whatever did Villiers say to you when he learned he was not to wed you, after all? He must have been outraged, at the very least."

She breathed a great sigh of relief. "That is the most amazing part of the story. You see, Villiers never arrived. have not heard from him either in person or by correspondence. I can only presume he had a complete change of heart. Perhaps his conscience began to smite him."

"Perhaps," the baronet murmured softly. He shifted his gaze to the fire and bent down slightly to again poke and push at the pile of burning logs. "I wish that I had known of your uncle's scheme to marry you to Villiers. I should have offered you all manner of support against him, for just as I told you I have known forever what that man is, having been his guardian at one time. Even as a lad he showed the most dreadful propensities to squander whatever monies were given to him. I confess I am still utterly confounded by your uncle's wish to see you married to such a man."

"Don't be distressed, I pray you. Neither you nor I knew of my uncle's plans. Besides, there was never a signing of marriage contracts, so Villiers can have no claim whatsoever upon me."

"Well, thank God for that."

He didn't seem very troubled at all about her marriage, which relieved her immensely. Recalling the news Mrs. Marycote had given her—that he had been a business associate of her uncle's—she broached the subject of the plantation. "I have come to understand, Sir Alan, that you and my uncle were more than mere acquaintances and rivals at the whist table, that you also were involved in trade together."

He smiled affably and said, "We were not in trade, precisely. Merely we counseled one another on likely investments as various opportunities happened along. But I thought you knew, these many years and more, that we have enjoyed discussing the world of economics."

She shook her head. "No, I did not, but then you must be aware to some degree how little my uncle concerned me in any of his interests, to say nothing of matters of business."

"He always showed a shocking lack of familial devotion. However, he was a genius when it came to creating a fortune. I had much admiration for your uncle."

Laurentia turned this over in her mind. "Would you happen to know of a plantation in which he invested? I believe it was located in the West Indies, but I have yet to come across the documents detailing this investment."

Sir Alan grew rather somber and puffed his cheeks a little. "I can't say that I'm aware of any such investment."

"I daresay it was years before you became acquainted with him."

"Indeed, you must be right for I have no recollection of ever hearing him speak of a plantation," Sir Alan mused.

She grew thoughtful, her gaze fixed away from the baronet. She had spent hours in her uncle's office, seated at his desk, reviewing dozens of papers. Not one of them alluded to a plantation. Perhaps it was, as Mrs. Marycote had suggested, merely a rumor, after all.

Movement near the doorway caught her eye. A feeling of affection and excitement rolled over her in the nicest way as Thomas entered the chamber. "Ah, here is my husband now. Thomas—that is, Mr. Swinfield—I should like to reacquaint you with an old friend of mine. If I recall correctly, you said you enjoyed a slight acquaintance with my guest, as well."

Villiers had entered the chamber ready to tell Laurentia he had made all the necessary arrangements for their trip to Bath, namely that he had spoken to the Head Groom about preparing the large barouche and had sent word to the White Hart in Bath that he would require two rooms for three days. His eyes had been all for Laurentia when he entered the chamber, especially since her visitor was bent over the hearth, and he had only casually glanced his direction.

However, the moment the gentleman turned around a chill swept over him. He had not seen Sir Alan in several years, and was shocked to find that his hair was now completely white. His features, however, especially his dark, narrow eyes, were all too familiar.

Redcliffe. The man he suspected of cheating him out of his inheritance.

And Sir Alan knew him and could expose him, possibly placing Laurentia in a terribly vulnerable position.

The shock that went through him seized his features in a tight grip, but he strove quickly to recover and paused only faintly in his steps before making his way to his wife's side. He spoke brightly. "You are quite right, my dear. I am already acquainted with Sir Alan, for we were used to know one another in London some years ago." He walked directly to Laurentia, took her hand in his and placed a kiss on her fingers. She beamed up into his face, and even in the midst of a truly wretched encounter he felt his heart skip a beat. He released her hand and remained standing beside her as he turned to face Redcliffe.

"Indeed," Sir Alan returned carefully. "I must confess I had forgotten your name until this very moment, but never your face or your skill at cards. Only tell me, where are your people from? I can't seem to recall. Swinfield. The name is quite familiar, yet I can't summon the connection."

So Redcliffe did not mean to expose him—at least, not just yet. "Somersetshire."

"Ah. Not unlike Villiers, himself. I believe he has an estate there. Are you perchance acquainted with his lordship? Your wife and I were just discussing him. It's very odd that he never arrived in Windrush to claim Miss, er, Mrs. Swinfield's hand."

"I am only remotely known to him," he responded evenly. "Somerset, as you know, is a large county, and I do not travel in such exalted circles."

Redcliffe smiled in a manner that brought Villiers hackles rising sharply. The baronet released a silken, "Ah. I suppose you would not be much acquainted with him, since he is commonly known to survive on the kindness of good friends and the purses of those so unfortunate as to fall into play with him."

Villiers could not let this pass entirely. "His skill as well as his fairness in play are well-known, of course."

"Yes, of course. How fortunate for you, a chance stranger, then, to have stumbled across your wife's fair hand—at such a propitious moment. I only wonder, was it difficult for you to agree to the arrangement?"

At that, Villiers seated himself in a chair near his wife and remarked easily, "I meant to refuse until I learned of certain attending circumstances."

"What were those?" he inquired. Villiers considered his response. He knew what he wished to say, but didn't want Laurentia to know of it. "At the time, I became convinced Miss Cabot was in some danger." ·

Sir Alan frowned slightly in response. "You mean from Villiers."

"Of course. Did you think I might have referred to someone else?" He stared directly at the man he believed to be his enemy, and bid him know his mind.

Sir Alan merely took on a rather saintly glow. "You are a man to be admired. It is no wonder Miss Cabot felt safe in placing her proposals before you."

"She is certainly safe with me, though I daresay as an old friend of my wife's you may have concerns of your own, in which case I hasten to assure you that I have already signed documents in the presence of Mr. Crabtree of Tewkesbury proving my intentions. If you wish to see these documents, you have but to journey to Tewkesbury yourself. You are acquainted with Mr. Crabtree, are you not?"

He wasn't certain, but he thought Sir Alan's eye twitched at the mention of the man.

"Yes, I am acquainted with him."

"As I said before, please avail yourself of these documents whenever it might please you."

"I wouldn't dream of it. I have been in the world many years, and have learned to know people just by looking at them. You are a fellow who can be trusted."

"Thank you. That was very kindly spoken. Tell me, in all this experience, do you also find that people change very much over the years?"

He shook his head. "No, I don't think so. Once the character is formed, in childhood no doubt, the true grain of a person remains fixed."

"I would have to agree," he answered stonily. He turned to Laurentia, who wore a perplexed frown between her brows. "But I am being excessively uncivil, for I have interrupted your *tete-e-tete* with Sir Alan. I came only to tell you that I have made the arrangements for our sojourn in Bath. All is settled." He rose to his feet. "I shan't intrude a moment a longer. I know how it is with old friends."

"You needn't leave us," Laurentia said.

"As it happens, I have promised a letter to an old friend, and wish to see it posted before tomorrow. You will forgive me. I will see you at dinner." He turned to the man he had once trusted with his life. "Are you dining with us, Sir Alan?"

Redcliffe shook his head. "Though your wife was very kind in offering her hospitality I had to refuse, for I have a previous engagement."

"Ah. Well, then. I'm sure we'll be seeing one another in the future."

"Indeed, I hope so."

Villiers inclined his head and left the drawing room. He made his way to the library, having decided not to leave anything else to chance. He penned the letter quickly, and sent a footman to the village with it fifteen minutes later. If Mr. James Dursley still resided in Bath, he wanted to make certain he would be in town to receive him. Now that Sir Alan had arrived before times with the ability to expose him to Laurentia and anyone else so nearly connected to her, he felt he could not afford the luxury of letting events unfold so casually.

Sir Alan once again commanded his postilion to ease away from the icy patches of Windrush's cobbled street. He was a careful man in every possible way. Now that he had passed the half century mark, he felt compelled to manage the physical safety of his existence with an even greater eye to his surroundings. He was not the athlete he had been in his youth, nor the strong fencer he'd been in his mid-thirties. No, he felt in every limb of his body the decline of life, a sensation he resented more than anything else he could think of. For one thing, if Villiers chose to attack him, how could he possibly defend himself against a man in his prime, a man who had only last Season succeeded in planting Gentleman Jackson as neat a rammer as he had ever heard of?

He shuddered to think of it.

Even today, he had seen by the manner in which the viscount had moved across the floor that he was as agile and as strong as ever.

He muttered a curse. "Damn you, Cabot, for bringing him here. What happened? Did you suddenly develop a conscience on your deathbed, so that you must attempt to marry your niece to the man we robbed?" He had never been more stunned than when he had heard Cabot's will read, fixing Villiers as the man his niece was to wed.

Of course he had known that my good Mr. Swinfield was Villiers once he saw him. What a shock he had suffered, but not less so Villiers himself!

As the coach turned into the lane leading to his home, he marveled at Villiers's audacity in adopting the masquerade he had. What had he been thinking, he wondered, to have placed himself in such an awkward, even scandalous, position? Surely he knew that one day he would be discovered. What was he thinking, then? Why hadn't he told Laurentia the moment he made her acquaintance of his true identity? Really, these questions were most intriguing. Did Villiers have depths hitherto unsuspected?

He remembered the callow lad of sixteen, deeply grieved by the loss of his parents. So cloaked in love had his life been that he trusted anyone and everyone—just like his father.

He smiled faintly, and tapped his cane lightly on the floor of the carriage. A warmth stole through his veins. He had taken only what by rights should have been his in the first place. He and the fourth viscount had both courted one of the wealthiest heiresses in the country. When Mary Pleasante chose Villiers over himself, he had promised a day of reckoning, a day which had come. The draining of Villier's son's fortune had, fifteen years later, made him one of the richest men in five counties—

with Cabot's help, of course. If his conscience ever troubled him, he ignored the occasional twinge. Yes, Villiers had been innocent, but so had he when a young man. And so the earth turned, and the sun shifted over the horizon, and the clouds formed into thunderstorms. Nothing remained the same. Yet, if one were clever, one could enjoy more sunshine than rain. Oh, and if he was nothing else, he was clever.

He chuckled faintly. How amusing it had been to watch Villiers's complexion drain of color as he recognized Laurentia's guest. How astonished he must have been. Now, what was he to do with Villiers's masquerade? That was the question. When should he alert Laurentia to her husband's charade? Or should he? By Jove, the chit seemed well settled on her course, a course on which naturally he could not allow to continue forever. However, if he remained mute concerning Villiers's identity he might just manage to avoid a confrontation entirely, with either of them. The divorce would proceed as planned, Villiers would leave the county, and he would one day marry the lovely Laurentia.

Yet, today she had asked him about the plantation. He frowned slightly. He shuddered. Cabot had kept her from society to prevent her knowing a deal too much about his business affairs. How, then, had she come to hear of the plantation? Who had told her of its existence? Had his own indiscretions several years ago in boasting alternately of the success and the failure of the plantation finally come home to roost? Ah, well. There was little enough evidence after all to prove the loss or the making of a fortune. To his knowledge, Cabot had destroyed his copy of the original paperwork which connected both of them to the plantation—just as *he* had, shortly after finding a servant of his perusing the damning papers so intently.

He drew in a deep breath. He had but to wait out the month of Villiers's marriage to Laurentia, and Cabot's will would work itself out tidily. Laurentia had shown amazing cunning in marrying as she did so that a divorce would quickly ensue, thereby making her mistress of her fortune. He found he was impressed, a circumstance which once again supported his intention of marrying her.

He nodded as the coach drew in front of the charming, picturesque home he had built several years past. How much he loved this home above the many others he owned! For him it represented his cleverness, this fine Gothic house swept with ivy over the numerous turrets. It was situated close enough to Laurentia to keep a firm eye on what he considered to be the rest of his fortune, and the stateliness of the architecture was a constant reminder that he was, indeed, a wealthy man.

From his perspective, as he descended the coach and entered the lofty foyer of his mansion, he decided there was only one aspect he could not quite see at this point—just what Villiers's game was, if any. Once he discovered his purpose, he would know if and when to end his masquerade. At present, he meant to enjoy his brandy.

"The usual in the green drawing room, Sir?" his elegant butler queried in soft politeness.

"Ah, yes, if you please, Felton. I trust a fire has been kept burning?"

"Indeed, sir. A strong fire."

He thought for a moment. "Will you send a man or two into the woods and find a Yule log, a fine, large log that we can keep burning until Christmas? I've a mind to restore that particular tradition to my home. It was a favorite of my mother's, you know."

"The entire staff will take to the notion, if you don't mind my saying so."

"I don't mind in the least," he offered grandly. "After all, what is Christmas without a Yule log?"

"Precisely," Felton murmured, as was expected of him.

Once settled in the green drawing room with a snifter of brandy cradled in his right palm, he sat in front of the fire, the smell of Christmas greens permeating the air from the mantel. He thought of Laurentia gracing both his house and hers as his beloved wife and the mother of the many children he hoped to enjoy from her womb. Only how to persuade the chit once she came into her fortune that she was destined to be his wife? Ah, Christmas, the time of beginnings. With Laurentia by his side, he would begin his life anew.

Dr. Ward sat across from Laurentia at dinner. He had called earlier to report on the fever at the orphanage, and brought nothing but happy news. He settled his fork on his plate and leaning forward slightly, addressed her. "I believe you saved at least half a dozen of the smallest children by your provision of proper blankets, food, and coal. We are, after all, quite fragile creatures. When our most basic requirements remain unmet, especially over a period of years, the toll on the body is dreadful. I have seen similar sufferings in the children who work the mines, their lives cut short by decades with each year spent laboring extraordinarily long hours underground. They grow up bent, malnourished. They don't live much beyond twenty, if they even survive to that age."

Laurentia leaned back in her chair. "I have heard of such things. Imagine in these modern times, in our very own country, sufferings which exist beyond our imagination." She grew silent. His words had affected her mightily, much as the local sufferings had affected her while growing up in Windrush.

She glanced at Thomas, who had listened attentively to the doctor's recounting of his trip to the orphanage. His expression had been grave throughout, and presently he was staring at his plate, pushing his peas against a bank of ham. In view of the good doctor's report, even her grandmother had been unable to relish the fine roast beef which Cook had prepared for the meal that evening.

Laurentia took a sip of claret, every thought sobered. She

believed Dr. Ward had brought her a message, not only of hope for the children of the orphanage, but also a pressing reminder of her original objectives in fulfilling her uncle's will by creating a sham marriage. She wanted more than anything to let her uncle's fortune be a balm to her country, to England, to restore to a state of health so much that had gone wrong in the past twenty years of war with France.

She addressed the doctor. "Then you believe that the danger of the fever is past?"

"Yes. I believe the source was the water barrels which had not been cleaned in some time."

"Then I am most grateful you responded to my request that you come to Windrush. I am not unaware of how difficult it is to travel at this time of year. If you wish for it, may I offer you a bedchamber for the night? Tomorrow, I shall have my servants prepare your carriage with hot bricks and a hamper of food."

"I must confess that I was hoping for just such an offer. The inn is quite comfortable, but,"—and here he smiled—"your gracious hospitality precedes you, Madame. I can think of no finer payment for my services than even an hour under your roof."

Laurentia smiled and chuckled. "You are trying to turn me up sweet, and I vow your efforts are having a proper effect. You may ask anything of me tonight or in the future, and I am yours to command."

Shortly after dinner, the good doctor retired early to his bedchamber. He had been tending the sick orphans for nearly fifteen hours, and confessed he wished for nothing more than a soft pillow for his head. Laurentia obliged him, adding to his comforts a cup of hot mulled wine which she knew would send him deeply into his slumbers.

In the drawing room, tea was enjoyed as the conversation turned to the happy effects of the doctor's visit to the orphanage. Mrs. Cabot took up a piece of whitework and began studiously picking at the thin fabric. "I am very proud of you, Laurentia," she stated, holding the small hoop to her eyes. The occupation of her fingers was an obvious delight to her. "You saw the need of the orphans and effected a change as quick as a cat could lick her whiskers. You are to be commended."

"Thank you, Grandmama," Laurentia said softly. "But it truly was the least I could do."

Thomas rose and arranged screens for them both against the chill of the outermost recesses of the grand chamber, and afterward brought a branch of candles to replace the single fat candle which had previously resided at Mrs. Cabot's elbow.

"Oh!" she cried. "No wonder I kept blinking at this ridiculous piece of cloth. Thank you, Mr. Swinfield. You are very kind. Laurentia, will you play for me a little, one or two carols and a little Handel? That would suit my labors wonderfully."

"Of course, Grandmama." She moved to seat herself at the pianoforte and immediately launched into the requested pieces. Thomas drew a chair forward to watch, not her fingers, but her face, a circumstance which several times caused her to play a wrong note.

When she had completed a second carol, she whispered, "Do you see how nervous you are making me! I winced my way through the last chorus."

He smiled and settled his elbow on the top of the pianoforte. "Do I distress you?" he asked, smiling a trifle crookedly.

"Yes," she murmured.

"Shall I move? Would you prefer I sat, oh, by the window?"

Since he gestured to the window facing the front drive, which was nearly thirty feet away, she giggled. "Of course not. You would become chilled, succumb to an inflammation of the lungs and perish, and I would be very sad, indeed!"

"Well, I wouldn't wish to make you sad on any count, so I shall remain fixed where I am."

She met his gaze, aware that their conversation bordered on flirtation, and wished not for the first time that she had not

been a great heiress, after all, but had been a simpler miss
who perhaps resided in Thomas's parish. She would have undoubtedly met him in more reasonable circumstances, at a local
ball or an assembly, say. He would have begged her to go
down a set or two. She would have let him make pretty love
to her over the following fortnight, and nothing should have
prevented her from tumbling madly in love with him. She
would have married him within a month of meeting, and afterward bore him a dozen children, or at least enough to fill
every chamber of the small cottage she would share with him,
so that laughter never stopped ringing from the rafters.

She drew in a deep breath, but did not let out the heavy
sigh which should have followed. She did not want Thomas
to know even in the smallest way the nature of her thoughts.
When he opened his mouth to pose the question which she
had watched rise to his exquisite blue eyes, she stopped him
by launching into a simple Handel *contredanse.* He laughed
and settled back in his chair, closing his eyes and enjoying the
progress of the music.

When the Handel drew to a close, she played a Mozart sonata. She concentrated on the action of her fingers against the
keys, on the shape the notes took as one line of melody sup-
planted the next. As she gave herself to the performance and
all its nuances, she forgot about Thomas, the doctor, the orphans, Sir Alan's unexpected arrival, the forthcoming trip to
Bath, her marriage, her hopes, her regrets. The music swelled
inside her and drove her arms, wrists, and fingers until she
was one with the instrument.

Time stopped, and only resumed when she had played the
last vibrant note.

She came back to earth after a time, aware that Thomas was
watching her and waiting. She breathed deeply, settled her
hands in her lap, and said, "I love playing that piece. You've
no idea."

"You are out there. I have a very strong idea how much

you enjoy it. You are utterly transformed when you play. Angelic, I think. Certainly, you were not here while you were running your fingers over the keys."

She smiled, the delicious lethargy of the performance still clinging to her. "You understand, then."

"Only what I can observe."

"Your observations explain my sensations precisely. I always wondered if anyone could detect how I felt." She rose from her seat and moved to stand near him. "Somehow, I am not surprised that you comprehend. From the first, you seemed to understand me."

A gentle snoring interrupted the conversation. Laurentia turned slightly with a smile to see that her grandmother's head was settled into the crook of the winged chair, her mouth slightly agape and an occasional rumbling issuing from her throat. "Poor dear!" she murmured. "She is fagged to death."

"Is this usual for her?" Thomas asked.

Laurentia laughed. "No, not at all," she whispered. "But you see, she is busy about some secret plans which she insists exist only in my imagination. I know that she is devising something, for she keeps covering up whatever writing she's been doing just after I enter the room. I daresay you and I will have to endure at least a soiree while we share the same roof. Will you have difficulty managing that?"

"Not a bit," he responded promptly, rising to his feet. "Come. Sit down and rest your fingers. Perhaps we can talk awhile."

"Quietly, mind," she said. "I do not wish to wake her."

"Of course."

He sat very close to her on the sofa, providing her with a footstool and behaving in every way, she thought, just as she would have wished her husband to behave. His consideration was everything she could want in a companion, and his conversation never lacked either sense or description. More than once she had to cover her mouth to keep from laughing aloud at something he said. More than once she found herself wishing that the hour was not advancing. More than once she longed to touch his face or take his hand in hers, to settle her head on his shoulder. Why she felt this way precisely, she could not say, except that Thomas was such an agreeable companion.

When the hour chimed ten o'clock, her grandmother awoke, signaling the end of the warm, delightful evening. Laurentia regretted nothing so much as the disruption of the sweet communion she had been enjoying with her husband.

He helped her grandmother to the chair, which would be carried upstairs as usual by the strongest of Evenlode's footmen, then summoned them. When Mrs. Cabot was mounting the stairs in queenly splendor, Thomas took her own arm and escorted her up the stairs following behind her grandmother.

After Mrs. Cabot was settled in her bedchamber, Thomas escorted Laurentia to her door, as was his habit. He lifted her hand to his lips and placed a lingering kiss on her fingers. She, in turn, quite spontaneously caressed his face with her hand, and surprised even herself by settling a gentle kiss on his lips. Her thoughts were drawn back abruptly to the passionate kiss she had shared with him in the music room. She wanted him to kiss her again, just in that way. If only he would!

She drew back slowly, willing him to kiss her, but saw such an anguished look in his eyes that her heart crumpled with sadness. Of course he couldn't kiss her. What good could come of such hopeless intimacies when they were destined to divorce in so short a time? "Goodnight," she murmured.

"Goodnight, Laurentia," he responded quietly.

She noted the tightness of his shoulders just as she closed the door, and knew he was making a great effort to control himself. She smiled sadly, and wished for the barest moment that he were not so disciplined. What would happen, for instance, were he to ignore their agreement and simply charge into her bedchamber and make her his wife, indeed? Would she deny him? Would she insist he leave before ever he touched her? Or would she welcome his advances? Would she then hope for the marriage to remain in place?

With these torturous yet not entirely unhappy thoughts running rampant through her mind, she tumbled into bed and hoped to dream any number of wonderful dreams in which Thomas would form the central player.

Swinfield. Suddenly the name had a familiar ring to it, as though she had heard it before, somewhere, sometime in the distant past. How strange. Why should the faint memory come to her now, and what could possibly be the context of his name?

When a long cogitation failed to bring forth anything more than a sensation she had heard of 'Swinfield' before, she fell into a deep sleep.

Eight

"No, you are mistaken entirely," Laurentia said. The sleigh glided across the newly fallen snow, the shushing sound of the rails a delightful counterpoint to the jingling silver bells dangling from the horse harness. "The Thomas's Day *fete* will not be for the gentry exclusively, but for the entire village of Windrush and the surrounding families."

"How very much like you," Thomas responded warmly, "to include everyone."

Laurentia loved the sound of his voice, and turned to look at him. Her heart seemed to melt a little bit more as he smiled down upon her and drew the thick, fur carriage rug more closely about her neck and chin. She still could not credit that her grandmama had had the sleigh restored sufficiently to afford her a long, leisurely ride about the countryside with Thomas. With hot bricks beneath her feet, she could not have been more comfortable had she been in the library. The daylight was fading swiftly, and as the sleigh rushed along lights began twinkling from every farmhouse and stone cottage they passed by.

In a few days, she would begin her first journey to Bath. Yet, even as much as she was eagerly awaiting the trip, she could not imagine being happier than she was now, bundled up in a sleigh beside her husband.

Thomas held her gloved hand in his, hidden secretively beneath the warm fur. What would he think of her, she wondered, if he knew her thoughts, that they were not at all fixed on the Christmas celebration she had been planning for years, and which very soon would come to pass? No, of the moment she had little interest in the festoons several of the village's needle-women were creating for the strict purpose of decorating for the St. Thomas's Day party in the village. Instead, even as she spoke, her every sense was fixed on the feel of Thomas's fingers gently gliding over hers as he appeared to be listening intently to her discourse.

"You cannot imagine how many times I had played the entire event over and over in my mind," she said, expanding on the celebration. "Who would be there, and under what circumstances, how ecstatic each villager would be upon receiving the invitation, the food that would have to be procured from Tewkesbury—I want oranges for everyone, which will mean a frightful expense, since they are grown in succession houses." Her mind drifted to her hand, and to the gooseflesh which rippled up her arm in waves as Thomas's fingers dipped over each finger in succession. She would never have believed that something so simple as a man's touch could make her wish to be kissed and hugged and touched a little more.

The moment seemed dangerous to her, somehow, as though hidden desires were making themselves known to her once more and threatening her careful plans.

Then she wondered how it was that neither of her former beaux had been able to arouse such odd feelings within her by merely holding her hand and toying with her fingers.

Thomas asked, "Do you think the gentry will attend if it is known the villagers have been invited? Sir Alan, for instance?"

Laurentia turned to him and met his gaze. She had heard his question, but the words hadn't yet made quite enough sense to be answered. Instead, she found herself trembling a little, and wishing that he would kiss her and toy with her lips in the same manner in which he was teasing her fingers. Was he aware of what he was doing?

His question began to form a proper sequence in her brain. Still, she would sigh, and her gaze fell to his lips, as though one part of her was continuing to enjoy his physical presence while the other shaped an answer in her head. Finally, she said, "Undoubtedly Sir Alan will attend, and I daresay the gentry, as well. Wealth is one of those curious entities which creates professed allegiances, no matter the varying views of the persons concerned. Because I, and thereby my uncle's fortune, have cast the invitation, many will come merely to court what I can give in the future. You mustn't think I believe myself ill-used, for it is nothing of the sort. I don't give a fig·why everyone comes, only that they do."

When had her voice fallen to a whisper? His face seemed indistinct, somehow. All she knew was that his lips were closer than before, and she was straining toward him. She found her head drifting sideways a little. The hand, so entwined with hers, suddenly withdrew. The arm, attached, slid up hers, and before she knew quite what was happening she was enveloped in Thomas's arms. His lips were on hers in the twinkling of an eye.

She sighed with deep satisfaction. The very thing she had wished for had come to pass. Thomas was kissing her again, as he had kissed her in the music room, warmly, deeply, passionately.

The sleigh hurried on as the coachman encouraged his team forward. The snow cushioned every lump in the road. Laurentia parted her lips and received Thomas's exploration of her mouth. Her own hand slid over his chest and rested in the vicinity of his heart to pluck at the fabric of his coat in a restless manner.

"Laurentia," he murmured hoarsely between gentle assaults. "I have been longing to kiss you again, so very much."

"I, you," she responded softly as she kissed him fully in return.

The kiss became an adventure as night fell over the countryside and the mounded snow became rippled with black shadows. Conversation was entirely forgotten. All that remained was an endless enjoyment of Thomas's mouth and his extravagant response with a tongue that searched and probed until she was certain he had thereby come to know every recess of her soul.

His chest and shoulders became a land to be discovered beneath her restless hand. His arms were muscled and strong, something she had noted before, given how nicely he filled out his coatsleeves. But this touching of the same limb previously admired by her eyes was unequalled, and served to prove the truism that experience far overshadowed mere observation.

His hand was not so much interested in her arm as her waist. He squeezed her and cuddled her, his fingers occasionally teasing her with a tickle until she giggled and made him laugh, as well. There was a gentleness in the entire forbidden exchange that appealed to her mightily, and made her want to repeat such mutual enjoyment many times before Thomas had to leave.

How much she wished that thought had not intruded into the series of kisses he was even now plying over her lips.

Thomas must leave.

Yes, indeed he must, but not now, not tonight, not with the stars sparkling in a bold, black sky and smiling down over the sleigh ride. She would, she decided, force the thought away— except that something in her embrace or the touch of her lips against his then communicated the sad nature of her thoughts.

"What are you thinking, my dear Laurentia?" he whispered.

"That you will leave in little less than three weeks."

He settled his forehead against hers tenderly. "I thought that might be what had disturbed you. I have striven for the past half hour to keep such wretched thoughts at bay, and had succeeded—until now."

"Well," she responded with a toss of her head. "I would have said nothing. Indeed, I meant to set aside such an unhappy cogitation, but you would ask me what I was thinking. So you see, it is your fault. By now, I daresay I should have forgotten all about the future." She slid her arm about his neck and leaned provocatively toward him.

He did not hesitate, but slanted his lips over hers, and once more she was sunk in the pleasure of kissing her husband and allowing him to kiss her forcefully in return.

Her husband. Now, *there* was a proper direction for her mind to take. For the present she meant to contemplate the joys of marriage as though there was no tomorrow, no contract to dissolve the vows spoken in Scotland, no need for her to protect her inheritance from the laws of the land.

He only stopped exploring her mouth and kneading the soft skin of her waist when the sleigh drew to a halt in front of Evenlode House.

As Thomas released her, Laurentia began to scheme for a goodnight kiss, but not at her bedchamber door—perhaps in the drawing room when her grandmother had departed for her bed, perhaps in the morning room—which was so beautifully decorated in the Christmas spirit and which she thought would be most romantic if lit with oh, perhaps, a score of candles—or perhaps the music room, and they could dance together again. How delightful that would be! Yes, the music room again!

"Look at what your servants have done!" Thomas exclaimed.

Laurentia dragged her eyes from his face, and for the first time since crossing the portals of her home she glanced around at the entrance hall. "Merciful heavens!" she cried. The entire staircase was twisted with greens, laced with yards and yards of red ribbon, and glittering with strings of clear glass beads. "Whatever was my grandmother thinking?"

Mrs. Cabot appeared in the doorway of the drawing room. "There you are!" she cried, moving slowly forward with her cane in hand. Laurentia quickly divested herself of her warm cape and velvet bonnet and crossed the hall to place a kiss on her cheek. Mrs. Cabot asked, "How do you like my surprise?"

"Truly, it is exquisite, and you know how much I wish every chamber could be dressed just as this one is. Grandmama, we really must scour the countryside for a proper Yule log."

Her grandmother's smile broadened.

Laurentia clapped her hands together. "You've already found one!"

Mrs. Cabot nodded. "Indeed, I have. The largest one I can remember." Her eyes suddenly filled with tears.

"What is it, dearest?" Laurentia asked softly, slipping an arm about her thin shoulders.

Mrs. Cabot pursed her lips together. "I loved my son and I have grieved losing him, but he was a complete spoilsport. I don't think he had an ounce of fun and gig in him and, though it is dreadfully disloyal of me to say so, I must confess this Christmas shall be the first to resemble my childhood since times out of mind." Her voice dropped to a whisper. "I don't like to mention the matter, but there was something unbalanced about Percival."

Laurentia had always thought so, but would never admit, even now, to such ruminations. Instead, she responded, "He was very careful with his pocketbook, and I know he did not like to see more than was necessary spent."

"You may speak of his fastidious nature, but every bit of greenery has cost nothing since it has been pruned from the gardens, and the ribbons and beads I have had laid by since my dear husband passed away. No, Laurentia, you do not need to soften Percival's memory for me. My son knew how to increase his wealth, but he knew very little about living or loving. Promise me, my darling, that you will not be such a one. Promise me that. I should die a contented woman if I knew that a granddaughter of mine would carry on the traditions much nearer to my heart than the acquisition of a fortune."

Laurentia did not know what to say to her, and found herself glancing longingly toward Thomas. He had remained a discreet distance away, regarding her lovingly. After a moment, she said, "I can promise you this much, Grandmama, that I will not set my fortune above the happiness of those I love."

"I can wish for nothing more than that," Mrs. Cabot responded. "But come. Even now one end of the Yule log has been set to burning in a most clever manner by Bream. If we are to keep it aglow until Christmas Day, we shall have to be very careful."

Laurentia felt tears sting her eyes. "Grandmama, I am so happy!" she cried.

"As am I," she returned, taking Laurentia's proffered arm and patting it gently. "As am I."

Over the next few days, Laurentia found herself in a glow of spirits. Her camaraderie with Thomas had grown with each passing day, and more than once he had taken her to the music room, quite secretly of course, to dance with her, to hold her in his arms, and to kiss her. How it was she had come to permit herself the enjoyment of such outrageous conduct she could not imagine, though she felt certain the magic of the season played a significant part in what was swiftly become a daily occurrence.

More delightful than just a nocturnal embrace or two," however, was the odd circumstance of finding how much pleasure Thomas's sudden appearance could bring to her, how a mere smile would set her heart to beating wildly, and how she cherished the times he would lay a comforting hand upon her shoulder.

Even now, as she scoured her uncle's ledgers once more for

some reference to the plantation Mrs. Marycote had spoken of, she heard the door to the office open with such a degree of hope springing up in her chest that she felt nearly giddy as she turned to watch Thomas enter the chamber.

A feeling very near to euphoria suddenly poured through her entire being. She was on her feet in an instant, and hurried to meet him halfway. He bore a tea tray with service for one. "I thought you might enjoy a little refreshment. Have you made the progress you had hoped for?"

She shook her head. "I don't understand how my uncle achieved his wealth," she stated. "I mean, I know that my grandfather enjoyed some eight thousand a year, but I have not been able to ascertain how, when he passed this inheritance to his eldest son, my uncle was then able to quadruple his wealth."

"What?" Thomas asked, astonished.

"Yes, well you may stare, but so it has happened. I have reviewed the figures a score of times, and it appears to me that his wealth began to increase approximately twelve, perhaps even fifteen years ago, quite suddenly."

Thomas whistled softly. "To quadruple one's fortune in fifteen years would require a keen mind of no small order. Are you certain?"

"Yes. Very much so. I have also been thinking that I would like to speak with Mr. Crabtree in Tewkesbury. Perhaps he may be able to help me comprehend the source of the increase to Uncle's wealth. Would you mind terribly if we paid him a call on our way to Bath tomorrow?"

"I think it an excellent notion. But now, if you please, sit down and enjoy your tea. Otherwise, it will grow cold in a matter of a few more minutes."

Laurentia asked Thomas to wait for her while she spoke for a few minutes with Mr. Crabtree. He obliged her readily by stating that he was hoping for a chance to admire the architecture of the ancient city. She made her way into Mr. Crabtree's office with a hopeful heart. Having found in her uncle's papers neither the source of his increased wealth, nor even a hint of the plantation of which Mrs. Marycote had spoken, she hoped he would have an answer for her.

When she made her inquiries, he said, "I'm sorry, Mrs. Swinfield, but I don't have the information you seek. In particular, I never drew up documents concerning a West Indies plantation, nor to my recollection did I ever heard your uncle speak of such an investment. In addition, though Mr. Cabot made use of my services to draw up any number of documents over the years pertaining to a large quantity of investments, I was not privy to the actual disbursal or accumulation of future funds. To my knowledge, he performed his own accountings of each investment, so that I am not even able to direct you to a banker or financier who would be able to help you."

"I see," she murmured, her hopes dimming. "His ledgers are in excellent order, and for the most part I am coming to understand the flow of profits which accrued to him over the years. What I have not been able to discover is what seems to be a large discrepancy occurring approximately twelve years ago in which his available funds for a number of investments seem to have simply appeared, without record. I find it most peculiar."

Mr. Crabtree frowned. "Perhaps there is a Missing ledger, then—one that accounts for the plantation about which you have inquired, and which might afford an explanation for the monies of which you speak."

"Precisely my thoughts, though I can find no reference to such a plantation in either his correspondence or his many financial documents. I was informed recently of the possible existence of the plantation by a dear friend who had heard only rumors of its existence over the years, which is why I asked you if you had seen a document to that effect. I, myself, am not certain one even exists."

"I'm sorry, Madame, but I have not. The larger investments, of which I have a general knowledge, include a canal, a trading company, and a cotton-spinning mill in Lancashire, but no plantation."

"I have found documents pertaining to the investments you've mentioned. The mill in Lancashire has been particularly profitable." She thought again of her conversation with Mrs. Marycote, and on impulse inquired, "To your knowledge, did my uncle have many business dealings with Sir Alan Redcliffe?"

"Yes," he responded promptly. "I believe nearly every venture involved Sir Alan in one aspect or another. Sir Alan, it would seem, had an eye to increasing his fortune, as well."

"Nearly every venture?" she inquired, stunned.

"Yes, Madame."

She felt uneasy suddenly, as though some truth long-suspected was beginning to make its way into her awareness. She had always held Sir Alan in great affection. His manners, so unlike her uncle's were not in the least boorish. He had spoken kindly to her since ever she could remember, and more than once had reprimanded her uncle for speaking crossly to her. For that alone, she had always valued his presence in her life.

Only this understanding of how nearly involved he was with her uncle made her nervous and uneasy. How could such a good man align himself so nearly with a man she considered to be base, and at times even cruel?

She had no answer for this question, and since Mr. Crabtree had responded to her numerous queries she felt obliged to rise, thank him for taking the time to speak with her, and bid him farewell. She found Thomas on the street staring up at the sky.

"What are you looking at?" she asked.

"Oh, you are finished, then?"

"Yes."

His glance trailed up the side of the building. "The construction. I believe this particular building to be three hundred years old, and the one across the street a little older. How many generations have passed through these doors? I wonder. It is quite remarkable, don't you agree?"

She looked at him and never once glanced toward the golden stone of the building. "Quite," she murmured softly.

He turned toward her, a quizzical expression in his eyes. Upon catching the meaning of her compliment, he completely disentangled his interest from Tewkesbury's architecture and turned fully toward her. "Are you flirting with me, Mrs. Swinfield?" he queried, smiling softly upon her.

"I don't know how to flirt," she responded with an answering smile. "So, you mustn't judge my conduct on that score. I was only thinking how very nice it was to be around a man who has a variety of interests. I rarely spoke with my uncle, but on the few occasions I attempted to engage him in conversation he seemed decidedly bored. I daresay unless I was speaking in terms of percentages and profit returns he had no interest in the subject, whatsoever. I recall once having mentioned that the monsoon season had begun in the China Sea, and his eyes actually lit up. I recall he said something about his stock being affected. Another time I mentioned the heat of India, and he declared that the northern mills, and an emerging array of English fabrics, would soon beat the Indian muslin industry all to flinders. Otherwise, he was silent, if not positively sullen."

Thomas took her arm and guided her toward the door of the traveling chariot. At the same time, the postilion mounted the leader. "From what you've told me he was certainly competent at his work."

"Having been for these past few days in the process of reviewing his ledgers, I would have to agree with you. Every tuppence seems to be accounted for." *At least in the past twelve years,* she thought, bemused.

She climbed into the carriage and found, much to her delight, that Thomas had procured a new pair of heated bricks for her. "Thank you!" she cried. "How very kind of you!"

"Nonsense," he replied. "Any *husband* would have done the same."

"From what I have observed," she responded, wide-eyed, "in that you are greatly mistaken. Chivalry has much departed England, though I do see something of it when Sir Alan is nearby. He has an eye to the comforts a lady enjoys most, just as you do." She felt the very air in the carriage change upon mentioning the baronet, and could not help but turn toward Thomas and eye him carefully.

He was not looking at her, but his hand was gripping the leather carriage strap tightly, and his complexion was whiter than it ought to have been. She said nothing, but watched him for a moment, remembering how he had looked the day he had met Sir Alan in her drawing room. The set of his jaw had been the same then as it was now—rather unyielding, she thought. She could recall being perplexed at what seemed to be a strain between the men at the time, but now she felt truly troubled. Was there some history between them of which she was not aware that would cause Thomas to fall so thoroughly silent? The men professed to know each other only slightly. What, then, had happened to create such a frosty degree of acquaintance between them?

As the carriage moved into the stream of coaches, gigs, carts, and heavily laden wagons, she said, "I hope I do not give offense, Thomas, but I don't believe you esteem Sir Alan as I do."

She watched him release the carriage strap as though with considerable effort before turning toward her. "I will not lie to you, Laurentia. There is some bad blood between us, something not yet reconciled. Indeed, when you asked me to wed you for a time one of the considerations was that Sir Alan resided in the vicinity, and I was hoping I might discover if there is any foundation for the trouble between us."

At these words, she brightened considerably. "Then you are hoping to be reconciled in your friendship?"

"I don't know if such a thing is possible, even were we to come to terms with the particular incident that has separated us these many years and more. You see, he was a good friend of my father's at one time, and I have felt that Sir Alan did him a disservice after his death some fifteen years ago. I have no proof, though, only a number of suspicions, one of which centers on a plantation he was said to have owned some time past."

"A plantation?" she asked weakly.

"Yes, but I know very little about it. I have been unable to locate documents in proof of his ownership of the plantation, or any other financial records concerning it."

The mere fact that she had only a few minutes prior requested information from Mr. Crabtree about her uncle's supposed plantation alarmed her exceedingly. Had the men at one time owned a plantation jointly? Fifteen years ago? Had Thomas somehow been connected to that plantation as an investor? Or Thomas's father? Sir Alan had refuted knowledge of such a venture. Had he lied to her, then? But why? Oh, if only she had some written word of its existence.

"I can see that you are overset," Thomas said, taking hold of her hand. "For the present, why don't we set aside my concerns about Sir Alan and enjoy our trip to Bath? Even in the winter we will be passing through some very pretty countryside."

At that, she felt enormously relieved. "An excellent notion," she said. She didn't want to hear anything further about Sir Alan or his connection to her uncle, at least not yet, and certainly nothing more about a rumored plantation.

Laurentia enjoyed every moment of the journey from Tewkesbury to Bath, which saw her traveling chariot drawing into the innyard of the White Hart after the sun had set over the Welsh mountains. Thomas confessed he had promised to call on a friend of his the moment he arrived in Bath, a call he did not expect to take much above an hour. Almost immediately upon arriving, therefore, Laurentia was left alone in her bedchamber, for which she found herself grateful. During the time he was gone she would be able to arrange her gowns to her satisfaction and order a dinner for Thomas and herself to be enjoyed in the privacy of their rooms once he returned.

Villiers was ushered into a well-appointed drawing room and offered a seat opposite the fireplace by his host, James Dursley. When he had first arrived at Lansdown Crescent—the direction given him by Mr. Crabtree—Mrs. Dursley had refused to see a mere Mr. Swinfield, unknown to her, and the maid had summoned a footman to eject him from the residence until Mr. Dursley himself hurried down the stairs. He had worn a haggard expression, and begged to know why he wasn't informed of his guest's arrival. The servants' belligerent responses gave considerable proof of the unhappy nature of the household.

Once in the drawing room, Villiers explained that a certain Mr. Crabtree of Tewkesbury had suggested he speak to him concerning Laurentia Cabot—presently his wife, Mrs. Swinfield—since she had been making inquiries about him in recent weeks. "Having learned of her former interest in you, Mr. Dursley, I was hoping I might be able to set her mind at ease about certain expectations she had once had but which had been terminated quite without warning some few years ago."

Mr. Dursley clamped his lips together. "So you have wed the beautiful Miss Cabot."

Villiers nodded.

"What would my life have been," he murmured to himself,

"had I not allowed myself to be persuaded to leave Windrush?"

"I beg your pardon?"

Mr. Dursley turned toward him, and for the first time Villiers could see the dark shadows of dissipation which colored the skin beneath his eyes. The man looked old far beyond his years. "I was just saying that I have been a great fool, and only recently have come to understand the depths of the errors I have made."

"You do not mind, then, discussing this matter with me? I realize it must seem impertinent on my part, but I wish to see my wife's mind laid to rest. She was uncommonly fond of you. She believed herself in love with you." He found himself angry in the presence of Mr. Dursley. If what he believed Mr. Dursley had done was true, he wondered if he could restrain his rising temper against a man he could only think of as a complete blackguard.

Yet, he had known such men before, who in their youth had traded on fine looks and the ability to sit a horse well for a place in society, rather than pursuing tenets of honor and character. What had Dursley traded for the privilege of marrying Laurentia? Mere money? The Egyptian furnishings in the elegant house spoke of wealth. Was this what he had gained in not wedding her? Yet, had Mr. Dursley married Laurentia, he would have been wealthy beyond his imagination.

"I loved her," he said. "Who would not have loved such a young woman? Who, upon having cast eyes on Laurentia Cabot, or upon having spent even one hour in her lively, innocent company, would not have tumbled head over ears in love with such a creature?"

"Then why, for God's sake," Villiers cried, "Did you leave Windrush without a word to her?"

"It was part of the agreement. I was to simply disappear." He turned anguished eyes upon Villiers. "I daresay you've no notion what it's like to love a woman to the point of madness yet know you can never possess her. But so it was. *He* came to me, and made it clear I could not stay. He sweetened his threats with a small fortune. I found I could do naught else but leave Gloucestershire."

"So you accepted Sir Alan Redcliffe's money to leave Windrush without a word to Miss Cabot?" he queried, forcing the point. He held his breath, waiting to see if Mr. Dursley would implicate Sir Alan.

"Yes, Mr. Swinfield. Redcliffe paid me handsomely to quit Evenlode, and made it clear that to stay would bring the full weight of his power and consequence against me. I was in no doubt of either his meaning or his ability to fulfill any threat he might wish to make against me. Even so, I should have been more courageous. I failed Laurentia, and I failed myself." He laughed bitterly. "But if it is any comfort to your offended sense of honor, I wish you to know that not a day has passed in which I have not regretted the path I chose." He crossed the room abruptly, poured himself a sherry, and swallowed the drink without blinking once. He offered a glass to Villiers, who refused with a tight shake of his head.

Villiers might have felt pity for the ridiculous youth, so handsome of face and figure, who had won Laurentia and lost her because of his own cowardice, had he not been consumed with a desire to plant the wretched fellow a facer for having brought so much pain to Laurentia's innocent heart. He knew quite well, given the man's obvious lack of character, that he was no match for her, and that she was well out of the bargain. However, the fact that he had hurt her as he had, abandoning her without a word of explanation, simply enraged him.

He felt strongly that he should quit Lansdown Crescent before he attempted to prove the worth of the many lessons he had endured in sparring with Gentleman Jackson himself!

He rose to his feet and thanked Dursley for receiving him with so little notice.

"I'm grateful you came to speak with me. I needed someone

to know of my perfidy. Perhaps, now . . ." His jaw worked strongly, and he could not complete his thought. After a moment he said, "I'll be at the Pump Room tomorrow at eleven. If you are inclined, would you bring Mrs. Swinfield there? I should like to make my apologies to her—in person."

"That would be the least you should do," he stated coldly.

Mr. Dursley nodded. "You have every reason to dislike me."

"No man, no gentleman, would have accepted such an arrangement."

Mr. Dursley laughed harshly. "There you have the right of it!" he cried.

Villiers stared at him for a long moment and finally said, "I will bring my wife to the Pump Room at eleven, but she does not know that I am known to you, and I would prefer for the present that it remain thus."

Mr. Dursley nodded, but his eyes narrowed at the same moment. "What are you about, Mr. Swinfield?"

"Merely to interest myself in all that concerns my wife."

"I see. Well, please let me assure you that in this instance she was completely without fault. I was entirely to blame."

At that, Villiers could only smile. "I have no doubt that you were." He turned to go and reiterated, "The Pump Room at eleven. Don't fail me. I shall afford you a moment of privacy with Laurentia. She will undoubtedly wish to hear from your own lips the exact nature of your, er, *perfidy.*"

"I shall consider it my duty to oblige you, sir."

Nine

The next morning, Laurentia stood at the entrance to the famous Pump Room, astonished that after so many years she was finally here. The chamber was quite thin of people, since the *beau monde* flocked to Bath during the late spring and early summer months. Still, the experience made her feel that somehow she had begun to live, finally, after so many years of isolation at Evenlode.

Many of those gathered about the counter, waiting to be given their three prescribed glasses of water, were bent with rheumatism, afflicted with the gout, or coughing in a familiar and unhappy manner. Since times out of mind, the Bath waters had been taken for their medicinal purposes. Laurentia intended to imbibe all three glasses herself, not to improve her health but to proclaim that she had, on one occasion in the winter of 1818, taken the waters at Bath.

"You must not listen to the various reports you've heard," Thomas said. "Indeed, I have found the waters quite refreshing, and not nearly so heinous as is frequently reported."

"Indeed?" Laurentia cried, glancing up at him hopefully. "You give me courage that I shall be able to endure the experience with a degree of equanimity I had not looked for. I have been told the waters are utterly vile."

"I won't allow it," he said. He then smiled on her and leaned down to whisper, "You look very fetching in your new bonnet.

That particular shade of blue velvet, quite reminiscent of the night sky just past sunset, sets your dove's complexion to extreme advantage."

For the moment, Laurentia forgot entirely about taking the waters. She turned her gaze upon her husband, and, with knees that began to tremble anew, thanked him. "You are very kind to say so, but do you not think it an extravagant creation with three matching ostrich feathers?"

"Quite. But then your hair is equally extravagant, and can certainly balance the entire effect."

Everything he said pleased her. "You begin to cause me to doubt your motives, Thomas. I do so enjoy what you say to me that I have been wondering for these past few days and more if you are hoping to remain in Gloucestershire beyond our agreed upon month."

She had meant the words to form a compliment, but she could see by the suddenly stricken look in his eye that he had misconstrued her thoughts entirely.

"I do not design my speeches," he responded quietly, "if that is what you mean. As for intending to continue my sojourn at your home, nothing could be further from my purposes, I assure you."

She could see that he believed she had questioned his character. She felt deeply chagrined, so much so that tears suddenly bit her eyes. "My words were drawn poorly," she said in a whisper. "I . . . I meant to suggest I would not find it at all an unhappy circumstance were you to, well, to find a home in Windrush or, or something of the like. I have come to value your friendship, your company, beyond anything."

He took her arm in his strong grip, and she was forced to look up at him. His eyes were blazing, and she feared what he would say next. "To what purpose would I live near you? To be tormented that I could never possess what has in this past fortnight become so very dear to me? Laurentia, you've spoken more cruelly to me than you will ever know."

She had become dear to him. Her heart turned over in her breast in several waves of pleasure. She was dear to him! Oh, happiest of days.

She wished of the moment they were not in the Pump Room, where so many could easily comprehend their exchange. She had so many things she wanted suddenly to say to him, yet couldn't. "Thomas, we must speak of this," she murmured.

"Again, to what purpose, my dear? I could never remain unless our marriage was other than the terrible sham it is, and yet I must leave because I vowed I would never wed unless I could offer my bride a proper home for our children."

Her gaze drifted away from his. "My house has sufficient room for a score of children." So much sadness welled up in her chest that she wondered if she would ever be happy again.

"Oh, not a score," he responded, attempting for a lighter tone. "No lady should suffer so."

She again met his gaze. "I grew up in a large, empty house, and I always dreamed of a score of siblings with which to play, or to do battle, or to converse. I am sorry, Thomas, for having spoken words that were as useless as they were unkind. I suppose you have merely reminded me of old dreams that must die if I am to achieve all that is in my heart. Pray, forgive me?"

She laid her hand on his arm. He searched her eyes and finally said, "I wish that I had met you years ago, when I had more to offer, and you were not fixed on this course."

She wasn't certain what he meant, since she knew him to be quite poor. Had he at one time expected an inheritance? She had no way of knowing, since the subject had never been amplified. "I, too," she responded. "And now, before we set all the tongues to wagging in this fine, old establishment by our brangling, shall we enjoy the waters?"

A few minutes later, Laurentia stared at a glass of Bath's famous water and took a sniff. The odor was horrendous. "Oh, my," she murmured.

Glancing up at Thomas, who was eyeing her calmly, she scrutinized his face carefully for some sign indicating he hadn't owned the truth to her, but his expression was completely innocent. Was it possible he had purposely misrepresented the taste of the waters to her?

"Henhearted?" he queried provokingly.

She scowled at him, but his words urged her on. She took a deep breath and began to drink. She squeezed her eyes shut as the first flavor of the water became known to her.

Vile! Oh, he had purposely told her a Banbury tale, the wretch!

She could drink no more! She drew the glass back from her lips and sputtered. Water dribbled down her chin, her eyes filled with tears, and her cheeks contracted painfully.

Thomas hastily offered her a kerchief, one she recognized from the Tump and Dagler Inn with the beautiful *V* embroidered in the corner. She grabbed at the kerchief as more of the water leaked from between her lips. She was never so mortified!

However, a faint chuckle could be heard issuing from her companion's throat.

She turned to glare at him as she settled the glass on the counter.

He bit his lip. He turned away from her. She watched as his shoulders began to rise and fall rapidly. He covered his mouth with his gloved hand. He began to cough.

Odious man that he was, he had purposely lied to her, to make her think she would be drinking something of no consequence, at all! Instead, she was convinced the water was prepared with a combination of mud and rotting beet tops.

She gently refused a second glass and tipped the pumper, after which she turned away, still pressing the kerchief to her mouth. She wondered if the awful taste would ever leave her tongue.

"You may stop laughing now," she stated curtly, "if you are

able." As he turned toward her, she extended the kerchief to him. He was, however, mopping his eyes with a second kerchief, and did not at first perceive the one she was handing to him.

"If only you could have seen your expression, my dear. Your eyes nearly popped from your head."

"That was a terrible joke to play on anyone, nonetheless your wife. But honestly, Thomas, I've never tasted anything so bad before. I vow sour milk is an aperitif to that horrid brew."

"Rotten eggs?" he murmured, still sniffing and chuckling as he began folding up his kerchief.

"Indeed! That is precisely the odor of the water, now that I think on it, though for a moment I was certain the creation had been constructed from Cook's compost heap!" She glanced at the kerchief he held in his hand and noted that the second one he possessed was also embroidered with an exquisite *V.* She recalled he had told her, or intimated, that a certain female acquaintance of his some years past had given him the kerchief. Had she, then, given him two? Or three?

As he took the one she held in her hand, she would have asked him about the odd circumstance of his possessing possibly three identical kerchiefs, purportedly from the same lady, when a man appeared at her elbow and addressed her.

"Miss Cabot. I wonder if you will remember me."

Laurentia turned and stared into a handsome and quite familiar face that brought a host of memories flooding her with equal parts of joy and pain. "James," she murmured, completely stunned. "Whatever are you doing here? How did you . . . that is, I cannot credit that you are here, before me."

"I am," he said, his dark eyes suddenly anguished. "When I saw you standing at the counter I thought perhaps I was seeing an apparition. How do you fare?"

She had flirted with him in the beechgrove, letting him chase her and catch her and kiss her. She felt so foolish now as she recalled how, after having proposed to her, he had simply vanished from Windrush. "You left so suddenly. You didn't even say good-bye. Friends ought to at least bid farewell before departing."

"I behaved in an excessively uncivil manner, I fear. I beg you will forgive me. Indeed, when I recognized you here today I had no other thought in mind but to offer my humblest apologies."

Laurentia found that there was so much she wanted to say to him, both of her anger and her hurt, that she could not order her thoughts.

"I don't mean to intrude," Thomas said quietly, "for I can see that you are old friends, but do let me make myself known to you. Thomas Swinfield, Miss Cabot's husband, at your service."

"Then you are wed?" Mr. Dursley cried swiftly, picking up Thomas's lead and taking a step nearer to Laurentia.

She nodded, appearing dumbstruck.

Mr. Dursley continued. "I am delighted, truly." With great politeness, he then turned to Thomas. "I do beg your pardon," he said. "Allow me to present myself. I am James Dursley, presently of Bath."

"You reside here!" Laurentia cried. "Not so far distant, then, from Windrush? I thought perhaps . . . well, I had thought a dozen things, but one of the most hopeful was that somehow you resided on the other side of England, or the world." Even to her own ears she could hear that her voice had trailed off.

"Perhaps—with your husband's permission, of course—we might take a turn about the Colonnade?"

Laurentia turned swiftly to Thomas. "You won't mind, will you dearest?"

He shook his head. "Not by half. I shall remain here and, er, admire the statue of Mr. Nash."

Laurentia only half heard him, for the moment he acquiesced, as she had supposed he would, she took Mr. Dursley's arm and hurried away with him. She didn't know which question to ask first. So many rose to her mind that very soon a cacophony of thoughts forced her brain to a complete stop.

He was silent, as well, this young man who, she saw as she glanced up at him, had aged considerably in the several years since she had last seen him. Dark shadows discolored the skin beneath his eyes, and his complexion was quite pale. She wondered what had happened to have destroyed his youth and vigor. "Have you been ill?" she asked suddenly, posing one of the vignettes she had arranged in her mind so many years ago by way of explaining his sudden disappearance.

He looked down at her, his nose growing pink from the cold. "No," he murmured, chuckling faintly. "I have been in perfect health since last we were together, at least physically. My soul, on the other hand, seems to have been partially destroyed by a sort of spiritual leprosy."

His words were full of bitterness.

She felt sobered suddenly and became uneasy, almost dreading what he might tell her next. "You did not love me," she stated abruptly.

"Oh, God," he groaned. "I was mad with love for you, Laurentia, violently so. I should never have offered for you otherwise."

Laurentia felt herself pale. "I don't understand. Please, tell me, if you can, what happened."

The Colonnade was a stone-paved, covered walk, supported by a fine row of Greek columns. Presently, it was swept free of drifting snow, and provided a private place along which she could walk and listen to Mr. Dursley's explanations.

"I intended to keep my promises to you," he continued. "I wished to marry you more than life itself. In truth, I was dissuaded against the union. I . . . I accepted a great deal of money to leave Windrush . . . forever."

"What?" she cried, aghast. "Whatever do you mean? No one knew of our . . . our love for one another. I kept my uncle entirely unsuspecting, as well as Grandmama, or at least I thought I had. How could he have discovered our assignations? He never gave a fig for my comings and goings. Oh, I can't believe he did this."

"Wasn't there someone else you told?" he asked gently.

She looked into his eyes, searching through the past. "Once, Sir Alan Redcliffe teased me about being happier than usual. I blushed fiercely. Perhaps he guessed at the truth, but I said nary a word."

"Redcliffe made me the offer, not your uncle."

She could not have heard him correctly. "Sir Alan?" she queried weakly. "But why?"

"He was very discreet. He assured me that your uncle would not countenance the match in a hundred years. He was quite persuasive." Again, he sounded bitter. "In the end, I found I couldn't resist the sum he offered. I was tempted, and I succumbed. The sum was so vast, at least from my perspective, since in accepting his offer I would know in that one moment more than I would receive from my own inheritance in a lifetime. He also said that your uncle was searching for just the right husband for you, that he wanted a handle to your name more than anything. He was adamant on that point in particular.

"However, I never stopped loving you. I still dream of you, of holding you in my arms. Laurentia, my darling, I made the worst mistake of my life when I left Windrush that day. I should have set aside all my misgivings, and I should never have permitted Sir Alan to dissuade me. I have regretted my decision a thousand times over. I was a coward, and I have been punished sorely for it!

She looked into his eyes and saw all his regret. She recalled her own pain, the tears she had shed when fortnight surmounted fortnight and still he did not come back to her.

He leaned toward her, his lips drawing near. She felt a sudden rush of affection sweep over her. She let him kiss her.

How familiar he felt. How much she had once loved him. And yet, nothing remained. Her soul was dead to him.

She drew back. "You shouldn't be kissing me. I . . . I am married now."

He seemed distraught, his hands still clamped about her arms. He leaned his cheek against hers. "Come to me while you are here. We can be together again, as we were, only this time . . . Laurentia, I need you. My wife is a wretched creature, terribly spoilt and lacking in affection. I should never have wed her! When I think of having given you up, I am miserable beyond words. But now you are here, and we are reunited. Say you will come to me, that you still hold in your heart some particle of affection for me."

"Stop, James, please. What are you saying to me? This is very wicked and . . . and besides, I have a husband of my own to consider. Oh, do stop pestering me, or I shan't ever forgive you for leaving me as you did!"

She struggled out of his arms. He lunged for her, and she gave a sharp cry as her feet slipped on the icy snow near the walkway. He caught her and attempted to drag her into his arms once more.

Suddenly, she felt his arms release her, and she stumbled back. "Oh!" she cried, turning to see that her husband had arrived to protect her from James's amorous assault. He spun James around and with a tight fist, planted him a hard facer.

James fell backward, stunned. He touched his nose. "You've drawn claret!" he cried. "Who the devil do you think you are!" He struggled to his feet.

"Mrs. Swinfield's husband. Make your apologies to the lady now, or by God I'll have you arrested for such brutish conduct."

Mr. Dursley rose to his feet unsteadily. He shook his head several times. "Good God," he muttered, appearing to come to his senses at last. "What have I done!"

Laurentia picked up her muff, which had become displaced

by James's groping, and jammed her hands within. She found she was trembling. "I—I never knew you, James. I am very sorry for you but I must confess of the moment I am glad you deserted me as you did. You have made known your character to me, and I will thank you for dispelling any regrets I once had at your abandonment of me so many years ago."

She turned away from him at that, and she could not be sorry. She might have been sympathetic at one time, but not now, not after he had said such terrible things to her, begging her to forsake her own husband and meet with him secretly! She was disgusted by his reprehensible conduct.

"Pray tell me you are unharmed," Thomas coaxed. He gently took her arm and guided her in the opposite direction, back toward the Pump Room.

"I am unharmed," she responded, blinking back several tears. "He . . . he is terribly altered. I am grateful you were not far at hand. I vow he meant to go on kissing me forever. He . . . he said such things to me, you cannot imagine!"

"He did seem a trifle ardent for a man who has a wife of his own."

At that she looked up at him and saw that his eyes were filled with humor. Some of the terrible tension of the moment left her, and she could not help but chuckle. "I don't know if I should be grateful, or offended that my husband has spoken in such an easy manner."

"To some degree you must accustom yourself to assaults of this kind if you are to be so very beautiful and wear your heart in your eyes, as you do. Undoubtedly he believed you still loved him. The moment you recognized him your face was lit with such joy."

As he guided her toward her traveling chariot, she stared at him wonderingly. "Is that how I appeared in the Pump Room? Am I so devoid of discretion?"

He gave her arm a squeeze, and met her gaze. "I would hope that you never gain discretion if that is how you interpret the word. One of your best qualities is that one is never in doubt of how you feel at any given moment, since every nuance of sentiment finds a resting place on one feature or another."

Laurentia found herself charmed by Thomas, as she had been from the first. James's unfortunate conduct was soon forgotten, the incident as far from her as Friday from Monday. However, she felt obliged to confess the nature of her conversation with him. "Mr. Dursley told me something dreadful about why he deserted me. He said that Sir Alan Redcliffe had paid him a large sum of money to leave me in peace because he knew my uncle would oppose the match. I am still so stunned I can hardly speak."

"What a dreadful business," he responded quietly. "I feel for you, most acutely. Although, I must say I don't know who I would blame most in this situation—your uncle, Sir Alan, or Mr. Dursley.

Her expression fell. "I blame my uncle, of course. Sir Alan was only acting on his behalf, of that I am certain."

Lord Villiers was silent. He could not agree with Laurentia, since he had a clearer notion of Sir Alan's true character and believed he had been acting on his own behalf the entire time.

"By the way," Laurentia interjected as Villiers handed her up into the carriage. "How did it come about you were so nearby when James accosted me? Not that I mean to complain, but I had supposed you meant to remain in the Pump Room. You said you intended to."

"I would have been a fool to have left my wife alone with any gentleman for an extended period of time, but most especially with one whose face rather put me in mind of the Roman statues one finds in the British Museum."

Laurentia sighed. "James is quite handsome, isn't he?"

"There can be no two opinions on that head."

"Only in his form, however. His character is decidedly flawed."

"Again, I would have to agree with you."

Laurentia's spirits brightened considerably once the coach was in motion, and Villiers happily took her on a tour of some of the more famous sights of Bath, at least the ones which were easily navigable by coach. Many of the hills were far too steep—especially with the paved streets wet with melting snow or slippery with ice—to ascend with ease. How lovely the ancient watering hole appeared in the winter, with the various landmarks bereft of greenery and draped, instead, with icicles. The Orange Grove, named after the Prince of Orange, was particularly desolate. The numerous sycamore trees had lost their leaves, and the white of the snow emptied the landscape of even a hint of green. Even so, Laurentia demanded to be set on foot in order that she might view the famous Obelisk for herself.

"Quite unexceptionable," she stated after contemplating the uniform edifice which had been placed in what were originally called the Gravel Walks. The obelisk commemorated a visit paid to Bath by William, Prince of Orange, in 1734.

"Quite."

She viewed it for a long time, finally turning slowly away and began walking toward the coach. "Have you been here during the summer months, when Bath swells with visitors from all over England?"

"Yes, of course. Some find the company rather insular and rigid, but after a rigorous London Season, with every manner of madcap chicanery evident from one ballroom to the next, I find the order of Bath restorative, not to mention the pleasures of taking the waters every day."

She trilled her laughter. "Of course, the waters! Let us never forget the waters. We will have to bring all our children here and force the vile liquid down their throats."

"What did you say?" He turned to her, astonished.

She blushed fiercely. "Oh, I am sorry, Thomas. Forget I said anything so nonsensical. I have been in the habit of creating these little stories in my head about us, so that we might truly appear to be married, just to make certain no one suspected our masquerade. That was one of them, I fear, or at least a variation on one, where I talk about what *our* children will be doing in a few years."

"I find it utterly charming," he said quietly, giving her arm a squeeze. The coach was hidden from view by a tree, and he could not resist the temptation of taking her up in his arms. "Would this be another of your little stories, how often your husband claims you and holds you in his arms?"

"Of course not," she murmured, blushing farther still. "That would be quite shocking."

"You don't even contemplate my kisses when I am apart from you?"

"Well, yes, I do that," she admitted. "But I try very hard not to make up too many stories. I don't want to confuse them with the several kisses you've already given me."

He was charmed, devastatingly so. The grove was empty. His wife was snuggled against him, and he was feeling amorous. Images of just how Mr. Dursley had violated his wife sprang suddenly to his mind as well as the pleasing sensation of his gloved fist having struck home quite handily. In that moment, he had felt Laurentia belonged to him truly, and the feel of her in his arms right then became a powerful elixir. "I dream of you," he whispered against her cheek. "I try not to, but every morning I awaken having been under your spell in some outrageous adventure only the night could create for us."

"Is this true, Thomas, or are you teasing me?"

"Both, for when I do not awaken remembering how you invaded my dreams then you come swiftly to mind, and I realize our time together has been like a dream. I am overcome with that sweet sensation of how time has stopped so that we could know something magical and romantic, if for only a short while. Dreams are like that, only a bit more intense."

His lips brushed her cheeks. "I have enjoyed every moment of this wholly inappropriate marriage to you, Mrs. Swinfield."

"I, too," she whispered in response. "I wish I had met you when I first came of age, or even as late as a year ago, for then nothing would have prevented me from tumbling head over ears in love with you and, hopefully, you with me. Then we could have eloped to Gretna in complete earnest."

He drew back. "I don't understand," he said quietly. "What are you saying? Would you have married a year ago?"

"I almost did, so my answer must be yes. I would most definitely have hurried off to Gretna with you a year ago, had you come calling."

"Good God, Laurentia!" he cried. "Whatever happened a year ago, then, that made you come to despise the married state so much, to distrust taking a husband of your choice?"

Ten

Laurentia felt herself grow very still inside as she recalled the dissolution of her second engagement. For a second time she had believed herself very much in love. Sir Alan had even countenanced the match, saying that he thought very highly of Matthew Cameron, though he had convinced her to say nothing to her uncle until she was absolutely certain she wished to marry the young man. How wise Sir Alan's counsel had proved.

For many years she had been in the habit of confiding her secret dreams to Sir Alan. Always he had nodded and approved of her various schemes, especially for those meant to alleviate the sufferings of the poor in Gloucestershire, especially in the Vale of Windrush. She hoped, for instance, to establish a foundation just for that purpose, and Sir Alan had immediately suggested how such a foundation could be created so that it would live in perpetuity beyond her own lifetime.

She was always stimulated by the many clever ideas Sir Alan presented to her, and he never criticized her enthusiastic dreams. She had always considered him a loyal and helpful friend. When James had deserted her three years prior to the arrival of Matthew Cameron in Windrush, she had even then told Sir Alan of his traitorous conduct. To think, however, that he was closely connected to James's quitting Windrush as he did—it all seemed so very odd.

She glanced at Thomas, and felt compelled to tell him of Matthew Cameron.

"My uncle did not know of my sentiments regarding Mr. Cameron. Sir Alan had suggested that I take a little more time before presenting our betrothal to my uncle in order that I might ascertain if Matthew was all that I believed him to be, in character and principle, especially since I had already had my most unfortunate experience with Mr. Dursley. I agreed, and have since been grateful for Sir Alan's sage advice. You see, within the next few days I discovered that Mr. Cameron had already brought a financial adviser to Windrush, his solicitor as well, to review my uncle's estate and to determine how best to manage so vast an inheritance once my uncle was no longer living."

"What?" Thomas cried.

"Indeed! Well may you stare. I was never more mortified than when Mr. Cameron assured me that he would be an excellent guardian of my fortune, that he would make every effort to increase my inheritance rather than to waste it, and that I would not have to bother my head about such things as percentages and the Exchange.

"Since I had for so many years determined the course for my inheritance, you may imagine my shock. I suggested to Mr. Cameron that we delay any such discussion until I could ponder his suggestion. That night I spoke with Sir Alan, who was as greatly shocked as I was that Mr. Cameron would propose anything so foolish, and helped me to see that I ought to be grateful he had revealed his intentions so completely to me. It would seem my betrothed was, as many gentlemen are, of the strong belief that a lady has no rights to her fortune, and that once we were married, he clearly intended to hold the purse strings. I know this to be true, since I pressed him on this point in particular and he admitted that he did not believe a woman capable of managing a fortune of any size, nonetheless an inheritance as large as mine one day would be.

"I was completely overset, as well you may imagine, but in the end I found I was indeed grateful. Knowing that the laws of England supported his view, I came to believe that somehow I was destined to live as a spinster in order that my own objects might be achieved.

"There you have my very sad tale in its entirety."

She had smiled when she spoke these last words, but Thomas did not smile in response. Instead, he gathered her up in his arms once more and held her tightly to him. She couldn't be in a way to knowing what his thoughts might be, but that his intention was to comfort her she could not be mistaken, not by half.

She reveled in the feel of his arms about her, wondering how it had come to pass that such a good, kind, honest man had come to support her in her transition from ward of her uncle's estate to heiress of his fortune. Between these two men, Thomas Swinfield and Sir Alan Redcliffe, she felt she had nothing more to want for in terms of counsel and assistance.

She sighed dreamily, aware that she was getting very cold yet not wanting the moment to end. She wondered if that was how Thomas was feeling, as well.

Lord Villiers felt as though ice flowed in his veins.

Treachery upon treachery, played out upon the innocent creature he was coming to love more and more. He believed he knew what had happened to Mr. Cameron, and would have staked a thousand pounds on the belief that Sir Alan had somehow managed to *advise* Mr. Cameron to make it clear to Laurentia that she would not have to be at all worried about the future, that he meant to take complete charge of her fortune.

How subtle it all was. Well, perhaps Sir Alan had been a trifle heavy-handed when he actually paid Mr. Dursley to leave Windrush, but then his skills had obviously increased with the years, and a mere hint in the proper direction to a young, inexperienced, and enamored Mr. Cameron had easily won the day—especially since Sir Alan obviously knew Laurentia as well as he did.

His only thoughts centered on just how he was to expose Sir Alan, given the fact that Laurentia did not seem inclined to believe ill of him.

He was disgusted and angry, so much so that the heat of his emotions kept the chill of the wintry afternoon entirely at bay. He could have remained holding Laurentia in his arms forever had she not shivered suddenly.

"Are you very cold, my dear?" he asked.

"Indeed, I fear I am."

"Come, then. We will return to the hotel and have a great fire built up in your room. Perhaps we can enjoy our nuncheon together before the blaze."

She leaned back and looked up into his face. "That would suit me to perfection."

Thomas stared down at Laurentia, struck as he had been from the beginning by her beauty, so full of innocence and goodness. "Shall I tell you what would suit me?"

"I think I know," she responded on a whisper, lifting her face to his.

He kissed her full, ripe lips and reveled in the warm feel of her body against his. He had never known love before. This he admitted now as feeling after feeling, of affection and passion, washed over him. Somehow, in the nearly twenty days they had been together, Cupid had shot him full of golden arrows, and his only object anymore seemed to be in what way he could be of service to his wife.

Winter could not stand in the face of the powerful emotions which surged through him. He was smitten as surely as apples fell from the trees when summer waned and autumn teased the countryside. His whole body glowed with the warmth of summer, showering his soul with ecstatic glimpses of heaven.

He was in love. He loved. His soul and his heart were fully engaged and utterly devoted. He would do anything for this trusting creature who seemed not to have a single disloyal bone in her body.

As he searched her lips and explored the gentle softness of her mouth, he sought for some way to express the depths of his feelings for her, to explain that in his journey to Gloucestershire he had intended only to refuse their betrothal on principle . . . and instead had married and fallen deeply in love with the very woman he was supposed to have wed.

The irony struck him deeply, as though forces not of this earth were strongly at work within him and around him, coaxing him down a path not of his choosing but most definitely suited to him. Only, how to tell Laurentia of the depths of his love for her, and to arrange such a telling completely apart from her fortune and his lack thereof? Most especially, how was he to reveal the awful truth that he was the man, *My Lord Villiers,* whom she had been taught to despise? He wanted her to know, to see, to feel, that he would lay down his life for her if need be, and that nothing on earth could ever destroy his love for her.

He drew his lips reluctantly from hers and at the same time cupped her face in his hands. He caught her gaze and let the beat of his heart speak from his eyes. She blinked, and her eyes seemed to grow hazy and drenched with feeling. Again, he silently spoke his love to her, in a wave of thought and profound sentiment. She blinked twice, and he felt her knees collapse. He caught her about the waist. She clutched at his lapel and touched his face with her gloved hand.

"Thomas," she murmured hoarsely.

He kissed her again, a violent assault that caused her arms to become tangled wildly about his neck. She clutched at him, and embraced him fitfully. He kissed her deeply, and in response a ripple of faint murmurs sounded in her throat.

At last she drew back, out of breath and appearing rather

astonished. "It is the strangest thing," she said. "I am not in the least cold anymore!"

He laughed and grabbed her once more about the waist, this time to twirl her in circle after circle until they were both laughing and falling into a soft bank of snow. Where his hat was he didn't know, and her bonnet was now slightly askew. Her cheeks and nose were pink. He drew close and gently touched her face with the back of his gloved fingers.

He knew an overwhelming impulse to confess his identity to her then and there, to end his masquerade as mere Mr. Swinfield, to inform her that he was Lord Villiers. He opened his mouth and his throat issued forth the air required to form the syllables, but suddenly it began to snow.

Laurentia squealed and rose abruptly to her feet. "It's snowing! It's snowing!" she cried. "For us. We are magical, Thomas. We made it snow, and very soon all the dirty wheel ruts of the city will be buried, and Bath will be a veritable wonderland. Come! I want to sit in front of that fire you mentioned and watch the snow from my bedchamber window, especially as evening falls and the lights of the city create a fairy world for us."

The moment was gone, lost perhaps forever. He shivered, knowing that a terrible day of reckoning would come in which she would learn who he was and she would never forgive him, not just for being Lord Villiers, but for seducing her in this way and turning her heart toward him.

She was running in the sweetest way toward the coach, spinning, her arms outstretched and flailing, all to make the snowflakes swirl about her. He followed behind on a quick half-step, wanting the sensation of despair to leave him but knowing that he had made a mistake just now in not speaking more quickly before the snowfall enchanted her. He understood something about life, then—moments came and went, never to return again. Such a one had passed, only in what way and when would it come to haunt him, he did not know.

* * *

Laurentia gave herself to the enjoyment of Thomas's company. The nuncheon was delightful, served as it was before a toasty fire and the table dressed with fine serviceware, dark green fir branchlets, and clusters of holly berries. The meal of thinly sliced roast beef, potatoes, green beans, raspberry jelly, cream, and a light cake was served with a peach-flavored Ratafia for her and a hearty Port wine for Thomas. A tea tray followed, replacing the meal on the bed of fir. The serving maid withdrew at last, and the snowy afternoon, warmed by a blazing fire, became a cozy corner in which conversation filled the remains of the day.

"Tell me of your home in Somerset," Laurentia commanded, sipping her tea and smiling just over the rim of her cup.

Thomas stretched out his legs toward the fire. As he settled his cup of tea on the companion saucer, his face took on a faraway aspect. "The house in which I was born was not a grand palace, but a fine old building of sturdy stone," he began. "The entire edifice has long since been covered with ancient, gnarled vines of broad-leafed ivy. The house is tucked away in a nest of hills, so that the worst of the Atlantic storms pass by unmolesting. To the west of the house is a grove of Spanish chestnuts. In one of them is my fort, in which I vanquished all the Continental armies time and again—especially the French, which have been a nuisance since times out of mind—and of course the Colonial armies, and even a few Indians when the occasion demanded."

"You must have been quite exhausted as a child, besides suffering from the numerous wounds you would have received from so much campaigning."

He chuckled almost dreamily, his eyes crinkling in that way of his which pleased her so much, for then she knew he truly was amused.

"My father would fetch me himself at dusk, knowing I

would be rampaging through the grove for hours into the night if someone did not disrupt my play."

"He did not send a servant?"

"Only when he had some pressing business to attend to. No, he came himself. Those were the days I remember best, for he would lay his arm about my shoulders as we walked back to the house and tell me of his life as a soldier when he was a lad, how he had fought at Concord and thought the rebels were either the least intelligent men that had ever been born, or the bravest."

"I can't believe he fought in what is now called the War of Independence."

"Yes. He brought home souvenirs of a sort, a rifle or two, that sort of thing. He was a lieutenant, and suffered a gunshot wound to his hip. He always had a limp. He sold out after a lengthy recovery in London. A few years later, he married my mother, and I was born in eighty-five. I grew up in that ivy-covered house."

"No brothers? Sisters?"

He shook his head. "Like you, I grew up only dreaming about them."

She nodded and sipped her tea a little more. Her gaze fell to the fire. Perhaps that would explain why she felt so at ease with Thomas—they shared something significant in common, and for that reason did not seem to need to utter a word.

"Do you spend much of your time at home, then? I mean"—and here she chuckled—"when you are not traveling into the wilds of Gloucestershire and rescuing quite silly women from very strange circumstances."

He chuckled in response, a deep rumble that always affected her, plucking at her heartstrings like an accomplished musician at a harp, with light, delicate snaps that made her smile and yet resonated throughout her entire being.

"Unfortunately, I have not seen much of Somerset in recent years. The house is very empty, and has been so since the death of my parents. I have not had sufficient funds to keep hearth and home together." He paused for a moment, and when he spoke again there was a reverence to his voice she had not heard before. "My father saved me, you know."

He had once mentioned that his parents had been killed in an accident at which he was present. "What happened that night?" she asked softly.

"The three of us, my father, my mother, and myself, were returning home from a visit to the mild harbors of eastern Cornwall. We'd done some fishing and a little yachting, and had just crossed the Devon border into Somersetshire. A storm, quite unusual for the season, appeared from nowhere. Our coach was sturdy enough, the horses extremely well-trained, the postilion one of our best grooms, but the rear left wheel hit a deep rut and splintered badly. The coach toppled into a ditch." He grew very silent and grave, his gaze fixed to the fire. She could see he was drawn inward, and that he was suffering.

She rose from her chair and crossed the small space between them to lay a hand on his shoulder. "Don't speak of it, if it makes you sad," she offered gently.

He covered her hand with his own and leaned his cheek against her fingers. "The odd thing is, I've never spoken of it before. Never. The memories, until this moment, have been kept locked away in some hard place of my heart, not wanting to come forward."

"Of course not," she murmured, tears stinging her eyes.

"Everything happened so quickly. I can hardly recall the sequence, it was such a blur. I remember my father pushing me toward the open doorway. The coach was quickly filling with water. I don't remember hearing a sound from my mother, not a cry for help or a word, not even a moan. Later, she was found with a deep gash in the side of her head. It was believed she'd been killed instantly.

"While my father was attempting to pull her from the coach,

with the storm beating down on the hillside, the side of the ditch and a great portion of the road near to where I was standing suddenly gave way and slid down the embankment. The coach, the horses, the postilion—who'd been trapped under the leader—slid with it. Everything was half-buried in mud. It was a nightmare.

"I scrambled down the hill, as well, not thinking of anything, of course, except trying to save my parents, but there was nothing to be done. They were so bruised and broken. My father lived for two hours, but he didn't know me. He kept calling for my mother, but I don't believe she had survived the first impact of the accident."

Laurentia leaned over and slipped her arms about his neck. She wept into the folds of his neckcloth. She felt him sigh deeply several times.

"I have never felt more helpless, before or since," he said. "At the time, I was only a lad of sixteen, but that night I must have aged a decade. I was alone with the broken carriage all night. How could we be seen from the road? And even if we could have been seen, who would have been about, traveling in a storm like that one? I have since learned that such things happen, that life is precarious at the very best. A wrong step, a wrong turn, a jaunt to Cornwall, and, well, there you are."

Laurentia's tears subsided more quickly than she would have supposed possible, except that she was suddenly rushed back to being a young girl of twelve, to bidding her parents farewell, never to see them return. She offered, "At least you were with them when they died, and in some way, as horrible as it might have been, you were able to say good-bye. My last memory of my parents was watching them drive happily away in our carriage, from Evenlode. I was told I should be grateful that my last memory was a happy one, but I vow there is not a day that has gone by that I did not wish to touch my mother's face one last time, even if it was cold in death, or to hold my father's hand to my cheek." She slid around him dropping to her knees by the side of his chair, and looked into his eyes. "Does that seem terrible to you?" she asked. "I have always been afraid to give voice to that thought. I was never grateful that they perished so far from me!"

He cupped her face with his hand, his eyes inexpressibly sympathetic. "Not so terrible," he murmured. "Come, let me hold you a while."

She rose up and slid onto his lap. She said nothing more, but held him close in return as he comforted her. For a long, long time, until the fire dwindled to a gray mass of coals, she was a child of twelve once more, and he a boy of sixteen— orphans, the pair of them. She wondered how their lives would have been different had their respective families not been so thoroughly disrupted by death.

Long after evening fell, she must have dozed in his arms, for he was whispering to her when she awoke. "You should be in bed. It is past midnight."

"Oh," she murmured sleepily, glancing toward the mantel, where a clock sonorously presented the hour in soft dings. "So it is. Have you been very uncomfortable, Thomas?"

"No, not a bit. I, too, must have fallen asleep. And now, to bed. Tomorrow, I will show you the Upper Assembly Rooms."

The time in Bath with Thomas had been infinitely sweet. As Laurentia laid aside her bonnet and her pelisse, settling them both absentmindedly on her bed at Evenlode House, she still felt caught up in the tenderness of her time with him.

For a long moment she was lost in a deep reverie as she considered the three days she had shared with him in Bath. At the same time, she began to gently review James's court- ship, as well as Matthew's. James had been four and twenty when she first met him, Matthew nearly three years older. She rather thought Thomas was a little past thirty. He was very mature, she realized of a sudden. His words were always considered—not in a stilted manner, but rather as those of one who has lived and who has adjusted his thoughts, putting everything in a proper order of meaning and sense.

She tried to recall something of James's rushed, passionate courtship. He had been devilishly handsome—but then, so was Thomas—but in such a loose, ungoverned style as would have appealed to any maiden, especially one locked away in the wilds of Gloucestershire, as he was used to say.

She had been completely enamored of him. He had read poetry to her for hours on end, nibbling on the tips of her fingers in a teasing fashion and professing to do so in order that he might restrain himself from taking her lips again and again and again.

Ecstasy had characterized her relationship with him. He had captured her imagination and driven her sails to the four corners of the earth, afterward exploring the heavens with her. He had chased her through the beechwood and kissed her. She had fancied herself in love. Instead, she had loved a fantasy, a man who had been all creative explosions of charm and airs but who had been driven from her side by a handful of guineas, swept away in the fashion that the dawn steals even the sweetest of dreams from memory.

Matthew had been a far more estimable gentleman. Handsome, intelligent, charming on occasion, he had wooed her over the season of Michaelmas, and by late January asked for her hand in marriage. He was in possession of an easy competence himself, so that he conducted himself as a gentleman would, without the pressures of securing a living to invade their time together. He had led her into the intricacies of philosophy, and the meanings of the poetry James had shouted at her. She had been intrigued, and had followed his lead down the path of his affections, willing to forget that James had abandoned her inexplicably. When he offered for her, she found herself completely willing to give him her hand and her heart.

When he had come to her with his plans for their future together, in particular his intentions to fastidiously manage her fortune, she had been brought to an abrupt realization of the truth—so long as she married, her money would not be her own.

With little effort at all she had bid him *adieu*. Was it possible she had never truly loved him?

Would she relinquish Thomas so easily?

Her heart constricted. She moved to the windows of her bedchamber and pushed back the drapes. The sky was a faint blue wisped with white-gray clouds across the entire horizon. She loved this time of year, for it seemed to her that the earth was taking a deep breath in preparation for a long, long sleep. The restfulness of the Yuletide season had always been a balm to her soul.

She breathed deeply, her thoughts fixing themselves on Thomas. As though she had conjured him up, he appeared on the drive below, his hat pressed firmly on his head, his greatcoat swinging with his broad walk. He carried a walking stick and wore strong, serviceable boots.

He had said he meant to walk for a time before dressing for dinner. She was grateful now that he had elected to do so, for she could watch him and ponder the meaning of this man who had chanced so suddenly into her life.

She recalled meeting him that first, stormy night, how he had appeared by the fire. She strove to recall his expression as she had burst into his parlor, how he had looked the split second before she had made herself known to him. Pensive.

No, not pensive.

A shudder of recognition went through her.

Sad.

She nodded to herself. His expression had been wholly sad. How odd that she would remember now.

He held his head high when he walked, stretching out his long legs. She had little doubt he meant to traverse several miles of countryside before returning to Evenlode.

A stray dog appeared from the side of the lane, glancing at him tentatively. Thomas stopped, and she supposed he was speaking to the ugly little cur. He slapped his leg with his hand, then turned and continued on. The dog followed after him. Thomas glanced back at the dog and smiled.

How her heart seemed to catch in her throat. Even at just a smile, her entire being would rise up and beg to know the man better. A man who would be kind to a stray dog—now, that was a man to know and to love.

She watched until the lane grew thickly covered in shrubs and so far away into the valley below that she could no longer see even Thomas's hat above the hedgerows. She drew away from the window, feeling completely and utterly bemused by her feelings.

Had she truly ever known love before? Had her feelings for James and Matthew been mere transient expressions of her loneliness, causing her to be far too eager to leap into an engagement without really knowing either man?

What of Thomas, then, and the powerful feelings she was experiencing for him? Was she only being fooled by her loneliness once more? How could she know whether or not she was truly falling in love with him, whether the tender feelings she felt for him were more than just her own restless need?

Perhaps when he left at the end of their month together, she would feel no more attachment to him than he was at present feeling for the little dog who had attached itself to a passing stranger.

The very thought lowered her spirits so much that only with some difficulty did she address the fact that she must call for her bath and begin dressing for dinner.

An hour later, she went in search of her grandmother and found her in her bedchamber christening her neck with fragrant powder and afterward donning her favorite diamond ear-bobs.

"And how was your journey to Bath?" she asked, turning in her chair and offering her cheek to Laurentia.

Laurentia immediately went forward and kissed her beloved grandmother's cheek, enjoying the bouquet of her powder and the softness of her wrinkled, aged skin. "I love you, Grandmama. How grateful I've been all these years for your companionship."

At that, Mrs. Cabot opened her eyes wide. "What on earth has prompted these very sweet, yet quite sudden admissions?"

Laurentia dropped down to sit on the footstool at her feet, and leaned her head on her knees. "I feel like a very foolish, very young woman, who does not know her right hand from her left. How is it I've grown up without having even a mite of understanding of the world?"

"Goodness. If I'd known you meant to open such a serious subject I should have locked my door and never permitted you to enter," Mrs. Cabot responded teasingly.

Laurentia giggled. "I do beg your pardon, but I am having an attack of conscience, I think."

"You mean you are just now realizing you should not have inveigled good Mr. Swinfield into your troubles?"

"At the very least that, but I think I've done something much worse." She lifted her head and met her grandmother's gaze. "I think I've made him love me." Her eyes filled suddenly with tears, and her grandmother's face took on an anguished appearance.

"Oh, my dear," she breathed, patting her shoulder several times. "You should have been in London all these years, at least for the Season. You are too untried to comprehend matters of the heart readily, to know when a man is flirting and when he is serious, to determine even the weight of your own sentiments. I blame my son for that as much as for everything else. In God's name, how did I raise such a self-centered creature!"

"It is a mystery, when my own father was such a loving

man. I can remember him still. He was always talking to me, taking me for walks, telling me about the trees and flowers, even teaching me the names of all the shrubs to be found in a hedgerow. He spoke of the future, too, that I would find my husband in London, during the Season." Laurentia giggled. "That was before I understood the proper meaning of the word 'Season.' I remember wondering to which season he was referring, winter or summer. Fall, perhaps? Then he died, along with Mama." She paused before adding, "Yes, I should have gone to London, for I am so confused." She then told her about meeting James in Bath and learning Sir Alan had paid him to leave Windrush when he did. She omitted telling her of his successive and extraordinarily unhandsome conduct in the Colonnade when he kissed her quite reprehensibly.

Mrs. Cabot frowned. "He told you as much, that Sir Alan had given him a sum of money to abandon you?"

She nodded in response.

"He never said a word to me. To own the truth, I find the whole of it quite inexplicable. However, what concerns me more in your unfortunate history is that Mr. Dursley, over whom you shed half a pot of tears—yes, I heard you crying more than once, my dear—should have proved not only faithless to you but mercenary, as well."

Laurentia sighed. "I was greatly mistaken in his character, and yet I had believed myself fully in love with him. Do you suppose Sir Alan had begun to comprehend his character, and had tested him by offering him the money? Oh, what does it matter! I have begun to think I do not know how to judge either a man's character or what love truly is."

"You mustn't be too harsh on yourself, my dear, truly." She appeared quite stricken as she continued. "For it is always that way, I think. Appearances can be so utterly deceiving, and a handsome face seems to possess the ability to rob us of our common sense. Oh, dear."

"What? What is it?"

"I was just thinking of something else, something most unfortunate. I wonder if I ought to tell you, since I now believe I have advised you at cross-purposes. Oh, what a tangle!"

"Grandmama, you must tell me! What is it?"

"I can't. It isn't for me to tell, only . . . my dear Laurentia, presently I don't think anything is as it seems. If I could give you one piece of advice, though, one truth upon which you should hang all your judgments, it would be this—watch carefully how a man conducts himself in all his ways, his relationships with friends, family, and foes. Only in this way can you truly ascertain if a man is worthy of your love or not . . . and you have so much love to give. Rely on this and you shan't go wrong, I promise you that much."

Laurentia searched her eyes and saw the depths of her sincerity. *Test a man in all his ways.* She nodded several times. She thought nothing had seemed so sensible as this. She hoped, however, that in matters of application, the same advice would be as easily put into action.

"Oh, and there is one more thing," Mrs. Cabot said. "I had wished to keep it a secret, but I realize I no longer can, for the simple reason that we do not have sufficient bedchambers in the whole of the Vale of Windrush to house two hundred people, especially if it should set on to snow."

Laurentia blinked. "Are you referring to my St. Thomas's Day party?" she queried. "For I can assure you that though I suspect there will be quite a number of personages present, hardly two hundred. Perhaps half as much, and most of whom reside in the village. What do you mean, then, by a secret?"

Mrs. Cabot touched her cheek gently. "I suppose there is nothing for it but to confess the truth, though I daresay you will be quite angry with me."

"What!" Laurentia cried. "Has something else gone amiss? Did my uncle purchase a factory in the last days of his life and turn two hundred people out of their houses, as well?"

"No! No!" Mrs. Cabot cried. "It is nothing of the sort, and

nothing at all to do with your uncle. The fact is, I arranged a wedding ball for you and Mr. Swinfield for tomorrow night, here, at Evenlode."

"What!" Laurentia cried, utterly horrified. "Is this what you have been designing so secretively, covering up your correspondence every time I would but enter a room? But Grandmama! We are to be divorced in less than two week's time. This is dreadful. You must pen all the letters required, and call it off! At once! Only think of the scandal once we are divorced. People will think it exceedingly odd in us, in you, to have celebrated our nuptials." Another terrible thought succeeded this one. "There will be gifts, as well! Perhaps two score, possibly even more! Oh, Grandmama, this is a terrible thing you've done, and you must undo it!"

Mrs. Cabot rose in a dignified manner to her short but forceful height and responded simply, "I will not undo it, nor will I continue to listen to your harangue. We are having a ball tomorrow night, and that is that! Now, please summon my footmen. I wish to descend to the drawing room and have a nice conversation with your husband."

Laurentia, from long habits of obedience, clamped her lips firmly shut and moved to the bellpull. She gave two rather vicious tugs on the poor strap and turned to glare at her grandmama. Finally, she said, "I see what you are about. You are half in love with Mr. Swinfield yourself, and intend to keep him here at Evenlode if you can."

At that Mrs. Cabot smiled, her face twinkling with merriment. "I believe you have the right of it! Oh, now don't come scratching at me. Mr. Swinfield is a charming man, and if I could choose a husband for you I would choose him. Yes, well you may stare, but there it is. I haven't lived so many years on the face of this troublesome island without having learned a thing or two."

Laurentia stared at her in disbelief. She had known from the start that her grandmother was disposed to favor Thomas, and she had even suspected that she intended to support the marriage. But this firm avowal of her fine opinion of Thomas stunned her.

"Y-you think he is a proper husband for me?"

Mrs. Cabot nodded once, quite firmly.

"Well!" Laurentia cried. "So you have set to scheming, have you? I will only say that Thomas will not like the notion of your ball, not by half!"

"We shall see. We shall see," was her grandmother's maddening response.

Eleven

Villiers was dumbfounded. "Tomorrow night? But Ma'am, you know of the arrangement. Do you really think a ball in our honor an appropriate—"

He got no further as Mrs. Cabot lifted an imperious hand. "I don't give a fig for your silly agreement with my grand-daughter, whether you signed papers drawn up by her solicitor or not! When two people decide to marry, regardless of the circumstances or reasons, they ought to remain married. I shan't discuss the matter further, with either of you. So, I suggest you accept the fact there will be a ball tomorrow night, in honor of your nuptials. Two hundred persons of both genteel and aristocratic breeding have agreed to attend, quite enthusiastically I might add, and you will undoubtedly be showered with a great number of expensive gifts. So, might I suggest that you both rig yourselves out in the finest style and make me proud of you? And that is all I will say on the subject! Now, please tell me, both of you, of your journey to Bath. Was there much snow on the ground?"

Villiers glanced at Laurentia, who appeared to be as stunned as he by her grandmother's sudden pronouncements concerning the future of their marriage. He could scarcely call forth even a single memory of his visit to Bath, and found himself grateful when Laurentia began, though somewhat haltingly, to speak of their few days together in the famous watering hole.

So, Mrs. Cabot felt he ought to remain married to her grand-daughter, even though she knew perfectly well who he was and Laurentia still did not! He watched the old woman carefully, wondering how it had come about that she had determined he was a proper match for Laurentia. She knew well that he was impoverished, and that a degree of scandal clung to his name. He felt flattered, suddenly, for there could be only one interpretation of her adamance concerning their marriage—she approved of him.

Well! This was an unlooked for turn of events. His gaze shifted to Laurentia, and he felt his heart soften in quick turns. The time he had spent with her in Bath, though entirely innocent in nature, he would always treasure. He had shared with her something of which he had spoken to no one before, of the horror of his parents' deaths. She had responded in the manner he had come to expect of her, with tenderness and understanding, which was undoubtedly why he had felt he could tell her of the event in the first place.

He wished Mrs. Cabot had not suddenly sanctioned their marriage, for he found in this moment that he wanted nothing more than to remain wed to Laurentia, yet he knew he could not. Too much separated them—his own unfortunate past, however innocent he was, her dislike of *Villiers,* his own distaste for marrying an heiress, and her strong intention to have command of her inheritance.

Oh, but she was a lovely creature. His gaze drifted admiringly over her red curls, which were dressed in a thousand lovely tendrils over the crown of her head and cascading past her shoulders. Her maid had tucked pearls among her locks. Her complexion was as fine as a Devonshire cream, touched on her cheeks with the blush of ripening peaches.

He drew in a deep sigh. He was more attached to her than ever, and knew he was caught in the throes of a hopeless love. His mind kept bending around and around the notion of remaining married to her, of loving her more and more each day, of making her his true wife, of having children with her, as many as she wished for.

He could see the future with her, that spring would rise with every dawn, even if the darkest of winter days was upon the land. She was the best of every season—the burst of life in spring, the warmth of summer, the delicate beauty of fall, and the strength of winter. Laurentia Cabot. He wondered again what her middle name was, and how many other small things there were to discover about her, and whether or not a lifetime would be sufficient to know her truly and fully.

"Tell Grandmama the very mean trick you played on me at the Pump Room."

"I beg pardon?" Villiers said. He had not been listening, not by half. She had said something about the Pump Room. He tried to focus on Laurentia's words, but his gaze was captured by the sight of her lips. He recalled kissing her in the snow, her cherry lips so ready for love. He wanted to kiss her again, a thousand times, a hundred thousand times. He would mark the value of each day by how many times he caught her up in his arms, completely unawares, and kissed her. He would keep mistletoe suspended from all the door lintels throughout the year. He would insist he must kiss her for tradition's sake. She would respond with that wonderful giggle of hers, the one that sounded like pearls warbling in her throat.

"Thomas?"

She was speaking his name. He didn't want to speak. He wanted to remain within the hopeful reverie Mrs. Cabot had given to him—that he would always be Laurentia's husband.

"Thomas, drink this! You do not look at all well, and you don't seem to be able to hear a word I've said to you! Please! You are frightening me!"

He took the small glass of sherry which she had quickly thrust into his hand. When had she crossed the room to fetch him a glass of sherry? He downed it quickly.

He rose to his feet, but before she could sit down he caught her elbow and tugged her in the direction of the door. "You must come with me," he said forcefully. "There is something I need to show you in . . . in the hallway."

"Thomas, you are behaving quite strangely, I must say. Besides, what will Grandmama think of our manners if we desert her in this wretched manner?"

Thomas turned toward Mrs. Cabot, who was beaming with something caught between amusement and joy. "You will forgive us, ma'am, will you not? I find I must speak with Laurentia."

"You have my blessing, Mr. Swinfield. Take her from the room at once!"

He drew her along with the force of his will and wrapped her arm about his. "There, you see! I told you she would understand!"

"But it is excessively rude!" Laurentia cried.

"Not in the least!" Mrs. Cabot cried. "I was young, once. Go! Even a fool can see that Mr. Swinfield means to tell you something of import. Go!"

"But Grandmama!" Laurentia cried, turning part way around to stare at her.

"Don't be silly, child. He has something he must say to you. I am perfectly capable of entertaining myself for a few minutes while you are gone."

Villiers took her into the hall, then stopped for a moment as a servant appeared in an antechamber some few yards away. He took her across the entrance hall, and knew then where he wished to go.

A few minutes more and they were in the music room. He looked up at the arched doorway which was hung with mistletoe, and said, "There. That is what I wanted to show you."

Laurentia glanced up at the curved lintel from which was hung a small bunch of mistletoe on a bright, red silk ribbon. "Oh, Thomas," she murmured. "You brought me here to kiss me? You made me abandon my grandmother, all because you wished for a kiss? But this is awful."

"I know it is. Terrible, in fact. Only, I knew that if I did not kiss you very soon, especially since your grandmother seems for some ridiculous reason to approve of me, I would likely suffer a fit of apoplexy."

"Apoplexy?" she murmured as he drew her into his arms. "That would be a dreadful tragedy for one so young!"

"Indeed," he returned. He said nothing more, but gentled his lips over hers in a series of kisses that very soon set her throat to murmuring and cooing. "I'm in love with you," he breathed at last. "Desperately and hopelessly. Laurentia, my darling, my dearest one, my precious wife."

The sherry seemed to have ignited his senses. Fire rampaged through him. He was devoid of the ability to order his mind. Only his soul could command him, commanding his lips to devour her mouth. He sought entrance, and when she parted her lips he tasted the depths of her mouth and claimed her for his own. He held her roughly as she leaned into him, the feel of her lithe body arousing husbandly desires.

"You can't be in love with me," she breathed over his lips. "You are mistaken."

"Oh, but I'm not." She kissed both sides of his mouth, teasing him. "You scarcely know me and besides, in just little less than a fortnight, we shall . . ."

He kissed her again. "I don't care about the future, not in this moment," he whispered. "Laurentia, pretend with me, even for just a time, that we will be together forever, that your circumstances and mine are an illusion. Tell me of your heart, my precious one. Do you kiss me because it pleases you, or because you cannot help yourself?"

She gentled her lips on his, then said, "I didn't want to be loved again. I didn't want to give my heart to any man. But Thomas, from the first it has been so easy to be with you, to speak with you, as though you understand my thoughts before ever I speak them."

"I feel the same way," he murmured, settling his head on her forehead. The tension in his mind twisted and seethed with a dozen warnings. He knew he should tell her who he was, should tell her now. On the other hand, what did it matter if he never told her? He would be forced to leave in two weeks regardless. Those dice had already been cast, and he didn't want the moment to end. He wanted to continue loving her and holding her in his arms, speaking his heart to her and listening to the musings of her soul, until his hand was actually forced. Perhaps he was being unwise, yet he felt this was the moment with her which would always belong to him, not the future, which had been stolen fifteen years ago. No, this moment was his.

He met her gaze fiercely. "Pretend with me that there is no future, only these moments, these final weeks. When I leave, I want to take all these memories with me, to hold in my heart as something true and wonderful our time together, so that the cold winters of Somerset will be as warm as a fine July afternoon. Please, Laurentia, do this for me. Pretend for me that you are not wealthy, that I am not lacking even a competence, that we never signed documents, either in Tewkesbury or in Gretna Green. Pretend that we are lovers who chanced upon one another in a place and time when all was perfect for a perfect union."

Laurentia became so utterly lost in his words and in the precious fire of his eyes that she did precisely what he told her to do. She closed her eyes and gave herself so completely to the masquerade of their love that all her fears and worries slipped away like ice melting under a hot sun. They were simply gone.

She opened her eyes and saw him without the least encumbrance of worry. Her heart blossomed quickly and brightly into an exquisite flower, opening to him and allowing the brilliance of his love to beat down on her, sun to earth. She wrapped her arms about his neck and spoke her heart. "I've loved you from that first moment I burst in on you at the Tump and Dagler Inn. Oh, Thomas, how easily you stole my heart. Even then I was enchanted by the amused glint in your eye, how you viewed such a silly woman with patience and interest, how you so gently took my cloak from my shoulders and offered me a cup of wassail. Whyever do you think I could have asked you to marry me in the first place? Did you think me a madwoman?"

"Only a little. I thought you beautiful and charming, a captivating imp in a woman's body and mind. Every day with you has been like a dream, being with you, knowing you, conversing as we do, as though we have known one another two lifetimes and have only just been catching up on the news from the past century or so."

She giggled. "Hold me close, Thomas, and kiss me again."

He obliged her. He took her to the settee near the windows, cradled her on his lap, and obliged her for a long time. Supper was forgotten, and Grandmama wisely forbade the servants to disturb them. Love was exchanged in a thousand professions of affection and attachment. She gave herself completely to the pretense, and allowed her heart to be spoken fully. He responded by reviewing their time together in detail, explaining how she had charmed him at the inn, at the orphanage, in the music room, on the sleigh ride, in Tewkesbury, in Bath—especially in Bath—while in the snow after seeing the obelisk in the Orange Grove. He told her he was satiated with his love for her because he had been able to speak of his love, to give voice to every nuance of his affection for her.

He kissed her a little more, and only ended the evening as the clock in the entrance hall chimed twelve times.

He lifted her to her feet and kept an arm slung tightly about her waist as he walked her toward the door. He kissed her as they walked, and sometimes the walking grew very still. Progress was made toward the entrance hall, and even up the stairs. The door of her bedchamber, however, grew very warm as he kept her pressed up against it for a long, long time. Only when the clock chimed one did she finally bid Thomas goodnight.

Laurentia dreamed strange, wonderful dreams that night, dreams that began full of white light and music and ended with racing horses and then a sword fight, though she could not tell who was doing battle. She awakened, then remembered the evening she had shared with Thomas, and the dreams were forgotten. Finally she slept deeply, and awoke near eleven in the morning.

Upon awakening, however, she found that her grandmother was just stealing into her bedchamber with one of her maids.

"Did I awaken you, my pet?" Mrs. Cabot queried softly.

"No. At least, I don't think so." She sat up slightly and saw that the maid was holding up a rather strange looking ball gown and smiling rather broadly.

Mrs. Cabot said, "There was something I failed to mention last night," she said. "I would have said something, but you both seemed rather overset by the notion of a ball, so that I felt I ought to keep silent. However, now that you've had some time to adjust to the forthcoming celebration I want to tell you the rest—the ball is to be a masquerade."

Laurentia, her mind still curling with sleep, squeezed her eyes shut. Was she dreaming? She opened her eyes and heard her maid say, "I believe it turned out quite well. Mrs. Soudley, in the village, has the finest eye. Her stitches are so small as to not be seen. Every seam as straight as an arrow."

"Indeed. The woman is a witch with needle and thread."

"Is that a costume, then?" Laurentia queried.

"Yes. Your costume. You must try it on soon, to make certain it fits properly."

"What about Thomas—I mean, Mr. Swinfield? What will he wear?"

"Coxwell has seen to everything. He is a wizard, that man. I believe he chose Sir Francis Drake, a little gold and black velvet. I saw the costume. Tights, of course, but Vill—I mean Mr. Swinfield—has such a good leg."

"What did you say? Grandmama, you almost called him Villiers again, didn't you? Why?"

Her grandmother shrugged. "I daresay because he looks a great deal like him, and because, though I don't like to mention it. I am getting very old. I have been confusing many things of late. Forgive me, my pet. I know that just mentioning that man's name gives you palpitations!"

"Oh, not palpitations, surely, Grandmama?" Laurentia cried, laughing. "I am not so hopeless a female as that."

Her grandmother smiled. "That you are not. And now, let's see how you will look as a water nymph."

Twelve

Late that afternoon, Villiers breathed a heavy sigh of relief upon learning the ball was to be a masquerade, and that for most of the celebration he would be costumed as Sir Francis Drake. He had been gone the entire day to Tewkesbury, having received an urgent summons from Laurentia's solicitor early that morning requesting his presence immediately. What he needed now, tonight, above all things, was a complete disguise, and the elegant costume Coxwell had created would perform the task beyond expectation. He was still reeling from the effects of Mr. Crabtree's communication, and what he had learned had completely changed his course.

He fingered the doublet of fine black velvet, marveling at Coxwell's skill. The front of the garment was stitched and cross-patterned to form diamonds over the entire front. The cape, also of black velvet, was lined with gold silk, and when thrown back over one shoulder appeared magnificent, indeed. The breeches were of a matching velvet trimmed with gold bands down each side. A ruff of gold lace, three tiers deep would surround his neck, and a black velvet hat, adorned with a single white feather, formed the headress. His tights were a thick knit fabric—quite sturdy, Coxwell assured him. Heeled, gold-buckled shoes completed the dashing ensemble. The costume was made perfect for the occasion by the clever half-mask Coxwell had created in black and gold, which dipped just below his nose and cut across his cheekbones at a sharp angle. He would be unknown to everyone, and if his luck should hold he would remain thusly until he could leave Evenlode, which he hoped would be sooner than he had planned—tomorrow, in fact, with his dear, sweet wife none the wiser as to his identity.

What he had learned from Mr. Crabtree had made it absolutely imperative he leave Windrush as quickly as possible. . . .

Upon his arriving in Mr. Crabtree's offices, the worried solicitor quickly disclosed the astounding nature of his summons. He had uncovered information which he felt Villiers would want to know immediately.

It would seem Mr. Crabtree had begun quietly seeking information concerning a certain plantation—of which had he heard rumors for years, and of which Mrs. Swinfield had asked him only a few days past. Rumors had long since connected both Mr. Cabot and Sir Alan Redcliffe to the plantation. His efforts had been rewarded, for he had found a former servant of Sir Alan's, who, after consuming a great deal of Christmas wassail, had been prevailed upon to open his budget.

After a time, the servant admitted quite bitterly having been dismissed from service by Sir Alan, on some pretext or other. This had occurred shortly after he had been in a room for some time where certain papers had been strewn about the baronet's desk. Yes, he had glanced at the papers. Well, yes, he had read some of the words of the uppermost. Well, yes, he could read. His parents had sent all four of their sons to the village school, and he could read a little, and write a handy scrawl if called upon.

To his recollection, the documents pertained to a West Indies Plantation by the name of Soledad, owned by a Mr. Percival Cabot.

Villiers had listened intently. In some dim recess of his mind he was aware that nearly every muscle in his body was knotted up as though to increase his hearing prowess. "How is Redcliffe connected?" he had demanded harshly. "Tell me this, and I shall be satisfied."

Mr. Crabtree had leaned forward in his chair. "There were numerous receipts for tens of thousands of pounds, paid by Mr. Cabot to Sir Alan, listed as profits for the operation of the plantation."

"All of this sounds quite legitimate."

"Yes, but there was a letter, as well, which explained where the 'profit' came from. The servant said he kept mum about it because he feared for his life, Sir Alan being a hard taskmaster and the information so damning. The letter was from Mr. Cabot, stating the exact nature of the relationship between the men and the false nature of the plantation. According to his best determination, it appeared that Mr. Cabot was receiving funds from one *Lord Villiers,* halving that sum, then paying an equal portion of it to Sir Alan Redcliffe in the form of plantation profits. Therefore, if Sir Alan was ever called upon to explain his sudden wealth, he would be able to claim that an investment in a plantation had proved enormously successful. Mr. Cabot, with no connection to the Villiers estate, would never be suspect."

Even now Villiers could recall the precise sentiment which had bolted through him at that moment, of hearing his name and his entire past vindicated by a letter a servant of Sir Alan's had once seen. He had known a sense of victorious relief so profound that every particle of his being felt alive and free at long last.

The sensation had been short-lived, however, for while his heart had been celebrating, his brain had made a quite sudden and quick calculation as another sentiment took possession of him. "The men split my fortune!" he cried, full of rage.

"So it would seem, for I must presume you did not make any such investment. Was this the misdeed to which you referred during our last conversation, then?"

"The very one. My father trusted Sir Alan implicitly, and

had assigned him to be my guardian. He had complete control of the purse strings. I can only presume, then, that he forged my signature."

"And paid Cabot handsomely for ignoring the forgery—half a fortune, to be precise."

"Half," he murmured, his thoughts drifting to Laurentia. She had recently told him that her uncle's fortune had increased rapidly from a point some twelve years ago when mysterious funds had appeared ready for investing. He was in no doubt now as to where the monies had originated. He also realized that the bulk of Laurentia's inheritance had been built on half his fortune.

Mr. Crabtree said, "The servant of which I have spoken resides in Tewkesbury, and I am convinced can be persuaded while sober to give testimony to what he told me. I am in little doubt that he would be pleased to inform against Sir Alan."

Villiers had fallen silent, the momentary exhilaration passing swiftly. His thoughts had turned to Laurentia, and to the ways in which their fortunes were so completely intertwined. His love for her seemed to rise in that moment, and to dominate all his senses. Of the many ladies he had known over the years, many of whom he had admired deeply, none had so touched him as Laurentia Cabot. In many ways he was still in awe of her, of the genuine sweetness and unspoiled quality of her temperament, the largeness of her heart in wishing to give so much of her inheritance to those in need, her dedication to righting what she believed were her uncle's many wrongs.

Were he to pursue the servant of which Mr. Crabtree spoke, were he to finally uncover sufficient documents to expose Sir Alan Redcliffe for the monster he really was, were he to demand from the Cabot estate what belonged to him, he would utterly destroy Laurentia's life. The scandal alone which would surround Evenlode was a possibility too horrendous to be born.

"Do you wish for me to arrange for a meeting with the man of whom I have spoken?" Mr. Crabtree asked.

Lord Villiers had turned to stare at the solicitor, his thoughts circling briskly about Laurentia and her future. He loved her so very much. Never in a thousand years would he do anything to harm her.

"No," he responded calmly. "You have done me a great service in discovering the truth about a situation which has dogged my heels for more years than I at present wish to contemplate. However, I see no reason to take this matter further."

"No reason!" Mr. Crabtree had cried. "But Sir, my lord . . . !"

Villiers lifted a hand and withheld a deep sigh. "Again, thank you for the trouble you have taken over this matter, but I wish to put the whole thing to rest at once. I ask that you refrain from speaking to anyone on this subject. Do you understand?"

"Yes, m'lord," he had said solemnly. He remained silent for a long moment, his jaw working strongly. Finally, he added, "You would do this for Miss Cabot, then?"

Lord Villiers shook his head rising to his feet. "No. I would do this for my wife."

Mr. Crabtree had appeared ready to speak, but then apparently decided against offering another word on the subject. Instead, he bowed to Villiers and expressed his desire that if ever he could be of service to him that his lordship had but to send for him.

"Thank you, Mr. Crabtree. You have acted on my behalf, and for that I shall always be grateful. Now, pray continue to act on my wife's behalf and *you* will have but to command *me*." He had bowed formally in return, intending for the solicitor to understand he wished the subject to be closed forever.

On the drive from Tewkesbury, Villiers had pondered the irony of the situation a thousand different ways. He had tried to create in his mind a different path for the future, one that involved the courts and justice, the return of his fortune, while somehow sustaining his marriage to Laurentia.

Unfortunately, even if she could bear the scandal which would arise were Sir Alan's and her uncle's perfidy to be disclosed, how could she ever forgive him for lying to her these many weeks about his own identity? After all, she had not been misinformed about *Villiers*. He was a gamester. He had lived by his wits and what he could win at a whist table in the various homes in which he resided in the course of a year's time. How could she love such a man?

Besides, he'd grown accustomed to his life, and still believed in his future. Had he not been able to save two thousand pounds, invested in the funds?

Once arrived at Evenlode, he had completely resigned himself to his course. He would never, *never*, involve his beloved wife in a scandal surrounding his inheritance. He had little doubt that were he to investigate fully Sir Alan's pilfering of his fortune and begin the process of prosecution, the notoriety of the event would be known throughout England as one of the worst scandals of the decade.

Now, as he watched Coxwell fussing over the Drake costume, his mind was dragged back even further, to his father's dying moment, how he had lifted his son from the wreckage and tried to save his wife, dying in the attempt as the carriage and horses slid down the embankment.

He would be no less heroic for Laurentia. He wanted the beauty of her innocent life to continue more than he wanted to be comfortable again, or to see his home restored to its former charm and warmth. He would see his way through the masquerade ball, and he would keep his identity a secret even if he had to disappear before the unmasking. Then he would leave Evenlode on the morrow.

A knock at the door and a whispered word from one of the servants informed him that Laurentia had descended to the drawing room. He dressed hastily and bid Coxwell settle the hat on his head—he wished to be going immediately. He wanted to see his lovely wife, to be with her, to enjoy her company for this one last evening together. He would leave off the mask, of course, until such a time as supper would be concluded and the guests began to arrive.

He found Laurentia alone in the drawing room. She stood near the pianoforte, craning her neck, apparently scrutinizing her costume in a mirror.

"Is something amiss?" he queried.

She started and blushed a little, then gave a delighted clap of her hands as she looked him up and down. "Grandmama said your man was a genius, but until this moment I doubted her enthusiasm for his skill! I shan't do so again. You look absolutely marvelous."

"As do you. Now, tell me why you were trying to see your back. Oh, and by the way, your costume is charming. A nymph, perhaps?"

Her eyes danced with merriment. "Yes," she breathed. "Isn't this the most delightful costume? I am completely sheathed in a mountain of tulle, although I feel as though a brisk wind could simply carry me away." She turned toward the mirror, and once more began craning her neck. "I wanted to see the wings again. I wish they'd been made larger so that I could see them, for they are so dainty and beautiful."

He drew up behind her and saw that she was right. Delicate wings, trimmed with thin threads of silver lace, were positioned in the center of her back and hung with more folds of the diaphanous material. "How very enchanting," he murmured, sliding his hands down her arms. "The wings, of course. The costume, certainly. But more than these . . . you."

She turned in a swirl of gossamer fabric and fell, as by habit now, into his arms. He kissed her deeply, placing his hand carefully at the small of her back and holding her to him.

"Oh, Thomas," she murmured breathlessly. "I missed you today. I wish you had not been gone."

"I, too," he whispered. "I had not meant to be, but there was some urgent business I had to attend to."

"What business?" she cooed. "What could be more important than continuing what we began last night?"

"Now that I see you again and have you in my arms, I don't know how I let myself be drawn away."

"Silly man," she breathed.

"Very," he responded, hoping for a light note he scarcely felt anymore. He wanted desperately to regain the sweetness he had enjoyed with her last night, but the events of the day had borne his spirits into a low place from which he still had not quite recovered.

As he looked into Laurentia's eyes, he saw a path by which he could leave behind the morass of his unhappiness. In the same way that he had begged her to pretend their love would abide forever, he summoned that sensation now, for this would be the last night he would ever be with her.

This thought filled him full to overflowing as he let his love for her dominate his senses. He leaned toward her and gently placed his lips on hers, tasting of her as though this kiss would be the last. She responded, as she always did, with warm murmurs, the sound of pearls caught up by her vocal chords, warbling in her throat.

His soul leaned toward her, touching her soul, begging her to understand the depths of his love for her.

"Thomas, you are crushing my wings," she whispered on a laugh.

"So I am," he said, sliding his hands away from the small, delicate creations and gripping her instead around her small waist. "Do you mind so terribly?"

"Oh, no, not a bit!" she cried. "To be loved in this manner, so completely. For a moment there I thought . . . I mean, I vow I felt, your thoughts touch my mind. I . . . I don't want you to go. I think, Thomas, I really think we ought to discuss the future."

"Are those tears brimming in your eyes, my darling? Pray don't cry, not tonight. We shall discuss the future, tomorrow perhaps, but not now, for I can hear Mrs. Cabot in the entrance hall upbraiding the servants who are carrying her downstairs."

She giggled a watery laugh. "So she is. But promise me that we shall discuss our future. I don't want our marriage to end. There, I've said it as plainly as I can. Thomas, I wish to remain your wife, forever."

"And I your husband," he responded sincerely. Not for a moment did he permit the truth of his situation to dim the joy he felt. For in this moment, they were married, truly, and in that he would be content. Let tomorrow come . . . tomorrow.

She leaned into him, her expression aglow. He waited for no further hint, but slanted a kiss across her lips, exploring her mouth deeply, his arms wrapped tightly about her waist and carefully avoiding her wings. He loved her dearly. He always would. And tonight, after the ball, he would keep her up long after the last guest had left Evenlode in order to share the dawn with her, kissing her and embracing her as he had on the previous night.

Then, after he had sent her to bed, he would quietly slip from Evenlode House and disappear from her life forever—believing, of course, that he could avoid those guests who were acquainted with Lord Villiers.

Laurentia stood at the top of the short landing which preceded the ballroom and wondered for the hundredth time why her husband was so tense. He had been perfectly amiable through dinner surrounded by a handful of the local gentry, but as soon as the remainder of the guests began arriving she had sensed a shift in his demeanor. Though he smiled with great politeness and conducted his manners, as always, with complete perfection, she had quickly detected a slight stiffness in his spine and could not help but notice the careful manner in which he answered each masked guest. She decided that at the earliest moment she would ask him whatever had happened to set his teeth on edge.

When all the guests had been introduced, she turned toward him and watched as he released a rather pronounced rush of air—not a sigh, precisely, but the closest thing to it. "Thomas," she whispered. "I've never seen you so ill at ease. Is anything the matter?"

Thomas's smile broadened. "Was it that obvious? And I was trying quite desperately to appear perfectly composed."

"I'm certain it was only obvious to me," she responded, taking his proffered arm.

He covered her hand with his own and gave it a squeeze. "I was only nervous about meeting your many friends and acquaintances. But now that I have, I can see I was quite foolish to have been distressed."

"Quite foolish," she returned gaily.

He patted her arm. "Come, I wish to dance a waltz with you."

"Oh, yes," she breathed. "I have been waiting the entire day to be in your arms."

"What a shameless thing to say!" he whispered across her cheek.

Her ear, quite exposed to his breath, caught the warm air, and a shiver went down her neck and side. She squeezed his hand in return and looked up at him, willing him to feel the depth of her affection for him and her desire that he never leave Evenlode. He had said they would discuss the future, and, however much she might enjoy a ball, of the moment she wished she was alone with him, in his arms, enjoying the gentleness of his kisses and begging him to believe that, whatever her previous plans, she somehow wanted him to be apart of her life forever.

"Oh, Thomas . . . I wish—"

"I know," he murmured in sweet response to her thoughts.

She saw the returned affection in his eyes through the slits of his black mask and felt her knees grow watery. She clung to his arm as together they began the descent into the ballroom.

All the joy and laughter of hundreds of happy guests rose to greet them, along with a mounting round of applause. Laurentia cast her gaze over the crowd and felt certain that with so much genuine well-wishing her life could truly want for nothing more. The ballroom, decorated in Christmas holly and glittering from the glow of scores of candles, reflected perfectly the best of the Yuletide Season. The orchestra, in an alcove above the floor, was poised to begin a waltz honoring their nuptials, a dance which they would commence quite alone for the first several measures, to be joined later by other guests.

The applause gently melted away. Laurentia took up her place opposite Thomas, and dipped a slow, graceful curtsy. He in turn bowed, then took her up in his arms. The orchestra, instruments tuned and readied, began the elegant, quite modern dance. As if in a dream, Laurentia gave herself to the enjoyment of the music, to the pleasure of Thomas's hand upon hers and his arm supporting her waist, and to the delight of moving as one with her husband about the ballroom floor.

The spectators were a blur as Thomas moved her up and back, around and around. Light from the three enormous chandeliers flowed over her in wave after wave of wonder and magic. She loved, and she was loved. The music became a stream of joy that poured over her head and swept her closer and closer to the man she had come to adore in only a scant few weeks.

Her eyes never left his face, nor did he withdraw his attention from her as the music swept her around and around.

Villiers looked into the face of love and was moved beyond expression. His soul expanded in his chest, and seemed to be reaching toward Laurentia with each powerful movement of his feet as the music took them both in a sweeping arc and circle, over and over. Others had begun to join them on the floor now, but he kept his beloved in the center of the ballroom, following a mental pattern of an oval that would permit no one to breach the sanctum of their dance.

He felt joined to Laurentia in a way that he could only describe as eternal. All the rest of his days he would remember this moment when he gave himself to her so completely that he knew he would never marry again, no matter what the future held. He was as certain of that fact as he was certain he was holding her securely in his arms even now.

He did not want this dance to end, yet at the same time he knew that something pure and holy had passed between them, something that would never end even though the music would soon draw to a close. She belonged to him, and he belonged to her. Even separated, as they soon must be, he would know a connection to her, and he would enjoy that connection the remainder of his life and, he believed, long, long after.

When the music stopped he gently drew her to him and, as though it was the most natural occurrence in the world, he placed a soft kiss on her lips. In some vague recess of his mind he could hear the rather shocked guests gasping and crying out hushed, "Oh, my!"s but he didn't care. He hadn't intended to kiss her, but the moment seemed to demand such an innocent display of affection.

By the time he released her, another round of applause was resounding through the ballroom. Could his marriage to Laurentia have been better honored than this? He thought not. That he would be leaving Windrush before the sun had fully risen in the sky was not something he pondered just now. The moment was demanding every particle of his attention, and he gave himself to it fully as he guided his beautiful bride off the floor.

Sir Alan Redcliffe, dressed as a Roman Senator, felt himself pale beneath his gold mask. All had been settled in his mind upon arriving at Evenlode. Villiers would be leaving soon, and he would begin his assault on Laurentia's heart. If her heart proved unwieldy, he intended to marry her out of hand once her marriage to Villiers had been dissolved.

But her unexpected display of sincere affection—no, of love!—in returning Villiers's unexpected and stunning kiss completely tore the foundation from his plans. He was utterly convinced there would be no divorce now, after seeing so much obvious mutual affection. In all his days, he had never seen a groom publicly kiss his wife. Never!

There could be only one explanation—Villiers was double-crossing Laurentia. He had never meant to keep his word to divorce her. He had wooed her and won her over the past few weeks, all to take what he wanted most—Cabot's fortune. The truth was, Villiers had enjoyed living a luxurious life in recent weeks and had no intention of letting Cabot's fortune slip from his grasp.

He should have known! Damme! He should have known!

Well! If Villiers thought he meant to keep his identity a secret now, he was fair and far off the mark. Only, how and when to inform Laurentia that instead of a courteous, gentle Mr. Swinfield making pretty love to her, the notorious game-ster, Lord Villiers, had sunk his talons into her?

At these happier thoughts he began to relax, and felt the blood begin to flow once more through his body. His cheeks tingled with the pleasure of the forthcoming revelation, and he began to circulate grandly among the guests proclaiming his blessings on Mrs. Swinfield's most excellent match.

Only, when to tell, when to tell . . .

Thirteen

Seated in a chair in the music room. along with a score of guests, Laurentia listened to the Christmas carolers perform a soft, gentle version of "Silent Night." Her heart seemed to slow to the elegant, lifting verses as the careful harmony of the choir swelled the old song. Was anything sweeter than the portrait of the Christmas story, of mother and child safe even in their poverty and protected by the quiet of the night?

Thomas, unmasked, stood by the fireplace. She glanced at him and found that he was watching her. He seemed deeply sad. She was a little startled by the melancholy of his expression, but a smile soon softened his features. She responded with a smile of her own, her soul filling full to overflowing once more.

She wondered now that she could ever have believed herself in love before. Her sentiments for Thomas Swinfield went far beyond either the violent infatuation she had experienced for James or the pleasure she had found in Matthew's company. Both of these aspects of Cupid's golden arrows she had experienced with Thomas. Yet, now, as she watched him, as the softened light in his eye permeated her being, she knew a sensation so intense as to be utterly possessive of her soul. Only one thought came to mind as she was filled with her love for Thomas—she would do anything for him, whatever he asked of her.

Anything!

How profound and mysterious! How was it possible that one day she could be thinking only of living a solitary existence, then the next day find herself insisting on a life married to a man she had known but a scant few weeks?

Yet so she was.

As the final verse was sung in a rising tide of Yuletide pleasure and wonder, she finally let her gaze be drawn away from Thomas. The faces of the carolers before her were aglow with the meaning and wonder of the song. The stillness of the chamber after the last note had drifted softly away reflected the impact the music had had on every heart present. A rippling of applause and murmurs of appreciation soon followed.

Laurentia smiled, ecstatic with the joy of both loving Thomas and being steeped in the warmth of the Christmas Season. She nodded to many others about her, who were obviously as enchanted as she had been enchanted. Her gaze finally came to rest on Sir Alan, who had unmasked, just as she had, a good hour prior. He was watching her, his eyes narrowed as though in dark contemplation.

She shivered suddenly, though she didn't know why. She thought perhaps someone had opened a window, permitting the freezing night air to rush through the heated chamber. She even glanced toward the windows to see if perhaps this had happened, but the fine, gossamer curtains of white Indian muslin were yet in repose.

Her gaze sought Sir Alan again. He was still watching her. Another chill wrent its way down her spine, forcing her to her feet. Instinctively, she turned away from him, hoping to capture Thomas's arm before he quit his position by the hearth.

Many of the guests, however, began to depart the chamber, and Thomas was swept along by a lively young woman who was insisting he go down the quadrille with her, for she had noticed what a fine dancer he was. Laurentia caught his glance over the tops of many cheerful bobbing heads. He shrugged and smiled, then took the lady's arm.

She was warmed by the sight and would have quit the room as well, but Sir Alan's arm was suddenly upon hers. "Stay a moment, my dear. A word, if you please."

Again, the odd shiver attacked her neck, her shoulders, her arms. "I oughtn't to stay," she responded carefully, uncertain why her good friend was disturbing to her as he was. "My grandmother expects me to attend to our guests."

By this time the last of the guests as well as the carolers had departed the chamber. He released her arm and quickly crossed the room to close the door. Then, with a brisk motion, he locked it against newcomers.

She gasped and felt herself grow oddly faint. "Whatever do you mean by locking the door?" she cried, taking a step forward but stopping abruptly as he turned toward her. His face was serious, even grave.

"I do so only to have a private moment. I assure you, what I feel I must tell you now I say only because I have begun to doubt Mr. Swinfield's intention of leaving Evenlode as he promised. If I truly believed he would actually leave Windrush, I wouldn't feel compelled to tell you what I now feel I must— as your friend, as your trusted adviser these many years, and as a constant business associate of your uncle's since times out of mind. Because of my sense of loyalty toward your family, I have for a long time made it a matter of my own dedicated concern to see your fortune protected from any who intended to wrest it from you."

"You refer to Mr. Dursley," she said.

"Have you become aware, then, about the circumstances surrounding his departure from Evenlode?" he queried.

"I . . . I chanced upon him in Bath, and he told me you had persuaded him to leave Windrush, and that you paid him a goodly sum."

"I was convinced he was not the proper husband for you, as was your uncle."

"Yet, my uncle thought Villiers would make a proper husband?" she asked.

"As to that, I truly believe your uncle was not aware of his reputation. He was attending instead to his desire to satisfy a request of his wife's to see you wed to someone who was related to you. At the same time, I believe he was ambitious for you, that he wanted a title for your name. Villiers, as a distant relation of Mrs. Cabot's, satisfied both requirements, at least that is my belief. I only wish he had consulted me before drawing up a final will. I was never more disheartened when I learned he had offered your hand to Villiers and Villiers had accepted of it."

He had drawn near to her and took up both her hands in his. "Oh, my dear Laurentia, how beautiful you are. To think when I first met you, you were but a child of nine. Now you are a woman grown."

She had not been so sheltered that she did not recognize the signs of an impassioned expression. She tried to withdraw her hands from his but he would not allow it, and her fingers soon ached with the effort. "You should let me go, Sir Alan," she cried on an anguished whisper. "This . . . this is most improper! I beg you, release my hands at once!"

"I shan't attempt to kiss you, if that is what you fear. I am not such a moonling as that. I am only trying to tell you that you have engaged my heart, quite fully, perhaps because I have known you and your sweet innocence since your were a child. You are the perfect woman to dress my table and adorn my home. I want many children, just as I know you do, for you once told me of your dreams to fill Evenlode with more tots than the village school. Now, with just a word, you can fill my home as well, fill them both, if you like. We shall be wed, you and I, one day, when this business with Villiers is finished at last. I promise—"

"With Villiers?" she queried, ice beginning to flow in her veins. "But that is long finished. It ended the moment I married Thomas—that is, Mr. Swinfield."

"Oh, but it did not, for that is what I mean to tell you—and so I shall now." At last he released her hands, though he remained standing very close to her. "Mr. Swinfield did not give you his complete name. Oh, yes, he is a Mr. Swinfield, but his full name is Thomas Michael Adolphus Swinfield, fifth viscount *Lord Villiers*. I know him well, because I was at one time his guardian. I am intimately acquainted with his propensity to gamble away every shilling that dares touch his fingers."

"I . . . I don't understand. I don't know what you mean."

"Swinfield is Viscount Villiers," he stated plainly.

"Villiers? The gamester?" she queried, incredulous.

"None other."

Laurentia shook her head, unwilling to believe what he was telling her. Yet why would he lie to her? "You must be mistaken," she said, stunned and weaving a little on her feet. *Swinfield*. Was that where she had heard the name, connected with Villiers? What a fool she was.

"I was his guardian," he reiterated. "I could never be mistaken."

"I can hardly believe it," she murmured, pressing her hand to her stomach. "But I don't understand. How . . . how long have you known?"

"From the first. He is much altered in recent years, but I knew him for Villiers that first day in your drawing room."

"You knew, but you said nothing?" she queried, a wave of nausea suddenly battering her stomach.

He nodded, his expression downcast. "I was shocked at first, particularly when I realized he had so completely duped you. At first, I didn't know how to proceed. I feared speaking the truth, since you were so *charmed* by him. Having understood the nature of your agreement with him, though, I decided to say nothing since I was convinced he would soon be gone."

Laurentia felt the room begin to spin. "But . . . but I love him. How could I love such a monster?"

"Undoubtedly, such men know how to cast a spell over the women of their acquaintance." His voice was low and confiding.

She nodded. Nausea once more pelted her. Sir Alan leaned toward her. His lips brushed her cheek. She tried to push him away, but her arms were weak and useless. He found her lips. The room turned upside down, and she fell into a place of infinite blackness.

Laurentia awoke slowly. Nausea clung to her, and her mind felt numb and strange. At first she did not know where she was, but then began to recognize in stages the decor of her bedchamber. She could not remember how she had gotten there.

She blinked slowly. The hearth was glowing a deep red with a mountain of coals. Beside her a single candle burned steadily, casting a strange glow over the figure of her grandmother, who was sitting very much asleep in a winged chair, her neck craned at a terrible angle. Poor thing! How uncomfortable she appeared.

She tried to lift an arm, to reach out toward her grandmother, but the numbness in her mind seemed to have spread throughout her whole body. She could barely swallow, and her mouth was horridly dry.

Laudanum. Someone had given her laudanum. She remembered now!

Other memories rushed back to her, as well. She had awakened from her swoon with a pair of lips upon hers, unfamiliar lips. She remembered hearing a strong pounding on the door accompanied by shouting. The door burst open and Thomas rushed in, but he was not looking at her. He pulled Sir Alan to his feet and threw his fist into his chin, landing a flush hit.

Sir Alan had fallen backward, writhing on the floor and clutching at his jaw. Thomas had picked her up and carried her from the room. She had felt too sick, too weak, to protest. She had begun to weep, almost uncontrollably, the masks of her guests passing by her in a long line of grotesque observers. When he was mounting the stairs, she remembered what Sir Alan had told her—that the man she had married was none other than that horrid gamester, Lord Villiers. She began to beat ineffectually upon his chest with her fist, calling him a liar and a cheat.

"You made me love you!" she had cried into his neckcloth. "Vile, vile man! You made me love you. You made me love you."

She must have fainted again after that. She remembered coming around once more, only to have a liquid forced down her throat.

As she glanced about the bedchamber, her head weak with the drug, her vision drifted to the draperies by the window, then to a pitcher of water by the door, to a chair, and then she saw him, in the corner. Or was the drug giving her another fanciful image to frighten her?

"Thomas," she whispered from her parched throat.

He approached her slowly. He appeared sad again, as he had in the music room while standing by the fireplace.

"So it is true," she said.

He nodded. "I meant to tell you, that day in Bath, but it began to snow and you became so excited. I let the moment slip away from me. I shouldn't have. I'm so sorry, Laurentia."

"Why did you pretend?" She could hardly speak, and now her throat ached with the constriction of a thousand tears begging to be shed.

"When you first approached me with your proposal, that

evening at the Tump and Dagler, I refrained from telling you who I am because you were so adorable, and I was charmed by your innocent trust in me. Later, however, it suited me to be anyone other than *Villiers,* because you held *him* in such abhorrence."

"You meant to take my fortune. Don't deny it's true. I know it is true, it must be true! What gamester would not want such a fortune to squander!"

"Never!" he cried. "But you will learn as much when you call upon Mr. Crabtree and begin divorce proceedings." His jaw worked strongly, and she could see that his eyes were moist. "I am leaving now. I had made plans for my departure before the ball, before you learned of my identity, for even then I knew the time had come for us to part. My darling, know that I love you, that I never intended to hurt you, and please, *please,* place your trust in your solicitor. He is a sensible man, and will know how to proceed. The only thing that I ask is that you allow your grandmother to guide you in the future. She will keep you out of harm's way."

"Grandmama knew you were Villiers from the first," she said, stating what she now knew to be the truth. "Twice she called you by your true name. I should have heeded such errors! Only why didn't she tell me?"

He shook his head and smiled sadly, "I'm not certain, but I believe she took a fancy to me."

Her head was swimming wildly, and tears had begun a swift march down her cheeks.

"Good-bye, my love," he whispered. "I return you to that which you desire most—to help those who have suffered so much in Windrush."

He backed away from the bed. Just as he disappeared into the hallway, she reached a hand out. "Don't go, Thomas . . . please."

She fell back against the pillows and disappeared once more into a deep, drugged sleep.

* * *

Two days later, Villiers walked into the library of his ancestral home, one of the few chambers of the ancient mansion that had not suffered from damp rot. Even now a small fire in a smokeless fireplace was burning brightly, and the chamber, if not warm, was dry and smelled decently, unlike most of the house.

He turned and surveyed the books lining the walls. During his childhood, this room had been the center of his world. His father had been an avid reader, and his mother not less so. Both had read to him since his infancy, and even now he moved to touch the fine leather bindings which were still in good condition despite so many years of neglect.

His aged butler, Simmons, lived there along with his wife, who had served as cook at Fairwood Hall since times out of mind. When his fortune had disappeared, he had kept these two retainers at the house with a request that the library and his bedchamber be kept in a state of repair and readiness against his occasional return. Simmons had honored his word, and whenever the world encroached a trifle too seriously on his peace of mind, there is where Villiers withdrew to recover his spirits in hopes of once again beginning anew.

"M'lord," Coxwell called from the doorway. "Simmons wishes to know if you will be dining in here or in the dining room."

He smiled and turned to his valet. "In here, of course, where I have dined since I was sixteen."

"It is a matter of form," Coxwell returned with an answering smile. "Do you wish for the horses to be readied on the morrow? Kent is not so far away. . . ." He let the hint rest in the air.

Villiers shook his head. "I shan't be leaving Somerset for a long, long time, I'm 'fraid, old man. We will winter here, though I will understand if you feel it time to seek a new position." He laughed a little harshly. "It is unfortunate, however, that Brummell is now in Belgium."

"I daresay you have the right of it, for he cannot possibly find a tailor as fine as Weston on the Continent. As for seeking another situation, I prefer to remain with you."

He understood him. "You are a good friend."

"Indeed, sir, I hope I am at least that," he responded with a lift of his groomed brow.

When the door closed and the sound of Coxwell's footsteps disappeared down the hall, he moved to the fireplace and began building a larger, more comfortable fire. He then settled himself in his favorite leather chair, a large, deep, square creation that had suited his father quite well and now suited him perfectly. He sipped a glass of sherry as the last of the twilight disappeared from the snowy sky and only a blackness filled the curtainless windows.

He would stay at Fairwood from now on, he decided. He had no stomach for the usual round of visits. He would become a laborer of sorts, and begin tending his property himself. Perhaps tomorrow he would begin clearing the dead wood from the forest of Spanish chestnuts. He might even chop the wood for Cook and for the few fireplaces his meager staff would require over the course of the winter. The roof needed repairs. He could ill afford to hire someone to do the job, but he was a strong man. Perhaps he would begin the repairs himself. He might even take up farming a little.

When Sir Alan's stripping of his inheritance included the selling off of most of the farms which had filled the family's coffers for centuries, he had been left with a few acres that might serve some use—sheep, perhaps, or oats.

He had a lot to learn, having once believed he would live out his years in strictly gentlemanly pursuits. Now, what was the name of that gentleman farmer? Oh, yes, Coke of Norfolk. Come summer, he might take a journey across the island to Norfolk and have a word or two with the man, who had concerned himself quite closely with the land and with improved systems of farming. Why the devil not! What was his life, anyway? Laurentia had called him a gamester, and that is what he had been for the past ten years, but no longer. Perhaps he would one day be known as Villiers of Somerset. . . .

Laurentia walked in a slow circle about the music room. Three days had passed since she learned that her beloved Thomas was none other than a man she despised—the infamous gamester, Lord Villiers. During those three days, she had kept mostly to herself, even refusing her grandmother's company. After all, her grandmother had been in league with Villiers. Well, if not *in league,* then certainly supportive of their marriage. Yes, Grandmother had most definitely taken a fancy to Villiers. More than once she had almost let the truth slip. Even quite recently, just before the wedding ball, she had hinted at Villiers's identity, and at the same time had advised her to examine a man in all his ways to see if he was worthy of her.

So, Grandmama had wanted her to examine Villiers in all his ways. Well, the dreadful man had lied to her! He had deceived her! How on earth could that ever make him a worthy husband?

Not that there was even a question anymore of remaining wed to such a man, not by half! She would be a fool and a simpleton to even contemplate the possibility of taking on the mantle of *My Lady Villiers,* no matter how fine a gentleman her grandmother believed him to be. No, it was absolutely imperative that she divorce him, and the sooner the better.

Except . . .

The very notion of being parted forever from Thomas—yes, from Villiers—made her absolutely heartsick. She ached to the depth of her soul and back again. She had come to rely on him as she had relied on no one before. His society, the wonderful ease and charm of his company, had taken a shape in her mind reminiscent of the Christmas star. He had become the light which guided her home to the quiet place in her soul which could always know rest and perfect peace in his presence. How could she live without him?

Yet . . . he had betrayed her, betrayed her confidence in him. He had proven that she was too naive to function properly in the world. She had misjudged James, then Matthew, and most certainly Thomas Michael Adolphus Swinfield!

Judge a man in all his ways. How was she supposed to do that? Villiers had gambled away his fortune. Sir Alan had told her so. Sir Alan had been his guardian, and would have known him as a young man, fifteen years ago. Thomas—*Villiers*—had told her that some conflict had separated him from Sir Alan, a conflict over a plantation.

She felt ill. The plantation again! When would she cease to be tormented by a plantation which Sir Alan denied and which only rumors had confirmed?

She glanced out the window. When had twilight faded to the blackest of nights? Dinner would be served shortly. How grateful she was for the homey routines of the house. The sun rose, breakfast was served. The sun took a high place in the sky and nuncheon quickly followed. The sun dipped in the west, and dinner settled heavily on the dining table. She had shed so many tears the day following the ball, especially once the laudanum had worn off, that her one comfort quickly became the steady drone of the staff which went about its usual chores, keeping Evenlode sparkling and comfortable.

Between bouts of tears she had been able to hear the servants at work, their laughter, the movement in the floors above, the steady march from one room to the next below. Meals were served at precise hours, and as she blew her nose over and over throughout the day, she had kept one eye to the clock. How very much the routines of Evenlode had soothed her lacerated sensibilities, so that by this morning—her third day of painful recollections—she had been much better equipped to begin·sorting out all that had happened.

Sir Alan Redcliffe had sent her a veritable mountain of succession-house roses, blood-red in color. The accompanying missive expressed his heartfelt hope she would recover quickly from so terrible a disappointment as she had so recently endured. She felt certain she should have been thankful for such an attention, yet she was not. Instead, a large, inexplicable uneasiness had grown within her. Some instinct warned her that something was amiss, something she could not give a name to. She even felt Sir Alan to be guilty of an unnamed misconduct, something larger than kissing her in the music room.

When she had learned of his intervention in James Dursley's suit, she had attributed the kindest of motives to his involvement—his desire to protect her. However, in reviewing just how and when he had told her of Villiers's identity, she began to see his conduct in general as supremely high-handed. For instance, he most certainly should have spoken to her about his suspicions regarding Mr. Dursley's character instead of offering him money to leave behind her back. And why had he chosen the eleventh hour to reveal Villiers's identity to her? Why had he not told her at the outset? She found she was angry instead of grateful.

Beyond the baronet's involvement in her romantic life, even beyond Lord Villiers's unhappy masquerade, she had become disturbed by another factor. Time and again as she continued moving slowly about the music room, her mind repeatedly took her back to her conversation with Mrs. Marycote about the West Indies plantation, something she would much rather forget about entirely. How aggravating that she had never been able to discover even a single reference to it in her uncle's papers. Not one!

In the last hour in particular, thoughts of the plantation had taken hold of her mind. She had become fixed on the rumors which had been surfacing about it, wondering if all the recent events of her life were somehow linked to what happened to the plantation. She couldn't explain why she believed this might be so, except that Mrs. Marycote had warned her not to proceed with her plans until she knew the extent of her uncle's activities. Until she had some knowledge therefore of the plantation, she decided she would set aside anymore thoughts of Villiers or Sir Alan. After all, she couldn't even continue with her philanthropic endeavors until she was settled in her mind about her uncle's affairs, in particular why she could not account for the source of his wealth.

Instantly, she made up her mind. She went in search of her grandmother and found her in the process of being carried down the stairs by her usual team of footmen. She waited for her at the bottom of the stairs.

Once the footmen had carried the chair away and disappeared down the hall, she said, "I must speak with you."

"What is it, Laurentia? Are you well? Perhaps you should return to your bed and rest. There is a light in your eye that disturbs me greatly."

"Grandmama, do you know anything of a West Indies Plantation? Did you never hear my uncle speak of such an entity or . . . or perhaps Sir Alan?"

She nodded. "Yes. Many years ago, when Sir Alan began construction on Windstone Manor, I inquired, most impertinently, how he had been able to afford to build such a large mansion. He told me that an investment, a plantation in the West Indies, had proved enormously profitable."

Laurentia stared at her. "Then he lied to me, for when I asked him about the plantation he said he knew nothing about it, and the worst of it is—Grandmama, I believe both Villiers and my uncle are somehow connected to this plantation. Yet, I can find no evidence of it in my uncle's papers, not one jot of ink so much as referring to it."

"In what way do you think Villiers is connected?"

"On our way to Bath, he told me that he and Sir Alan had suffered a rupture in their friendship—for at the time he had not told me he had been Sir Alan's ward—and that this rupture had occurred because of a plantation."

"Indeed!" Mrs. Cabot breathed, her eyes as wide as saucers. "Oh, my dear, if what I begin to suspect is true—and you think my son was connected, as well?"

"I believe he was," she said. "Only I have no proof of anything. Yet, why, if some terrible crime was committed, did my uncle bring Villiers to Gloucestershire to wed me?"

Mrs. Cabot's eyes filled with tears. "Perhaps in his last days he realized the terrible thing he had done and repented of it. Oh, but this is all too incredible to be believed."

"So you are beginning to think as I do, that Villiers was robbed?"

"Laurentia, we must find some means of proof. I know that Percival was careful in his records, and I know he would have been equally as careful in accounting for such an investment. The documents must be somewhere in the house. We should begin searching for them in my son's office, I think. Perhaps . . . oh, I know this will sound absurd, but perhaps there is a hiding place within."

"There must be!" Laurentia exclaimed. Her heart grew suddenly very light as she turned on her heel and began hurrying to the office located just beyond the library.

Once in the library, she seized a large branch of candles and carried it into the office, settling the weighty object on her uncle's desk. She turned to peruse every panel of the small chamber and began a slow, delicate examination of each board, pressing and tapping, pressing and tapping, trying to feel for anything out of the ordinary. She was soon joined by her grandmother, who began at the opposite wall and slowly performed the same careful explorations.

An hour passed as together they covered the walls of the office. Mrs. Cabot finally slid into a chair and sat down, exhausted. Laurentia felt tears of frustration bite her eyes. "There must be a panel somewhere. What about the floor? Do you think it possible?"

Mrs. Cabot shrugged. "I don't know. I suppose it might be worth a try."

Laurentia eyed the floor, covered by a thick Aubusson carpet. She was about to drag back one corner of it when a servant arrived informing them that dinner had been served.

Laurentia ordered her mind to a calmness she hardly felt. She slowly escorted her grandmother to the dining room and felt her arms tremble as she helped her into her chair. "The task was too much for you, Grandmama," she said.

"Yes, I admit it was. I only wish I could help you continue after dinner."

Laurentia watched one of the servants stirring up the coals with a heavy poker. He thrust it deeply into the bed and flames leapt in the fireplace. She blinked several times as the butler began serving the first remove. She smiled suddenly. "I know what I shall do," she said, not caring that any of the servants would hear. "I shall take an axe to the walls."

"What?" her grandmother cried, sputtering over her wine.

"I have to know. I am convinced the documents exist somewhere, and I mean to find them. I believe as you do that as fastidious as my uncle was in his record-keeping he would not have failed to make a strict accounting of the plantation. Good God, just thinking about how he squeezed every groat from the orphanage and detailed the whole of it, convinces me!"

She turned abruptly to the butler, who was settling a fine piece of roast chicken on her plate. "I wish you to instruct four of your strongest footmen to find axes, large ones, not the small ones used for kindling, and to meet me in the library in one hour."

"A—axes, Madame?" he inquired, astonished.

"Yes, axes. Four, large sturdy axes, and your strongest men!"

The butler paled, but compressed his lips tightly together and withheld even the smallest complaint of Laurentia's bizarre order.

With dinner concluded, Laurentia once more escorted her grandmother to the library. Mrs. Cabot was greatly restored by the fine meal, but wisely took up a seat on the opposite side of the room, away from the office, where she could rest while observing what next happened.

Laurentia gathered the men together and suggested they remove their livery coats since they would be engaged in some rather strenuous labor for the next hour. The men eyed one another warily but responded with quiet, "Yes, Ma'ams," as befitted their stations.

"Now," she began with her hands clasped before her. "This is what I wish you to do." She then outlined in simple detail that she wanted all the furniture in the library pushed to the far side of the room so that a large space could be created in which all the furniture from the office was to be placed. Once the furniture, the paintings, and the rug were removed from the office, every plank of wood was to be torn from the walls. "I am looking for a packet of papers which I believe my uncle kept in a secret place, and which is missing from the rest of his documents. Proceed with care, but leave no inch of wall in place."

The globe of the world was the first article to be removed from the office, followed by three chairs and the large desk. The paintings and rug were the last.

When the chopping began, Laurentia took up a seat by her grandmother. She found her own limbs were trembling. She still could hardly credit, even if they discovered the documents, that she would find any answers to the questions which plagued her, but so strong was her belief that when the first of the fine wood panels was hacked into terrible pieces, she felt nothing but a mounting sense of relief. She was convinced the papers were hidden in the office, somewhere.

An hour later, however, a servant emerged, perspiring from his labors. The walls had revealed nothing.

"Tear up the floor," she commanded without the smallest hesitation.

A half hour later, after every bit of flooring was removed, the same servant announced their failure to discover anything.

Laurentia moved to the office and stared at the gaping holes. The men had done their work well. Still, there appeared to be no secret hiding place.

She turned around and stared at the desk. "Take this apart, as well. Hack it to bits!"

She returned to her place beside her grandmother, who gripped her hand hard. As the axes fell, Laurentia murmured, "What if it is not there? Will I have to tear Evenlode down stone by stone?"

"Yes," her grandmother responded succinctly. "I believe you will."

When the desk was nothing but a pile of scrap wood, Laurentia moved to stand over it shaking her head in disbelief. "How could it not have been in here somewhere?"

She rubbed her temples, utterly frustrated.

"Do you wish we should commence cutting up the ceiling, Ma'am?"

Laurentia turned to the servant, then glanced into the darkened office. She shook her head. "I can't believe that he would have put the papers in the ceiling when it is fully twelve feet high. He would have had to use a ladder. Only where in the world did he secrete them?" Her uncle had business interests not just in England but all over the world. Perhaps the papers had been hidden in another location, an office in London, or Paris, or even Calcutta . . .

An odd chill spattered gooseflesh over her arms. She

whipped around and stared at the globe. She pointed a finger at it and commanded, "Break it apart—now!"

The nearest footman disengaged the round globe from its stand and settled it on the floor. With careful aim, he raised his axe and brought the flat side down hard. The globe disintegrated. The servant pushed the largest pieces aside and there, in the middle of the debris, was a tidy packet of papers.

Laurentia picked up the packet. Inscribed on the front paper were the words, Plantation Soledad, West Indies, 1803. 1803—the year Villiers's parents died.

Fourteen

While the servants began hauling away the debris from the office, Laurentia and her grandmother removed themselves with the mysterious documents to the drawing room. Laurentia seated herself on the sofa near the fireplace, while her grandmother took up a place beside her. She fingered the tattered black ribbon, noting the stains on the outer parchments and all the while shaking her head. She felt her entire life had been building to this moment.

"Courage, dearest," her grandmother remarked softly. She laid a white, wrinkled hand on her arm and gave it a gentle squeeze.

"I am afraid," Laurentia whispered. "I know something horrid lies hidden in these papers."

"We must know the truth. There have been rumors for years concerning the source of my sons wealth. Perhaps this plantation is the key to understanding how he came to acquire so much in so little time." She paused and added almost as an afterthought, "And Sir Alan's, as well."

Laurentia turned to meet her gaze. "They were business associates," she added. "Mr. Crabtree told me that nearly every investment was a joint endeavor between the men." She saw her own fears reflected in her grandmother's soft blue eyes. Taking a deep breath, she returned her attention to the packet and gave a brisk tug on the old ribbon.

So tightly had the packet been bound, however, that instead of unfolding before her, the papers remained tightly crimped. She carefully began pressing them apart, and at first could only ascertain that the document was of a legal nature concerning the plantation, that a company owned the West Indies operation, a company which included upon its board both her uncle and . . . Sir Alan Redcliffe.

That meant nothing. Sir Alan had confirmed his connection to her uncle many days earlier. "I believe this will take a great deal of scrutinization to properly ascertain all that is contained within. I begin to think I should travel to Tewkesbury tomorrow. Do you wish to attend me?"

"It is far too cold for my old bones to be going anywhere. No, I fear you must go alone."

Laurentia nodded, rising to her feet and pulling apart the document a little more. She glanced down the length of it, as well as the subsequent five pages. At the very end of the document she found three signatures—she drew in a sharp breath—Redcliffe's, Cabot's, and . . . Villiers's! But that was impossible! In 1803, Villiers would have been but sixteen. Even had he signed the document, surely his signature would not have been legal.

At the very bottom was a brief note, addressed to her, the ink still bright from its recent addition.

> *Laurentia,*
> *By now I hope you are Lady Villiers, for then I shall rest easily in my grave. I behaved badly, but your marriage will restore what I took and a great deal more.*
> *Cabot*

She dropped down beside her grandmother once more. "Do but look! You must read this! Then it is true!"

Mrs. Cabot quickly read the note penned by her son and

covered her mouth with her hand. "I knew it. I knew something of good was in him. Oh, Laurentia!"

Laurentia read the words over and over. Though the message was cryptic, she understood enough to comprehend that her uncle had robbed Villiers. But how? She didn't have enough information to draw a proper conclusion.

That settled the matter for her. She would have to travel to Tewksbury, the sooner the better. Had darkness not fallen, along with a light snow, she would have ordered the horses put to at once. As it was, she had to content herself with informing the Head Groom that she would be needing the barouche tomorrow morning, at six o'clock, sharp!

Laurentia was exceedingly grateful that Mr. Crabtree had obligingly set aside the remainder of his appointments that afternoon to attend to her concerns. He read through the document, aloud, and explained point by point the nature of the language employed, the location of the plantation—which upon examination seemed to be somewhere in the middle of the Atlantic Ocean, as far from the West Indies as England was from Italy—and finally that the partners who had formed the company included the three men whose signatures were witnessed at the bottom of the document by a financier named Alexander Quince—the very one she had seen arriving at the Tump and Dagler on the morning after she had met Mr. Swinfield—Villiers—for the first time.

"But what does it all mean?" she asked. "I want to understand everything perfectly. I want to know exactly what happened."

"Redcliffe was Villiers's guardian when his parents died. Somehow, Redcliffe used the plantation to drain the Villiers's fortune into this company,"—here he tapped the document—"known as the Soledad West Indies Plantation, a company which, by the way, ostensibly became insolvent in the year eighteen oh eight."

"The year Villiers attained his majority." Understanding dawned on her, and of such a magnitude that she felt quite ill and quickly searched in her reticule for her vinaigrette. "I am generally not such a frail creature," she said, her senses swimming as she held the small silver box to her nose, "but I fear I have never been more shocked save when I learned that my husband was Villiers, himself."

"Yes, I imagine you must have been astounded when you learned his true identity, but I hope not entirely disapproving."

She took a whiff, her eyes watering a little from the strong aroma, then shot a searching glance at Mr. Crabtree. "You knew, then?" she asked, astonished once more.

"Yes, from the first. I recognized his signature from correspondence he had conducted with your uncle concerning your nuptials. If you will recall, that first day when you arrived together, you had both quit my office but he returned ostensibly in search of his gloves. He did me the very great honor of confiding in me."

"Were you not shocked, then, by his masquerade?" she asked, astonished.

"Only a very little, but, forgive my saying so, not nearly so much as by *your* decision to wed a complete stranger."

"It was all madness," she admitted. "yet, why did you say nothing to me? Why must everyone suppose I should be protected at every turn?"

"An instinct, I suppose, though I do beg you to believe that had I thought for even a moment he would harm you I should have summoned the constable and had him arrested. It is unlawful for a nobleman not to declare his title, especially in legal matters. I believe your marriage could be annulled on this point alone."

"He said you would know how to dissolve the marriage," she stated.

He nodded. "But before you undertake anything of the sort I wish you to know that when he returned to me the following

Wednesday week, he signed an entirely different set of documents which he intended you to have on the day he quit Windrush. From the first it is my belief he had no intention of accepting your original payment of seventy-five thousand pounds. I was to give this to you when I saw you next. The present hour seems suitable."

He was holding out to her a sealed document which she took with trembling fingers. She broke the seal and began to read. It would seem Thomas—Villiers—had long since returned the money to her, or to a charity of her choice. The document was dated the twenty-fifth of November. "You say he had you make up this document nearly three weeks ago, then made a journey to Tewkesbury in order to sign it?"

"Yes. As I said, he gave me the instructions the very day you began your journey to Scotland to be married. When you returned to Evenlode after your trip to Gretna Green, he came to Tewkesbury, that very Wednesday, and signed them.

"I see," she murmured, her heart warming suddenly. "And tell me, what is your impression of Villiers—generally, I mean. Does he strike you as the sort of man who would waste his fortune in the East End Hells, as Sir Alan assured me he had?"

"No, not by half, though I do believe he has subsisted these ten years and more as a gamester of sorts. Rumors among men of commerce tell me that he has saved his earnings and has invested two thousand pounds in the funds. Such a figure may not seem like a great deal, but given the nature of his employment and the fact that more than one of his friends has assured me he is completely honest in his play, I am impressed by his determination to right his fortunes as well as to make the best of what I am steadily coming to believe was a terrible wrong done to him by a very powerful man."

"My uncle," she breathed at last.

Mr. Crabtree shook his head, but said nothing.

She tilted her head and eyed him closely for a long moment. "It has been Redcliffe all along, then, has it not?" Her mind began bending and whirring and moving in swift darts and turns. She had for so long a time viewed Sir Alan as a dear friend and confidante that she had never allowed herself to consider a dozen circumstances of his conduct in the unhappy light which the documents before her suggested. She had even gone so far as to forgive his role in separating her from James, yet now his motives seemed wholly suspect. Indeed, how could she see his involvement in any other light? He wanted her for himself. He had told her as much. She even began to wonder as well in what way he had encouraged Matthew to assure her he meant to take excellent care of her fortune!

"I am too naive," she murmured, "Too willing to believe everything I am told. Are you of the same opinion, then—that Sir Alan is to blame? Am I comprehending all the facts before me in the proper light?"

"You are," he returned solemnly. "Though there is something else I feel I ought to tell you. Villiers knows of the plantation."

She glanced at the documents before her detailing the creating of Plantation Soledad. "Has he seen something like this, then? Another set of documents, perhaps?"

"No, but just before your journey to Bath, you asked me about the plantation. I decided to begin a very quiet investigation which resulted in the discovery of a former servant of Sir Alan's who saw what I believe to be a companion set of documents pertaining to the plantation."

She nodded. "I once asked Sir Alan if he knew anything about such a plantation, and he told me he did not. He lied to me."

"So it would seem," he agreed. "Presently, I believe you have sufficient proof to bring charges against Sir Alan if you wish for it."

"If I wish for it?" she exclaimed. "Of course I do. This, this villainy perpetrated against his ward, a young man who trusted him implicitly! He must be made to rectify this terrible wrong, to suffer for it!"

"I hope you will consider the matter carefully, for if I am not mistaken I believe your husband quit Evenlode House for the strict purpose of avoiding prosecution. He did not confide his purposes in me, only said that he meant to protect his wife."

His wife. How her heart began warming to the sound of that particular appellation. *Villiers's wife.*

"What do you think he meant by wishing to protect me? I don't understand precisely. Protect me from what?"

"It seemed to me that he wanted to spare you the sort of scandal that the prosecution of his guardian would bring down on your head, given that your uncle was in collusion with Sir Alan."

Her heart grew warmer still as she began to consider how nobly Villiers had behaved toward her, even from the first, even when he was masquerading as mere Mr. Swinfield. She wasn't mistaken in having given her heart so fully to him. She had loved well, and properly. She had chosen a man worthy of her fortune, after all. This was what her grandmother had been warning her to do, to test a man in all his ways.

She thought of Sir Alan and his ways—he had lied to her about the plantation, he had kissed her when she had fainted, he had stolen a young man's fortune while that young man was under his protection. For all his superficial gentlemanly qualities, for all his protestations of understanding, he was a liar, a cheat, and a hypocrite. Villiers might have pretended to be mere Mr. Swinfield, but Sir Alan's was the true masquerade. All these years he had carried out the charade of a gentleman and friend. She found she despised him more than words could express.

He had done a terrible wrong to his ward, but in the end her uncle's conscience had brought that wrong to light. Her uncle had summoned Villiers to Evenlode as a husband, and therefore master of at least part of the fortune which had been stolen from him.

She smiled suddenly, for there seemed to be a fitting unity to the quagmire of Sir Alan's villainy and her uncle's greed, for she had fallen in love with the very man to whom the inheritance truly belonged. "How odd," she murmured, her hands clasped tightly on her lap as she reviewed the past few weeks. "The money belongs to my husband, not to me! And to think I was holding to it so tightly."

"Not all of your uncle's fortune belongs to your husband, of course, but I would venture to say that the bulk of it does. Although, one could argue that his own careful management of the assets, as well as his wise investments, could accrue to you in the form of a management fee plus interest, if that is the route you would choose."

"Of course it is. In this matter, there is only one honorable path, and now I understand fully why Mrs. Marycote warned me not to proceed hastily with my numerous schemes for apportioning my fortune. Perhaps even then she knew it did not belong to me. Oh, I must think, I must think!" She leaned forward and pressed her gloved fingers to her forehead, squeezing her eyes shut. She was grateful that Mr. Crabtree remained silent while she gave herself to reviewing the horrendous nature of all she had just learned.

After a time, she straightened in her seat and begged him to recommend an inn for the night, since she intended to spend the evening carefully considering just how she ought to proceed.

"The Bear has excellent accommodations. You will be quite comfortable there, I'm sure."

She rose and thanked him for his attentiveness. She begged to meet him again on the morrow, at which time she hoped to have a sensible plan framed in her mind for the future disposition of her fortune, as well as just what action she should take against Sir Alan Redcliffe.

He bowed quite formally to her, his smile warm as he assured her that his services, as well as those of the legal community in Tewkesbury, were at her service.

Once ensconced in her bedchamber at the inn, she read the document through once more by the afternoon light from the window. She pondered Villiers's conduct, as well as her uncle's and Sir Alan's. She estimated the true worth of her husband's fortune at this juncture, and could not restrain whistling low. Regardless that both men had behaved vilely in stripping Villiers's of his fortune, as well as ten years of the comforts such an inheritance would have brought to him, each man had done exceedingly well in investing the fortune. Villiers, once his inheritance was returned to him, would be quite one of the wealthiest men in England.

Ah, but that was the rub. She knew him well. He would not want such a fortune were it to mean her own ruination, either financially or through the scandal attached to such a measure.

She therefore made the prompt decision not to involve him in the matter until she had set her course in motion. He wouldn't allow it otherwise, which she supposed was why he had left as he did. He must have thought she would never learn the truth, and therefore she could continue in her belief that she was a great heiress and mistress of enough blunt to redress all the historic wrongs in Windrush, that she had accidentally married a vile man she was fortunate to be rid of! Foolish man that he was!

She honored him for his sentiments toward her, but she was rather dashed that he thought so little of her intelligence to believe that she would never guess at, or by any other means come to a full knowledge of, her uncle's perfidy. She chuckled at the thought, and once more folded up the document and retied it with a new black silk ribbon.

The only question which truly remained was how precisely to deal with Sir Alan Redcliffe.

By the next morning, Laurentia knew what she had to do, and

returned to Mr. Crabtree's office at the appointed time. She requested that he pen a letter, not to Windrush and Sir Alan, but to Lord Villiers of Fairwood Hall, Somersetshire, bidding him return to Tewkesbury on a matter of some urgency.

Two days later, Lord Villiers opened a letter from Mr. Crabtree in the presence of Coxwell, who was watching him carefully. He was suspicious at once, since Mr. Crabtree was quite vague about the *matter of some urgency* which required his presence immediately in Tewkesbury. The non-specific letter said nothing at all of Laurentia, yet had she been a more conniving female he would have said that the request had the smatterings of female witchery written all over it.

As it was, he could not imagine Laurentia behaving in such a fashion, and could only drop into his comfortable leather chair and peruse the brief missive a dozen times in hopes of determining Mr. Crabtree's purpose.

All the while, Coxwell moved restlessly about the chamber, straightening a book here and one there, sweeping the hearth no less than three times, and once attempting to pour sherry into an already brimming glass. He stopped himself just in time and muttered an oath as he returned to the table by the door.

"Oh, very well," Villiers cried. "If you must know it is a request from Laurentia's solicitor in Tewkesbury that I attend him in two days' time on a *matter of some,* though unspecified, *urgency.* I am loathe to go. I have no wish to leave Somerset. I just now settled in my rooms, and there is a great deal of wood to be chopped before another heavy snow sets in to make the task formidable in the extreme."

Coxwell's shoulders slumped a trifle. Villiers noted the unusual posture, and could only conclude his valet had been hopeful of returning—to Windrush? "Did you leave something at Evenlode?" he queried. "Something of *inestimable value?*

I could not help but notice of late that you have seemed a trifle out of sorts, but your manner just now seems . . . *rather blue-deviled."*

"Indeed?" Coxwell returned stiffly. He removed a kerchief from the pocket of his finely tailored coat and began buffing the glass decanter in quick jerks.

"Yes," Villiers responded. "Quite blue-deviled, in fact. Come. Out with it, man. You've tumbled in love with Mrs. Bourton."

Although Coxwell was turned away from him, Villiers could see that the tips of his ears had turned pink. The viscount drew in a deep breath. So that was the lay of the land. "I see. You know, you may leave any time you wish. You are not obligated to me—certainly not now, when my prospects are dismal in the extreme."

Coxwell turned around slowly, his color much heightened. He took a deep breath and plunged in. "I was hoping to enjoy a holiday just past Christmas, if you would oblige me, m'lord. I confess that when I departed Evenlode, I had thought to be at ease in Somerset, but such has not been the case. I have formed an attachment, and I am wishful of making my affections known to the lady, before, er, her interest becomes engaged elsewhere. However, if it is at all likely that we might be returning to Gloucestershire, I would be grateful if you would permit me to be absent for, let us say, two days, when we reach Tewkesbury?"

"Of course, if we *were* going, I should be happy to oblige you. Unfortunately, we are not. I see no reason why I should go. I intend to send a polite letter in response that I am unable at present to leave Fairwood."

He held the missive up, and his mind began plaguing him. He wondered suddenly if something had happened to Laurentia. Perhaps his worst fears had been realized, and Sir Alan had been able to force himself upon her, after all. Good God! He couldn't bear the thoughts which began bombarding him one after the other as he recalled seeing Sir Alan holding Laurentia in his arms the night of the masquerade ball.

"Oh, the devil take it!" he cried, crumpling up the letter in frustrated fingers. "I suppose I must go! *We* must go. And you may pay your visit while I see what urgent business has forced Mr. Crabtree to send for me in this wholly suspicious manner! Yes, yes! We shall leave at first light, just as you wish!"

When Villiers arrived in Tewkesbury, two days later, he entered Mr. Crabtree's office in an ill humor. "You had best tell my why the devil you sent for me in this wretched manner, without a word as to what has gone amiss! Only tell me, is Lauren—is Mrs. Swinf—is my wife well? Has harm come to her? Speak, man, or I shan't account for my conduct! Well, why do you stand there gaping at me like some farmhand watching a procession of gypsies pass by? You sent for me. Now tell me why, this instant, or be hanged!"

"M'lord. No! Everything is well with Lady Villiers. However, she wanted very much for me to give this to you, and to tell you that you must be at the crossroads near Sir Alan Redcliffe's home by five o'clock this evening or all will be lost."

Villiers took the papers Crabtree had thrust at him. As he glanced down at the document the words, *Soledad West Indies Plantation,* jumped out at him. "My God! She found the documents!" He snapped his gaze to Crabtree. "She hasn't done anything foolish, has she? Does she mean to confront Sir Alan? Tell me, man, or I shall take your spectacles and shove them down your throat! He is a hard man! Has no one taken his measure properly?"

"She will await you, she said, at the juncture of the main highway and the lane which leads to Windstone Manor. But I would suggest you go now. She fully intends to force a confession from him."

Villiers did not wait, but quit the room in a trice and ordered the postilion to Windrush. "And spring 'em, my good man. There will be five sovereigns in it if we are at the Tump and Dagler before half past four!"

"Wery good, me lord!" the eager young man cried. As soon as Villiers had seated himself, the coach gave a hard jerk, and was soon moving swiftly through the heavily trafficked streets on the road to Windrush. Glancing out the window, however, he could see that the clouds had grown heavy. Damn and blast! If he was correct, the horses would be dragging their way through deep snows within the next hour.

Fifteen

The snow had begun to fall heavily two hours earlier, and Laurentia now knew she could not keep the horses standing much longer. She felt she had been foolish to have insisted on waiting for Villiers in the first place, much less in the cold, unpredictable weather. The late fall day was proving as brisk and uncomfortable as an early February afternoon, and she shivered with cold as one of the horses lifted his head and blew a nostril full of warm, steamy air over the head of his harness-mate.

Yet she was certain she had arranged the matter in the best manner possible in order to force Villiers's hand. Had she requested his presence at Evenlode, he would never have come. She knew him well enough not to have even asked. When the snowflakes began to gather in heaps on the horses' backs, she leaned her head out the window and commanded the postboy to take her directly to Windstone Manor. Sir Alan would not know why she had come, and would probably welcome her visit.

She would then wait for Villiers to arrive.

But would he come? She had left far too much to chance, after all. What if he had already sent word to Mr. Crabtree refusing his request to come to Tewkesbury? What if he read the document and, even after learning that she meant to confront Sir Alan, had returned to Somerset?

Once more she regretted infinitely that she did not have more experience of the world.

When ushered into the expansive library where Sir Alan sat quite at his ease enjoying a glass of sherry, she saw his every glance and movement in an entirely different light. He was still quite handsome, even though he was past fifty and his hair was completely white. He cut a dashing figure in his coat of dark-blue superfine, striped waistcoat, and buff breeches. His black shoes were polished to a shine, and his smile was all that was generous, warm, and affable.

She had trusted him so completely!

"Ah, Laurentia! You cannot imagine how happy I am to see you on this bleakest of winter days." A strong feeling of misuse rose within her so heatedly that it was all she could do to bear his attentions to her now. He rose from his chair, crossed the room to her, and possessed himself of her hands, kissing them both lightly, then examining her complexion. "But you are quite pale, my dear. I trust you are well. It snows so fiercely that I wonder you had even put your horses to, much less made the journey across the vale to pay this most unexpected visit. Not that I am not pleased. Believe me, I am!"

Laurentia understood completely how Villiers, as a lad of sixteen, had been duped by his guardian. Sir Alan's words, the tone of his voice, were everything they ought to be. Indeed, had Villiers never entered her life she strongly suspected that one day she would have given herself in marriage to Sir Alan, so exceptional were his persuasive abilities.

"My setting forth this afternoon has proven quite ridiculous," she remarked carefully. "You have spoken truthfully, as you always do, and I admit I am the most foolish of females. However, Grandmama was not feeling well, and the house, as you may imagine, is become quite empty again since Villiers so wisely chose to leave Windrush. I felt I should soon go mad if I did not leave Evenlode, even for a time. To my credit,

I will say that when I left it was not snowing quite so forcefully as it is now."

Since during both his speech and hers he had not released her hands, she gently withdrew them now, which afforded him the opportunity, to take her arm instead, and wrap it about his own. "Come to the window with me. I wish to see the snow fall, for I had been engrossed in my book for so long a time that I hadn't paid the least heed to the weather until my butler informed me of your sudden arrival." She walked beside him the length of the room. The chamber was decorated *en suite* in shades of gold, and the smell of new leather permeated the air. Most of the volumes present were obviously recent purchases, and must have cost him a fortune—more of Villiers's fortune spent by the odious man at her side.

He began, "I can't tell you what a delight this is for me, my dear. I have been hoping that once Villiers quit Evenlode, you and I might become better acquainted. Although, I do believe I must offer you an apology for my conduct at the masquerade ball. I should never have kissed you as I did."

He caught her eye in a teasing fashion, and she could see he never doubted for a moment she would do naught else but forgive him. Many times, especially in the light of her knowledge of the baronet's true character, she had shuddered in repulsion at the memories he had just culled forth. She could not do so now, however, and strove to keep her sentiments at bay. It would not do at all for Sir Alan to learn how completely her opinion of him had altered in recent days.

She swallowed the biting retort which rose to her lips and lowered her gaze. Attempting as light a tone as she could manage, she said, "Of course I have forgiven you. Compared to Villiers's horrid masquerade, your slight indiscretion seems but a feather of a misdeed."

"You are too generous, for I behaved quite badly, and I now confess it to you. Only, pray believe that I would not have done so had I not been so completely enamored of you in that moment. I am still dumbfounded by the odd shift in my own sentiments. For so long I had viewed you merely as the charming niece of a dear friend. Now, however, you have but to enter a room and I am become a simpleton. Oh, but you are trembling! Are you chilled, or does the subject distress you?"

"Both, I fear," she responded on a whisper. Her anger was threatening to undo her completely. She had never known such a blackguard as Sir Alan Redcliffe, and his honeyed speeches were causing her soul to cry out within her. She hastily reached for a kerchief and covered her face. She then left him standing by the window as she sought refuge in a chair beside the fireplace.

She heard him follow after, expressing his concern for her. Then he added in a tender voice, "I will not speak of my feelings, if you do not wish for it."

She could only nod as she pretended to be overset on points of delicacy.

"Let me build up the fire," he added.

"Oh, yes, please do!" she whispered. "The drive to your house was frightfully cold, and twice we nearly slid into a ditch!"

"My poor child!"

He immediately turned to the fireplace and began rearranging the logs in preparation for adding another to the tidy blaze. She watched him, with wonder that he could be such a well-cloaked monster. That Villiers had been able to keep his true identity from her she could understand, for she had not known him before. But how had it been possible that Sir Alan, with whom she had been acquainted for years, had been able to disguise the evil hidden in his heart for so long a time? Indeed, if she didn't know the truth, she would still believe him all that was good, kind, and honorable.

He straightened up and turned slightly toward the doorway. "Someone has arrived," he stated with a faint laugh. "How odd to be receiving visitors on such a day as this."

Laurentia was suddenly filled with exhilaration. Surely Villiers had arrived! He had responded to her request that he come, and any moment he would be crossing the threshold of Sir Alan's library!

She felt quite safe, even powerful now, as she rose from her seat and faced the baronet. As he turned to smile upon her, she straightened her shoulders and began, "You have believed me to be overcome with modesty these past several minutes because you chose such a time to speak of your supposed feelings for me. Allow me to say, however, that in the past few days I have come to know you for who you are, a veritable serpent. You are no friend of mine, and if my guess is correct the next person to cross that threshold will be a man you have wronged since he was a lad of sixteen!" Strong, booted footsteps were heard in the hallway beyond, and she dramatically extended her hand to the doorway.

Sir Alan's complexion moved from a pink hue to a chalky white in a matter of seconds.

Laurentia had never experienced so strong a sense of triumph in her entire existence. Ever since she had learned of Sir Alan's horrendous abuse of his ward's finances, she had been aching to see his entire existence destroyed in the same manner he had obliterated Villiers's future. Her cheeks were warm with confidence as she glared at Sir Alan, for hidden in her reticule was a copy of the damning papers she had found in her uncle's study.

The baronet, much to her great pleasure, turned to watch the door with apprehension pinching his aging features.

The butler entered the chamber solemnly.

Laurentia knew the moment of vindication had arrived. Her heart swelled and beat out an infinitely strong cadence.

"Mr. Quince to see you, sir."

"Mr. Quince?"

The butler seemed a trifle confused as he glanced back at

the person waiting in the hallway. "Y-yes, Sir Alan. Mr. Alexander Quince, lately of Tewkesbury. Indeed."

Sir Alan let out a hearty laugh and waved a hand at his servant as he turned back to Laurentia. "By all means, Felton. I have been hoping to see Mr. Quince. Do show him in."

Laurentia felt foolish, dumbfounded, and frightened all at the very same moment. She was in no manner used to arranging confrontations, not to mention one so significant as this, so it was to her considerable dismay that Mr. Quince, the very man she had seen so many weeks ago at the Tump and Dagler Inn, entered Sir Alan's library.

"Well met, Quince!" Sir Alan called to his friend. "Only, tell me, old chap, is it true that I have wronged you since you were a lad of sixteen?" Though he had posed this question to his financier, his gaze was directed quite malevolently upon Laurentia.

Her knees having grown quite useless, she sank back into her chair, drawing her reticule, which she held with whitening fingers, into a tight ball on her lap. What had she done? Of course Villiers did not mean to come, and she had given him so little time to respond! Besides, a snow storm had set upon the village of Windrush with nothing short of a vengeance. Even if he had wanted to rush to her aid, perhaps the roads had become impassable!

She was trapped at Windstone with a man in possession of as low a character as any she had ever known or heard of. Her heart was again beating hard in her breast, yet no longer from exhilaration. She had erred, she knew she had erred, and was in a trap of her own foolish making. She averted her gaze from Sir Alan and turned instead to place her attention fully on Mr. Quince. He seemed considerably perplexed, and for the first time she wondered what had brought him through a terrible storm to Sir Alan's home.

"I don't know what you mean," he said in answer to what

must have seemed to him a riddle of sorts. "I don't believe we were acquainted when I was a lad."

"No, to be sure we were not," Sir Alan stated, his spirits reviving in quick stages. "But what the devil brings you to Windrush in all this snow? You must have been mad to have left your lodgings in so comfortable a town as Tewkesbury."

Mr. Quince glanced at Laurentia. She smiled faintly upon him, but the perplexed frown on his brow deepened. "A matter of some import. I would have a word with you, if your charming guest would be able to spare you for a few minutes?" He bowed politely to Laurentia.

She inclined her head, and a sense of deep foreboding began to settle within her. She thought it likely Quince had heard rumors in Tewkesbury about the Soledad Plantation, and had come to warn Redcliffe.

"Have you not met my dear young friend? No? Allow me, then, to present Mrs. Swinfield to you, previously Miss Cabot of Evenlode."

Mr. Quince seemed startled, but again bowed. "I am honored, Mrs. Swinfield."

Laurentia could not speak. She was trembling nearly from head to foot. She did, however, manage to incline her head once more.

Sir Alan turned to her. "I'm afraid I must leave you for a few minutes, my dear. I won't be long. Then we can discuss in some detail these extraordinarily ridiculous notions you've taken into your head. I'm sure we'll be able to sort everything out to our mutual satisfaction."

With that, he ushered Mr. Quince from the chamber.

Laurentia did not hesitate. Once the door snapped shut she jumped to her feet, determined to save herself from the horrid situation in which she had placed herself. She carefully opened the door and listened for the footsteps of the men. When she heard another door close with a hard snap, she entered the long hallway and immediately ran toward the servants' stairs.

She had many allies among the serving classes of Windrush, and she was certain someone among the staff of Windstone Manor would know her and, hopefully, would lend her the assistance she required.

She hurried to the first floor and had slipped inside the music antechamber when she heard the butler's voice, and footmen at the end of another hall. Her heart was pounding in her chest. If she could leave the house and get a horse, a single horse, she might be safe.

From upstairs she heard a sudden shout. Then, quite near her in the hallway beyond, a young female voice whispered, "Wat is the master shouting about now!"

Relief suddenly broke over her. She leaped into the hall and grabbed the young serving woman by the arm, pulling her into the antechamber. "Penny!" she cried in a hushed voice. "You must help me! You must save me!"

"Miss Cabot—I mean, Mrs. Swinfield! Whatever are ye doing in the music room?"

"Hush, please! Lower your voice, or I am lost!" Heavy footsteps could be heard on the stairs. "Oh, I hear him coming. Do not reveal my presence here—please!"

Penny blinked several times quite rapidly, then dipped a nervous curtsy. Laurentia hid herself behind the table near the door.

"You there!" Sir Alan barked. "Have you seen Mrs. Swinfield? Well, tell me, have you? Speak, you stupid creature! Why do you stare at me as though you've seen a ghost! Then you have seen her! Tell me now where she is, or I'll have you turned off immediately! Tell me!"

Laurentia felt tears sting her eyes. Surely Penny would not be able to withstand such badgering.

"I don't know wat ye mean, sir. I 'eard Mrs. Swinfield was come to Windstone, but isn't she in the drawing room, as a proper young lady ought to be? If not, why would such a lady be charging about yer 'ome? 'as she aught to be frightened of?"

"What insolence is this!" he cried. "By God, if I weren't— get out, at once! Do not even speak to the housekeeper. I am discharging you myself."

"As ye wish, Sir Alan."

Laurentia was smiling, even though tears now touched her cheeks. Penny obviously knew what Sir Alan was, and if his display of anger and violent words were any indication of the usual treatment of servants in his home, she thought it likely she would find more than one friend within the walls of the house. She heard Penny's footsteps shamble off in the opposite direction, ostensibly heading toward the housekeeping quarters.

Sir Alan called to the butler and issued orders to search the house, to find Mrs. Swinfield, who he said was suffering some sudden derangement of the mind, and to bring her back to the library at once. She waited for a long moment, for she could hear the butler conferring with several of his footmen in the entrance hall.

Suddenly, Penny was before her. "Come, now, Ma'am, and be quick afore Felton or the others see ye."

Laurentia did not hesitate, but let Penny lead her on a run down another set of servants' stairs which brought her summarily to the kitchens. Once there, she saw several astonished servants, many of whom she knew by name, for she had grown up with them.

She did not hesitate. "I am in the gravest danger. I need to leave immediately. Can any of you be of assistance to me?"

Everyone seemed frozen for a long moment. Then they slowly began staring at one another, as though afraid to utter a word. All eyes finally shifted to a tall, matronly figure in the corner.

Oh, dear God in heaven, the housekeeper! Where would her loyalties lie?

She did not know the woman, and by all reports believed her to be rather severe, even punishing at times.

The lady pinched her lips together and clasped her hands tightly and properly in front of her. "Mrs. Swinfield," she stated in her firm voice though her lower lip trembled, "I have endured much at the hands of this master, but never did he try to keep a lady against her will. You there!" She shifted suddenly to bark at a lad who had just come in from the storm. "You will saddle a horse and have it waiting for Mrs. Swinfield, and another for yourself. Can you see Mrs. Swinfield to the Tump and Dagler?"

"That I can," the lad answered, his eyes wide. "Even through the snow. I dun it a 'undred times, I 'ave! I could do it blindfolded!"

Penny squeezed Laurentia's arm. " 'e can, ma'am."

"Come to the buttery," the housekeeper stated brusquely. "The rest of you, attend to business as though you know nothing of what is going forward."

The pounding of feet was heard coming down the stairs, but the housekeeper whisked Laurentia into the musty room where the wines were stored, possessed herself of two bottles, told Laurentia to remain still and quiet, then left quickly.

"What is this meaning of this!" she snapped as she entered the hall. "Mr. Felton! I am astounded that your men are disturbing the kitchen staff. What do you mean, what am I doing with these bottles? The Clarks are very ill, and I have taken it upon myself to see their sad circumstances relieved. You may be sure that I shall have the price of these wines deducted from my wages, but at present you must explain why you are setting the house on its ears. I absolutely forbid . . ."

The lady's voice faded, and Laurentia was left to wait in the cold of the buttery. She listened hard to the movements above her and around her. Occasionally she heard the housekeeper complaining loudly about the ridiculous nature of hunting for a Lady of Quality in the kitchen. Suddenly the door burst open, and a footman appeared.

Laurentia extended a hand to him. "Oh, please . . . no!" she whispered. "Please, tell them the chamber is empty. Please. beg of you!"

She did not know the young man.

"Be ye Miss Cabot of Evenlode?" he inquired.

She nodded.

The young man's mouth worked strongly. "I were raised in the orphanage. I heard wat ye done for the children there. Bless ye!"

He backed out and reported loudly. "No one 'ere!"

"Then she must still be hiding in one of the antechambers. Step lively, lads. Sir Alan is waiting!"

The thunder of their footsteps pounded outside the door and beyond. After a moment, she heard them mount the stairs.

Laurentia took a deep breath and covered her face with her hands. Tears broke from her eyes. For the moment she was safe.

Ten minutes later, the housekeeper returned with a set of warm, winter coverings for her—a woolen pelisse, a wool cap which surrounded her face completely, leaving a small hole from which to see where her horse was going, a heavy cape, thick mittens, and a dark scarf. She was soon dressed and being led out-of-doors. The snow swirled about her. A few steps more and she found a horse waiting for her, along with the young man who would lead her to Windrush.

She did not hesitate, but mounted the poor beast, and giving a solid kick, began at a trot down the drive.

Laurentia did not slow down until they had covered a considerable distance. Only then did she have the courage to turn her head to see if there were any signs of pursuit. As it was, she observed only a steadily falling snow and the shadows of white-covered trees flanking the lane. Windstone Manor was entirely hidden in a wall of white.

"But are you really certain you can find your way to the Tump and Dagler?" she asked nervously, turning back to the young man who was guiding her.

"I'll 'ave ye there in a trice, ma'am."

"Thank you," she murmured.

She felt foolish, but above all fortunate that so many kind persons had helped her leave Sir Alan's home. Given the nature of the orders he had issued to his servants, as well as his harsh words to Penny, his true nature was once more affirmed. She had only one wish now—to be as far away from him as possible.

A half hour later, she dismounted stiffly from her long-suffering mount, thanked the servant, and entered the backdoor of the inn much as she had so many weeks earlier on the evening she had first met Lord Villiers. Even the hour was not much different, for night was nearly upon the hamlet, and the rush of warm air which greeted her as she opened the door was as welcome as it had been then.

The landlord smiled warmly upon her. "Thank God that yer well! We've been that worried, we 'ave. All of us, once we learnt ye meant to travel in this weather, 'ave been nigh on sick with worry. But never fear. He's 'ad a fire ready fer ye, and a bowl of wassail, too, this past hour."

"Who?" she cried hopefully.

"Why, yer 'usband, 'o course. Lord Villiers." He smiled broadly and sighed with something very close to a deep satisfaction.

"Then you know," she murmured.

"O' course we know. Yer grandmama is that proud, she is, as we all are. She told us it were only 'is way, that 'e wished to make himself properly known to us all afore venturing to take on the mantle of his station. I always liked 'im, not more so than now."

She shrugged off her cape and with trembling fingers unbuttoned her pelisse. The landlord took both in his hands and waited to receive her hat and muffler. "I must look a sight," she cried, dropping her voice to a frantic whisper. "I shan't enter the parlor without at least having run a comb through my hair. Is Betsy here? She will be able to help me."

"Aye, that she is."

Laurentia forced herself to become calmer as Betsy took her upstairs and arranged her sadly flattened hair. The maid could do little more, however, than brush out the tangles and tie a ribbon about her long mass of red curls. She was, if nothing else, presentable.

With a final tugging on a curl or two and a smoothing out of her wrinkled, dark blue, velvet skirts, she descended the stairs. She did not scratch on the door, but gently pushed it open and entered the chamber slowly. He was seated in the very same place as on the night she had first met him.

So many treasured sentiments coursed through her that it was all she could do to keep from running to him and throwing herself into his arms. Her heart beat erratically. "Hallo, Villiers," she said, her voice barely more than a smokey whisper.

He jerked around, caught sight of her, and immediately was on his feet. Before he had taken more than three strides, or so it seemed to her, she was fully taken up in his arms as he pelted kisses over her face in the most delightful manner. When he found her mouth, she wrapped her arms tightly about his neck and held him close. The kiss, or assault, or whatever his attentions might be termed, seemed to last forever. The day's misadventure was entirely forgotten as she gave herself to the sweetest communion ever. She knew herself loved, and let that love flow in warm waves over her body. The chill of the ride to the village passed out of her limbs. Even her fingers and toes were tingling with renewed heat.

After a moment, he drew back. "I feared the worst when I could not reach you. I sent a messenger to Evenlode believing, hoping, you had returned when I could not meet you at the crossroads. Five minutes ago I was informed you had been gone from your home since early in the afternoon. Tell me you are well, that you are unharmed. Tell me!"

He shook her gently and the fear writ in his eyes put her forcibly in mind of the peril she had faced once Mr. Quince had entered Sir Alan's library.

"I am perfectly well, though I will admit Sir Alan's servants aided my escape. I behaved so foolishly, only I wanted so very much for that monster to know that he was found out, that his horrible schemes had finally come to the light of day. I was sure you would arrive at any moment, and I made the worst blunder. I—I accused him of his crimes, believing you were in the hallway. Instead, it was Mr. Quince."

"Come to warn him, no doubt."

She nodded. "He seemed most anxious, and it was highly unusual for him to travel in a snowstorm."

"But come to the fire, my darling, my adorable, wonderful Laurentia. Will you have a cup of wassail? Good. Please sit down and I'll serve you."

Laurentia took up a chair opposite him. She was warmed by the belief that somehow the situation would now resolve so she would never have to be parted from Villiers again. When he handed her the steaming cup, she sipped slowly and carefully, savoring the spicy brew.

"I am so glad you came," she said. "For we have much to settle, specifically how we are to make certain that your fortune, plus interest, is returned to you."

He sat down slowly and his expression grew decidedly grave, so much so that she refrained from dictating that they must repair at once to Tewkesbury, as soon as the roads might permit, in order to make the entire transaction legal and binding. Instead, she sipped her wassail and watched him carefully.

"You don't know what you are saying," he stated at last. "To begin such a proceeding would involve a scandal so outrageous as to be spoken of from one end of England to the other. Your name, so precious to me, would be ruined forever, your future shattered. There is no good that could possibly come of it. None. You must trust me in this."

She met his fierce gaze and saw the strength of his opposition as a formidable wall she would be unlikely to breach by the usual arguments or even tender persuasions. She took another sip and averted her gaze. For one thing, he would never believe, even though it was true, that she could endure such a scandal if it meant she could live forever as his wife. For another, she doubted he would believe she would be willing to forgo all her former schemes. She had for so long made these activities a large matter of importance, that she could scarcely say they had no meaning for her—he would never believe it.

"And there is Grandmama," she murmured, adding to his arguments. "Until you mentioned what scandal might ensue, I had not thought of how the whole business would affect her, nor all the good people of Windrush whom I meant to help."

"Precisely," he stated firmly. "Laurentia, you've no idea how your saying these things in such a logical manner has relieved my mind. I had not thought, nor believed, I could persuade you so easily to the way things must be."

"I am not without some intelligence," she said sadly. "I suppose I was merely caught up in the excitement of having come to know the truth, and meant to remedy the situation as quickly as possible. You must know, then, of the existence of the sham plantation?"

"I learned of it the day of the masquerade."

"Then you left Windrush entirely for my sake?"

He nodded.

She rose and settled her cup of wassail on the mantel, then turned to face him. She smiled, bent over, and placed a kiss on his lips. "You are far too good to me."

"Oh, Laurentia, this must not be, either," he said.

She ignored his remark, and dropped to her knees to cradle

her head on his lap. He petted her hair, and she gloried in the sweetness of his touch and in the joy of being close to him.

Her mind began to whir and hum once more. One scheme after another began popping in and out of her mind as to how she could bring the situation about to her satisfaction. She now understood that Villiers would never act against Sir Alan. Therefore the task must be hers, and hers alone.

The following morning, Lord Villiers rode in his carriage, greatly subdued. Leaving Laurentia this second time was the hardest thing he had ever done, yet he believed completely in what he was doing. Laurentia must have the future she always desired for herself, to be of service to the many unfortunate inhabitants of the vale who had been wronged by her uncle for the past fifteen years. He would not take that from her.

The more he considered, however, just how close to mischief she had come in calling upon Sir Alan the day before, the uneasier he grew. What was there to prevent the baronet from harming Laurentia if he was not there to protect her?

Just before the carriage turned in the direction of Tewkesbury, he lowered the window and called out to his postilion, "Take me to Windstone!"

The horses immediately veered to the right, making sluggish yet steady progress through the snow-covered lane toward Sir Alan's home.

Once in the green drawing room, Villiers stared at the man who had robbed him of his inheritance. So many thoughts came to mind, so many things he wanted to say to the vile man before him, that he found he could not at first speak.

"I suppose you know the truth, then?" Sir Alan queried, all affability having fled his features. What was usually a portrait of kindness and nobility now was nothing but brutish self-interest.

"That you stole my fortune from me—yes. I knew it the

day of the ball—I had proof the day of the ball—and had you not interfered and revealed my identity to Laurentia, all would be well."

Sir Alan's brows snapped together. "What are you saying? That you had no intention of prosecuting? You expect me to believe that?"

"I expect you to believe it still. Last night Laurentia told me that her uncle had summoned me, not at his wife's behest, after all, but because his conscience had finally gotten the better of him and he wanted me to have what was rightfully mine, by wedding her. The pair of you were such fools, though I must say that is the kindest thing I will ever say to you, for you are much worse than that."

"What does it matter? I took what your father stole from me when he married your mother. She was mine, and he took her from me."

"What are you about?" he cried. "How dare you desecrate either his name or hers by invoking them now! My father took nothing from you. It seems to me my mother took your measure and chose the better man!"

He watched a fury encompass Sir Alan's face like nothing he had ever witnessed before.

"By God, if I weren't twice your age—!" he cried.

"You aren't twice my age, so why do you hesitate? Nothing would afford me greater pleasure than planting you another facer—or better yet, facing you with a sword! What do you say, Sir Alan! Will you face me? Or how about pistols at twenty paces!"

Sir Alan moved away from Villiers, toward the windows. He remained with his back to him for a long time, obviously struggling to regain his composure. Finally he said, "I wouldn't dream of doing anything so foolish as to engage in a duel of any kind." After another pause, he managed, "So, you intend to let matters rest, for the sake of Laurentia's foolish plans?"

"Yes. She deserves nothing less."

Sir Alan turned around. His lips were clamped, and his eyes were cloudy. "Very well. I suppose I should be grateful, then."

"Don't bother yourself with expressions of gratitude, or I will show you just how well Gentleman Jackson has taught me over the past ten years."

"I've little doubt you would," the baronet muttered.

"I shall leave now. I merely wanted you to know that I intend everything to remain just as it is, which includes your leaving Laurentia in peace. If I hear even a whisper of an intention on your part to make her your wife once we divorce, I shall return to Windstone and end this business once and for all."

For the first time during the interview, Sir Alan paled. "You love her that much?" he queried.

"More than my own life," he responded. "So I suggest you take care how you conduct yourself in the future. I shall have a long discussion with Mr. Crabtree before returning to Somerset, just so that others are informed of how I wish to see matters unfold in the coming years. Do you understand me?"

"Of course I understand you," Sir Alan muttered bitterly.

Sixteen

Lord Villiers returned to Somerset with a heavy but determined heart. He was very grateful that his wife, who was soon not to be his wife, had listened to reason, for now he could resume his labors at Fairwood knowing he had done his duty by her. had she not been so nearly involved he would have enjoyed nothing so much as seeing Sir Alan Redcliffe brought down from his high horse. Indeed, for so many years he had thrived on the vision of one day seeing the job done that to leave it behind a second time was a matter of no small degree of courage and conviction on his part.

Seeing Laurentia once more, holding her in his arms, kissing her, however, had not in the least undermined his determination. On the contrary, he was convinced now more than ever that this perfect, innocent, pure-hearted creature deserved every penny of her fortune, even if it had been created on the back of his own. Indeed, he could not have chosen a better vessel for it.

With these thoughts, therefore, he strove to content himself.

On Christmas Eve, he was chopping wood when a barouche and four drew into the stableyard where he was working. He stood at the woodpile nearby, in his shirtsleeves, with his coat hanging from a peg on the outside of the building and a scarlet muffler tucked about his neck against the ever-present wintry chill. The snow, though much present, was melting steadily beneath a weak December sun as thin high clouds trailed over the sky. The day was perfect for the work he had undertaken in clearing the chestnut wood of a great deal more of, the unwanted growth which had taken ten years to accumulate. He was utterly astonished when, upon slamming the tip of his axe into the chopping stump, he witnessed Laurentia emerge from the elegant coach.

She called to the postilion. "Attend to the horses yourself, Will, for I have been given to understand that there is naught but a single stableboy residing here."

"Wery good, ma'am," the postilion responded cheerfully.

She descended gracefully from the large conveyance and moved to stand at the edge of what was a thick circle of wood chips. She was incredibly beautiful in a dark green, velvet pelisse, a matching hat with a long, curling ostrich feather arched over the crown, and her hands tucked deeply into an elegant muff of white fur.

"How do you do, Lord Villiers?" she greeted him, her smile saucy and far too adorable to be endured with equanimity.

"What the devil are you doing here?" he cried, irritated that he could not run to her, twirl her in a circle and kiss her soundly. Had the chit come to torture him, to flaunt what could never be his?

Her forehead grew puckered. "I had hoped for a warmer greeting from a gentleman I count as one of my dearest friends."

"Friends!" he cried, prepared to take umbrage. However, a single glance at the postilion, who was presently struggling with the horse harness, brought his manners about in full force. "Yes, of course. Do forgive me, Laurentia. Are you taking your grandmama to Cornwall? The eastern coast is remarkably mild during the winter, and she would enjoy, I think, a holiday in such a fine locale."

"Not precisely," she responded, beginning to advance upon him, her boots crunching softly on the wood chips. "At present, she is in Bath, taking the waters and happily abusing her four footmen, who I daresay even now are carrying her up every steep hill she can find merely to make them puff and sweat and mutter curses beneath each breath."

He smiled in spite of himself. "Will you come inside? The house is in a miserable state, but the library, my own principal receiving room, is tolerably comfortable, and the buttery is well-stocked with excellent wines from years past."

"I would be delighted, truly. However, will you not show me your fort first? From the moment you first mentioned it to me I have been agog to lay eyes upon it."

"My—fort? You mean the one in the woods?"

She nodded. "If you please."

"Very well, if you indeed wish for it."

"I do. The weather has become quite mild, and I should prefer to walk about a bit before again taking up a seat."

He chuckled. "The roads are not precisely well-maintained in this part of the county."

"I vow I was bounced from Somerset to Devon and back with every jolt. I even hit my head once, but dear Will, so solicitous of my comfort, shouted his apologies."

After shrugging on his coat, he offered her his arm, and she accepted. He guided her in a southerly direction and very soon they reached the edge of the wood.

"So this is the chestnut grove," she remarked. "I see you have begun hauling dead timber out. Goodness, but you are right. Only a severe pruning will bring this forest about."

"The trees have been here forever, it would seem. You should see them in the summer, magnificently leafed."

"I hope one day I might do just that. I believe I begin to see your fort! Oh, Thomas, it's so grand. Did you build this yourself, then? I vow you should have been an architect."

"The thatching is in need of some repair, and I had to hire a couple of cats to clear the rodents from a score of nests. Otherwise, it is much as I enjoyed it as a child."

"I love it," she cried, "every inch of it. And there are your cats now, perched on the roof! What are their names?"

"The black-and-white one is Sparky, and the black one is Frisky," he said, chagrined. "Yes, I know. Terribly unimaginative, but they don't need excellent names to hunt mice well."

"No, I suppose not," she responded, laughing. "Well? Do you intend to help me climb the ladder?"

"You will need to set aside your muff," he said.

She shook her head and frowned slightly. "That I refuse to do. I have not been separated from my most important source of comfort since I departed Evenlode." She withdrew her hands carefully and, unbuttoning her pelisse, stuffed the muff against her chest. She then rebuttoned the pelisse in two places at her waist and laughed heartily. "Don't I cut a ridiculous figure?"

"I refuse to admit to any such opinion, though I will say you have certainly solved the problem as to how to take the muff up with you."

She nodded briskly. "I believe I have become quite good at solving problems of late. Indeed, it would seem the more troublesome and perplexing the dilemma, the better I am at finding a most excellent solution." She took a firm hold on the ladder and began an awkward ascent, since her muff-swollen pelisse tended to inhibit her progress. Finally, she arrived at the entrance and stepped onto a solid porch.

She moved away to allow Villiers a little room and at once began a march about the porch, which encircled the small building entirely. Only in one place was the floor a little shaky.

"The board is rotten there," he said. "But the rest seem to have suffered little over the years."

"The view is wonderful, and I'm sure at night you are able to watch the stars make a lovely path across the sky."

"The moon, as well, during certain parts of each month."

"Now, *there* is a sight I should like to see. Will you show it to me one day?"

She heard him sigh quite deeply. Laurentia turned toward him and knew full well that her words were causing him pain. She changed the subject quite abruptly. "You have not asked me how my St. Thomas's Day Celebration fared."

He smiled politely. "I have little doubt it was a rousing success."

"It was," she answered promptly. "Only a few people were unable to attend because of some illness or other, and the rest, because they have been friends since childhood, served to remind me of why I have always loved Christmas best. I was showered with every manner of homemade gift, cake, or biscuit, even several of some of the finest jars of honey one could ever find in all of England. The dancing lasted until the wee hours of the morning. My slippers were nearly worn through, and I must say the only difficulty I experienced the entire evening was in explaining your absence."

At that his expression fell. "Everyone will know soon enough."

She sighed and nodded. "I suppose you are right."

"I don't imagine Sir Alan had the effrontery to attend."

She shook her head. "He had quit Windrush some few days earlier. He is not expected to return. Windstone, if you must know, is being sold off to pay a number of his debts."

He eyed her narrowly. "Laurentia, you did not—that is, never mind. My thoughts were foolish of the moment. I am not surprised to learn he had acquired debts which forced him to sell one of his houses."

"Is this your opinion, then?" She unbuttoned her pelisse and released the muff from its warm prison. She immediately settled her hands deeply within.

"How else ought I interpret his sudden need to sell Windstone?"

She withdrew a bundle of papers from her muff and extended them toward Villiers. "That he has at last come to his senses and is returning both your fortune to you, as well as all accrued interests and investments. I must say, however, that though he is an extremely vile man, he certainly knew how to judge a sound investment."

"What nonsense are you speaking!" he cried, staring at the papers. "We agreed! You told me you would abide by my wish to pursue the matter no further."

"Actually," she said. "I merely nodded and smiled while you ranted at me. If you recall, I agreed to nothing. I knew it would be of little use to argue with you when a sapskull could see you had quite made up your mind. But even as you spoke of how *good* I was and how I didn't deserve to be sunk in scandal, I was configuring in my own mind some means of turning the entire situation about. I have succeeded to my satisfaction, and hereby return from both estates what always belonged to you. Merry Christmas, Thomas. This is my gift to you."

His complexion had paled as he stared at the bundle of papers. "I want nothing of this."

"You have no choice. No, that is not true. If you wish to reject the whole of it, the fortune will pass into a trust, to be administered by Mr. Crabtree. Your fortune, then, would find its way into a great many charities. So, either way, I will be content."

"Are you saying you are penniless, Laurentia? Tell me you have not been so foolish as that!"

She shrugged. "Of course not. Both Sir Alan and I retain approximately two thousand a year, which is a fortune by many standards. I, of course, have already made it known that I intend to sell Evenlode. I could not keep such a large house even on two thousand a year. Grandmama and I will be searching for more accommodating quarters somewhere in the west. So far, I believe Somerset to be my favorite place in all of England." She eyed him hopefully, fully intent that he should take up her meaning and ask her to remain with him at Fairwood.

Instead, he slapped the papers on the palm of his hand. "This is not what I wanted. You know it is not. Besides, how can you even think of selling Evenlode? No, this is a great absurdity—the whole of it. I refuse to hear another word on the subject."

"The matter is no longer yours to decide," she said softly. "Only whether you wish to keep what is rightfully yours or give it to the poor."

He took a step toward her. "You did not go back to his house?" he inquired softly, his expression troubled.

"Yes, as it happens, I did, but not without an entire army to support me. Mr. Crabtree is so well-connected in Tewkesbury that he was able to summon precisely the right blend of solicitors and several rather bruising men—from the Bristol docks, I believe. Our descent on Windstone had precisely the effect I had hoped for. We found him packing a valise in his office with a great many papers. Apparently, his financier, Mr. Quince, who had arrived at precisely the moment I believed you were to make your appearance that dreadful day, had come to warn him of his doom. Rumors were rife in Tewkesbury. I suppose had he actually succeeded in fleeing England he would have been able to take a substantial part of your fortune with him. As it was, Mr. Crabtree carefully searched through the papers and found all the incriminating evidence necessary concerning the Soledad Plantation.

"With so many legal minds present, the squadron of solicitors landed on the numerous documents like blackbirds feeding in an autumn hayfield. Sir Alan tried to dissuade me, but I gave him so furious and scornful a stare that he immediately perceived there was nothing to be done—especially since I then told him in no uncertain terms that I had no desire to base even my charitable works on a fortune so vilely obtained and built.

"By the next day all the figures had been assembled, and a final agreement made to which Sir Alan was forced to acquiesce. He will be able to keep his ancestral home and lands, of course, plus a rather modest manor in Surrey. The rest will be sold eventually, and the money returned to your estate."

"You don't know what you've done, Laurentia," he said, obviously overcome.

"Oh, but I do. I've done what is right, what anyone in my place would have done."

He laughed bitterly. "There you are out. Although I know a great many people, I can't imagine but a handful who would be so kind and generous."

"Nonsense," she replied softly. "You were so wretchedly ill-used by your guardian, a man your father trusted implicitly, a man *I* trusted implicitly, that you cannot conceive of how right-minded most people are."

He met her gaze and shook his head. "My dear, sweet, innocent Laurentia," he murmured. He slipped his hand about the back of her neck, closed the distance between them and settled his lips on hers. Laurentia heard the papers fall with a thump on the faded wood of the porch as he gathered her up in his arms and kissed her properly. She let her muff fall, as well, whereupon she returned his kiss, holding him tightly, afraid that even though so very much had been resolved, something might arise to separate her from him. After all, now that he was quite wealthy there must a dozen young ladies from whom he could choose one to grace his table and fill his halls with all the children he could desire.

After a time, she drew back. "There is something I feel I must tell you, Villiers. You see, Mr. Crabtree believes that we may not be legally married, since you wed me without the use of your noble name. I daresay you are quite free of me, and you may now reenter your society as you ought to have so many years ago. In a few months, little more than three, you will be able to return to London in the style you were born to. You will be a great favorite among the ladies, I suspect."

Lord Villiers saw the hopeful glint in her eye, and the small lines of worry beside her lovely mouth. He couldn't help but tease her a little. He released her and turned away from her, walking rather dramatically to the railing of the porch. He stared into the distance and began, "I hadn't considered that! I am very grateful you brought the matter fully to my attention." He stole a glance at her and saw that all hope had fled her face and she was now chewing on the inside of her lip. She could not know how adorable she appeared in that moment. She was such an innocent, and her lack of guile in any aspect of her sweet being pulled at his heartstrings even more than her beauty or her generous nature.

However, he could not resist continuing. "I should like to enter the city in a coach and six, each horse, if not beribboned, certainly sporting fine feathers atop each head and all the harness embellished with gold. I have for so long taken a lower seat among my peers that I am determined it shall be so no longer. And what a good thing that we are not truly married, for you were very right to point out to me that I will soon become the object of every matchmaking mama in London. Scores of young ladies will somehow break the strings of their sandals just outside my door, quite by accident, and require that good Lord Villiers accompany them home so that they might be returned to their mamas safely. The prettiest of the ladies will set their caps for me . . . ah, I shall experience no greater happiness."

"What gammon!" she cried. "I see now that you are funning."

He whirled on her and again caught her up in his arms. "You deserved every word of it, telling me, essentially, that now I may cut a dash in London. What nonsense."

"I didn't mean that precisely," she murmured.

Once more he kissed her quite thoroughly. He was about to ask her to become his wife again, only this time under the auspices of the Church of England, when a great commotion was heard near the stables. "What the deuce is that?" he cried.

Laurentia brought her fingers to her chin. "Oh, dear. They have come beforetimes. I told Grandmama that they were to wait in Bath until I sent for them, but she must have ordered them on, anyway. How very vexing, yet how very much like her!"

"Who?" he inquired. "Who has come?"

"Well, dearest," she began uneasily. "I knew that you did not have a great number of servants here, so I took the liberty of hiring a few on your behalf."

Since the noise near the stables was growing louder and louder, he turned to his wife who was not exactly his wife, and inquired, "How many servants?"

She swallowed visibly and blurted out, "I had to bring them. They would not leave me, nor my grandmother, and besides, I believe the housekeeper has formed a certain *attachment.*"

"Laurentia, you did not bring the entire staff from Evenlode?

"Of course not," she said. "Only half of them. The others had families in Windrush. The rest! How could I turn them off without having situations readied for them?"

"Half the servants! Are you saying you brought thirty servants with you?"

She nodded. "The Head Groom and his grooms. A number of the footmen, most of the maids, the housekeeper. Most of the gardening staff, which is quite formidable, since I was well aware that the grounds here were in great need of pruning. My abigail, as well as Grandmama's. I would say thirty, perhaps a few more."

"Good God."

"You need not keep them," she stated firmly.

He laughed outright. "Of course I must, else I shall offend my bride irrevocably, and I don't think that is how I wish to begin my marriage."

She smiled softly, "You will have me, then, with all my flaws?"

"If you will have me, with all of mine."

"Oh, yes, Villiers, for the only flaw I could ever detect in you was too great a propensity to protect me from the harshness of life. That manner of flaw I believe I could tolerate for many years to come."

Even though the noise from the stables was rising ominously as the hubbub of the unloading of coaches wafted steadily into the air, Villiers once more kissed the woman he adored with all his heart. He wondered if he would ever tire of dragging her into his arms and letting her know with the search of his lips how much he loved her and adored her. Just how much longer he might have continued this assault, he wasn't permitted to discover, since he heard his name called.

He released Laurentia and glanced down to the ground below. "What is it, Coxwell?"

"It is come to my attention that we are to be overrun by guests from Evenlode, and I haven't the faintest notion where they are all to stay."

"They are not guests," he said, laughing. "My wife has come with *a handful* of her servants to make her comfortable in her new home."

"A new home, here?" Coxwell's face took on a sudden glow. "The housekeeper, as well?"

"She is among those present, is she not?"

He nodded, his complexion turning a lovely shade of pink.

Villiers said, "Arrange matters as best you can. Simmons will be completely overwhelmed, though I am certain Mrs. Bourton will know precisely what needs to be done."

"That she will. Such a commanding female as she is."

"We will be along shortly. Make certain that Cook knows she may obtain whatever she needs from the village to feed such a large staff—it appears we are in funds again, Coxwell, at long last."

"I am very glad to hear it, m'lord."

Once Coxwell left the chestnut wood, Laurentia slid her arm

about Villiers's. "You do wish me to remain?" she queried quite seriously. "I realize I have completely thrust myself upon you, my servants as well . . ." She regarded him with tears in her eyes.

Though he knew an impulse to tease her a little more, he saw that there was a serious light in her eye which he felt he ought to address. "More than life itself, my darling. I would have happily given up everything that you might be able to live as you had always lived, but this is far better, for I truly did not know how I was going to endure my life without you."

"Oh, Thomas, we are magical together, aren't we? I mean truly magical together?"

He nodded. "Yes, but I begin to see the bloom of another love which might soon outshine our own."

Laurentia giggled. "I wish Coxwell and his love much happiness, but their affections for one another will never outshine my feelings for you."

Villiers let the past fifteen years rush past him in a blur of examination and wonder. He decided that after all the disappointment and pain he had endured, because such a terrible road had led him to Laurentia and to a love as large as the sky he could be downcast no longer.

"There is one point I must argue, however," he said. "I cannot permit you to sell Evenlode."

"I cannot afford to keep it."

"Then with our joint fortunes we will manage, for I am beginning to believe that such a fine house would be an excellent dowry for our eldest daughter."

He watched as tears leapt to her eyes. "Oh, Thomas! I could think of nothing better for her."

"Nor I," he murmured softly.

He gazed lovingly into her face, wanting to know everything about her, even the smallest details. "So, tell me, Laurentia, what is your middle name? Will you not now entrust me with that knowledge?"

He saw the color rise on her cheeks as she began plucking at the lapel of his coat. "You must remember that I was born very close to the New Year, just a few days from now, and I believe there were numerous church bells pealing at the time of my birth. Mother always said that I stopped crying immediately upon hearing the bells. I have never believed her for a second, but she chose to mark the occasion with my middle name." She paused, apparently not wishing to continue.

"Dearest, you have put me in the gravest amount of suspense. Tell me what you are called."

She looked up at him, the color deepening in her face. "Laurentia Merrybells Cabot. There. Now you may laugh all you wish."

"Merrybells—as in, *merry bells?*" he queried, smiling.

"Precisely."

"I think it charming," he said, chuckling softly. "I only wish I had known your delightful parents, my dear Merrybells."

"Please don't ever call me that. You cannot imagine the nuisance such a name can be."

"But it expresses your entire person so beautifully."

She would have protested, but at that precise moment the chiming of church bells could be heard in the neighboring village. Villiers chuckled again, but his wife was not amused. "I am beginning to believe there is no escaping it—or you!" she cried.

"Now you have the right of it. Oh, my darling, you have made me the happiest of men." Once more he drew his wife into his arms and kissed her.

Put a Little Romance in Your Life With
Janelle Taylor

__Anything for Love	0-8217-4992-7	$5.99US/$6.99CAN
__Forever Ecstasy	0-8217-5241-3	$5.99US/$6.99CAN
__Fortune's Flames	0-8217-5450-5	$5.99US/$6.99CAN
__Destiny's Temptress	0-8217-5448-3	$5.99US/$6.99CAN
__Love Me With Fury	0-8217-5452-1	$5.99US/$6.99CAN
__First Love, Wild Love	0-8217-5277-4	$5.99US/$6.99CAN
__Kiss of the Night Wind	0-8217-5279-0	$5.99US/$6.99CAN
__Love With a Stranger	0-8217-5416-5	$6.99US/$8.50CAN
__Forbidden Ecstasy	0-8217-5278-2	$5.99US/$6.99CAN
__Defiant Ecstasy	0-8217-5447-5	$5.99US/$6.99CAN
__Follow the Wind	0-8217-5449-1	$5.99US/$6.99CAN
__Wild Winds	0-8217-6026-2	$6.99US/$8.50CAN
__Defiant Hearts	0-8217-5563-3	$6.50US/$8.00CAN
__Golden Torment	0-8217-5451-3	$5.99US/$6.99CAN
__Bittersweet Ecstasy	0-8217-5445-9	$5.99US/$6.99CAN
__Taking Chances	0-8217-4259-0	$4.50US/$5.50CAN
__By Candlelight	0-8217-5703-2	$6.99US/$8.50CAN
__Chase the Wind	0-8217-4740-1	$5.99US/$6.99CAN
__Destiny Mine	0-8217-5185-9	$5.99US/$6.99CAN
__Midnight Secrets	0-8217-5280-4	$5.99US/$6.99CAN
__Sweet Savage Heart	0-8217-5276-6	$5.99US/$6.99CAN
__Moonbeams and Magic	0-7860-0184-4	$5.99US/$6.99CAN
__Brazen Ecstasy	0-8217-5446-7	$5.99US/$6.99CAN

Call toll free **1-888-345-BOOK** to order by phone or use this coupon to order by mail.

Name _____

Address _____

City _____ State _____ Zip _____

Please send me the books I have checked above.

I am enclosing	$_____
Plus postage and handling*	$_____
Sales tax (in New York and Tennessee)	$_____
Total amount enclosed	$_____

*Add $2.50 for the first book and $.50 for each additional book.

Send check or money order (no cash or CODs) to:

Kensington Publishing Corp., 850 Third Avenue, New York, NY 10022

Prices and Numbers subject to change without notice.

All orders subject to availability.

Check out our website at **www.kensingtonbooks.com**

Put a Little Romance in Your Life With
Fern Michaels

More Zebra Regency Romances

Merlin's Legacy

A Series From
Quinn Taylor Evans

__**Daughter of Fire** 0-8217-6052-1	$5.50US/$7.00CAN
__**Daughter of the Mist** 0-8217-6050-5	$5.50US/$7.00CAN
__**Daughter of Light** 0-8217-6051-3	$5.50US/$7.00CAN
__**Dawn of Camelot** 0-8217-6028-9	$5.50US/$7.00CAN
__**Shadows of Camelot** 0-8217-5760-1	$5.50US/$7.00CAN